# HEART OF
# THE PACK

# By the Author

A Royal Romance

Heart of the Pack

Visit us at www.boldstrokesbooks.com

# HEART OF THE PACK

*by*
Jenny Frame

2016

**HEART OF THE PACK**
© 2016 BY JENNY FRAME. ALL RIGHTS RESERVED.

ISBN 13: 978-1-62639-566-4

THIS TRADE PAPERBACK ORIGINAL IS PUBLISHED BY
BOLD STROKES BOOKS, INC.
P.O. BOX 249
VALLEY FALLS, NY 12185

FIRST EDITION: MAY 2016

THIS IS A WORK OF FICTION. NAMES, CHARACTERS, PLACES, AND INCIDENTS ARE THE PRODUCT OF THE AUTHOR'S IMAGINATION OR ARE USED FICTITIOUSLY. ANY RESEMBLANCE TO ACTUAL PERSONS, LIVING OR DEAD, BUSINESS ESTABLISHMENTS, EVENTS, OR LOCALES IS ENTIRELY COINCIDENTAL.

THIS BOOK, OR PARTS THEREOF, MAY NOT BE REPRODUCED IN ANY FORM WITHOUT PERMISSION.

---

**CREDITS**
EDITOR: RUTH STERNGLANTZ
PRODUCTION DESIGN: STACIA SEAMAN
COVER DESIGN BY MELODY POND

# Acknowledgments

There are a great many people I need to thank for this book. First and foremost Radclyffe, for continuing to give me a platform for my work and creating a wonderful writing community that, just like the wolf pack, supports and allows its members to be the best they can be.

To the Bold Strokes Books staff, Sandy, Cindy, Connie, Toni, Sheri, amongst many others, who work extremely hard behind the scenes to support us as authors and make everything run smoothly, thanks for everything you do.

Big thanks to my editor, Ruth Sternglantz, for helping me grow as an author, helping me develop my writing style, being hugely supportive, and answering my endless questions and worries. I couldn't ask for a better editor.

Thank you to my good friends Amy, Gova, and Christine, who are always ready to give me an encouraging word whenever I need it.

To all the readers who have supported me and taken the time to contact me about my stories, I'm extremely thankful for every email and message you have sent. You all keep me inspired and writing.

As always thank you to my family for helping me so much on a daily basis and for their continued support in all that I do.

Finally, my own little Frame pack. Lou, the Alpha of our pack, you do so much for me, more than you should have to, but you do it gladly. I'm forever thankful that you swaggered into my life and gave me the strength and confidence to be myself and taught me what real love looks like. A special thank you to our own little wolf, Barney boy, who keeps me company each and every day, stays by my side as I write, and teaches me so much about wolfie behavior.

For Lou, as always
The Alpha of our little pack

## Prologue

Two wolves ran through the dense, snow-covered forest at breakneck speed. They leaped over fallen trees and rocks blocking their path with ease. They were both fevered with the need to hunt down their prey and move in for the kill. The Alpha wolf in front, with a thick gray, white, and black pelt, began to slow and sniff the air.

Behind the Alpha, the pack Second caught the scent of their quarry more strongly than before. She communicated telepathically to Dante, her Alpha, *Alpha, we must be close.* Every nerve ending under her dark brown, white, and black pelt tingled, now they were closing in on the prey.

*Yes, she is so close I can almost taste her blood on the air, Second.*

She followed the Alpha as she padded up to the edge of a clearing and peeked through the thick undergrowth. There licking her wounds was the pure black wolf, the Alpha of the Lupa pack, who had attacked the Alpha's mate.

*Second, I'll head into the clearing on my own, and you circle around to the rear.*

*Yes, Alpha.* As she rounded the perimeter of the trees, she watched her Alpha walk calmly out into the clearing. The Alpha had five or six inches on the black wolf and was more powerfully built.

The black wolf, Leroux, said, *The mighty Alpha has arrived, and your Second, Caden, too. You can come skulking out of the undergrowth, I can smell the stench of a Wolfgang at five paces.*

Caden walked out and stood defensively to the side, waiting for her Alpha's orders. The two rival wolves circled around each other, Dante baring teeth and demanding submission.

*Once I'm done with you, Dante, I am going to tear all your whelps to pieces.*

Dante snapped and snarled. *You will never get near my cubs.*

*I managed to get to your mate though, didn't I, Dante? Once I kill you, I will kill your cubs, take your mate, and seize your pack lands.*

Caden felt her Alpha's fury in every cell of her body and wanted nothing more than to rip Leroux apart, but this was Dante's fight. Leroux had attacked her mate so first bite went to the Alpha.

*You think you can beat me?* Dante snarled. *My mate, a small submissive wolf, ripped your face open. What chance do you think you have against me? You are pathetic. The Lupa pack must be in a sorry state if you are the best wolf to come from them.*

Leroux replied, *My pack is strong—we live in the old ways, living off the land, ruling by power and slaying every human that crosses our territory, not growing fat on piles of money and selling our kills to them.*

Leroux roared and launched herself at Dante, but the Alpha easily dodged her opponent. *Is that the best you've got?*

*You are arrogant just like those that bore you. My grandfather was killed by your grandmother, and I swore I would one day control this pack and all it had. When I saw your mate...she was an added bonus.*

*Well, good luck trying to take what's mine, Mutt.*

Leroux went for her again, and this time Dante met the strike head-on, and they rolled over on the ground, each looking to gain the upper hand. They fought and snarled and bit, until a bloody Leroux was near collapse. Her flanks were covered in deep claw marks and there was a bite on her hip.

Caden scented another wolf heading toward them, and as they got closer, she recognized the scent of Dante's daughter, Dion. She was being chased by a second Lupa wolf. Caden ran around to the spot where Dion would emerge from the trees and growled. *Get behind me.*

The Lupa wolf was no match for Caden, but she was joined in seconds by Dante, who had sensed the danger to her cub. Caden brought the wolf to the ground, and Dante snapped at its neck, ripping the wolf's throat out.

She and the Alpha howled to proclaim their victory to the pack, but they turned back to the middle of the clearing to find Leroux gone.

As if in an instant the clearing was gone and Caden found herself watching a chaotic scene in the middle of a freeway. People screamed, and the smell of acrid smoke permeated the air. In the middle of the road a car lay mangled where the big rig beside it had plowed into its side. Caden stood paralyzed, trapped in her own nightmare, unable to move with the fear of utter helplessness inside.

Smoke was billowing from the car, and someone shouted, "Get back! That rig is carrying oil."

She felt the whoosh and heat of the fireball before she heard the explosion. Someone pulled her back from the carnage, and she screamed and kicked trying to break free, but it was useless. Everything that ever mattered to her or loved was gone in those few seconds.

Caden woke up gasping for air, with sweat running down her body. She threw the bedsheets off and ran to the bathroom. She turned on the faucet and splashed the cool water over her face. As her breath calmed slightly, she looked at herself in the mirror above the sink, and a pair of angry yellow eyes looked back at her.

"Never again. I swear by the Great Mother's word, I will never allow pain or harm to touch the people I love."

## Chapter One

Selena Miller looked around her empty apartment and felt the familiar foreboding slither around her stomach. She had lost count of the number of times she had nearly changed her mind about this move, and every time she had to fight so hard to overcome her deep-seated fears and let her logical mind win out.

*I am doing the right thing, aren't I?* But before she had the chance to answer her own question, the moving supervisor interrupted her.

"Ma'am? That's everything in the truck. Is there anything else you need before we head off?"

Selena pushed her glasses up on the bridge of her nose nervously. "No, you can go now. I'll be a few more minutes."

"Sure thing. It'll take around two and half hours for us to get to Wolfgang County, but you'll probably make better time than us in that sports car of yours."

How embarrassing. She hated her new car, which was unusual for someone with a top-of-the-line Porsche Cabriolet, but she hated to stand out in the crowd. She had been happy with her mid-range Ford, but her father didn't think it reflected well on the family position, so she was given the hot-pink Porsche for her last birthday. She had more important battles to wage against her overbearing parents, so she'd accepted the unwanted gift. But it had the effect she'd feared: people stared everywhere she went.

"I drive slowly and carefully, so you'll probably make it before me, but you have a set of keys. Please just start unloading when you arrive."

"No problem," he said. "Next stop, Wolfgang County." He headed outside to the truck.

The fear of leaving the protective bubble she had built here in Salt Lake City was terrifying, but she reminded herself, as she had many times since she'd applied for this new job, that this was her chance for independence, a chance to move out from under her mother and father's control and spread her wings.

From the very second she had read about this transfer opportunity on her company's internal website, the prospect of moving to a farming community in Utah had both excited and terrified her. Not only had she to fight her own internal fears but her mother's and father's too. When she told them she would be moving away, they were horrified, but the prestigious reputation of her new employer forced them to put up with it.

Selena looked over to the teddy bear sitting beside her purse, and the man who had given it to her came vividly into her mind. Uncle Joel.

Her mother's brother was the black sheep of the family and loved it that way. She was the only family he connected with, and he'd seen past her many failings. After he died a few months earlier, she knew she had to make a change in her life. As he lay in the hospital toward the end, he had urged her to follow her heart. *You're not like my sister, your father, or your brothers. You're a kind, gentle soul who deserves a loving, happy life. Selena, get away from here, or they'll suffocate you. Follow your heart, and follow the moon. You are its Goddess, after all.*

This would be a new chapter in her life. Time to be brave and take the chance.

❖

Caden Wolfgang strode purposefully into the head office of Venator, one of the most successful meatpacking and distribution companies in America. Dressed in her jeans, boots, and Stetson,

Caden stood out in this corporate-suited world. Everyone who passed her either bowed their head respectfully or thumped their fist to their chest in salute.

She took off her hat and smoothed back her hair as she approached the reception desk. "Morning, Kyra. You're back with us? How was your trip?"

The young receptionist lowered her eyes submissively and blushed. "Morning, Second. Yeah, I'm back. Just a few more months and I can start my teaching job at Wolfgang Academy. I can't wait."

Caden always had a soft spot for Kyra. She was a close friend of Kyra's family and she'd watched her grow up.

She smiled and reached out to cup Kyra's cheek. "You've done so well at college, Kyra. We'll be lucky to have someone like you teaching our youngsters. Just remember to have some fun while you're home. Don't work too hard, okay?"

"I'll try, Second," Kyra spluttered nervously.

Caden gave her a nod and walked on toward the elevators. After a quick ride to the tenth floor, the CEO's PA, Marcy, was waiting for her.

"Morning, Marcy. Is she in yet?"

"Can't you hear the shouting from here, Second?" Marcy said.

"Problems as usual, huh?" Caden slowed her long stride so the older woman could keep up.

"The usual inefficiencies. You know she has very little patience for mistakes. You're to go straight in."

"Thanks, Marcy."

Caden found the Alpha of the Wolfgang pack—the CEO of Venator, and her friend—at her desk wearing a headset, shouting at someone on the other end.

Her own casual attire was a contrast to the executive-suited Alpha. As pack Second, Caden's job was managing the ranch, slaughterhouses, and pack land. She loved the outdoor life and couldn't imagine being cooped up in an office all day, like her Alpha.

She knew the Alpha's preference would also be for the outdoors. Until Dante's father's death, she'd spent most of her time with Caden down on the ranch, but as Alpha her job was to run the pack and the business empire. This one business and its offshoots supported their small county, and Dante took that very seriously.

Caden could tell the Alpha was angry as her claws lengthened at the ends of her fingers.

"I don't care what kind of staff problems you have, Marshall. I want that shipment delivered, and on time. Get it done." Dante ripped off the headset and threw it onto her desk.

"Alpha?" Caden brought her fist to her heart.

"Cade, come in. Sit."

She sat and waited for the Alpha to speak first.

"What is it about humans, Cade? They tell you they will do a thing and then they don't. A wolf would never do that."

Caden smiled and said, "You can't expect anything else from humans. Shall I go and bite him for you?"

Dante stretched and appeared to let go of some of her tension. "Humans aren't all bad, Cade—just this one is particularly frustrating." Dante gave a low growl. "I wish I could just rip off this suit and go running."

"Why don't you? We could go up to the deer park and hunt. There's a surplus of them at the moment."

The carefully managed habitat around Wolfgang land was the pack's pride and joy. The Wolfgang pack had settled in America generations ago, for the freedom to live as they wanted, and to have enough land to hunt without fear of detection. They began with a small network of ranches under the leadership of the Alpha, and then as time passed, they'd evolved into meatpacking and distribution, making the Wolfgang pack very wealthy.

Dante sighed. "If only I could. I need to get through some paperwork if I'm to come out on the ranch with you tomorrow."

"Fair enough, I've got a lot I want to show you. Things are going well. Flash has made changes to the breeding programs that have been very effective."

"He's excellent in handling the animals, but I couldn't do it without you, Second. Come out running this evening—I promised Dion I'd take her hunting, and give her mother a break. She's at that age that tries every parent's last nerve."

Caden always enjoyed running with the Alpha and her oldest daughter. She was fifteen, but convinced she was an adult wolf, and very keen to show her wolf skills to her hero, Dante.

"Of course, Alpha. How is the Mater?"

Caden, like the rest of the Wolfgangs, adored Eden, the Alpha's mate. She was mother of the pack, in name and in deed. Eden's guidance and care of her wolves earned her great loyalty and love from them, not only because she nurtured and loved so devotedly, but because that love gave Dante the strength to lead the pack fearlessly.

As always when asked about her family, Dante's usual gruff commanding aura of authority fell away. "Eden is fantastic. I don't know how she copes with three cubs running around all day. It would drive me insane, but she runs our den like a military operation, I might be the Alpha of the Wolfgang pack, but when I walk through our front door, I say *Yes, ma'am, no, ma'am, whatever you say, Eden*. I think if she was Alpha, the Wolfgang pack would have taken over the world."

"No doubt." Caden picked up the family pictures on Dante's desk and looked enviously at them. One showed Dante, tall and dark, holding the smaller fair-haired Eden on their mating day. They both looked so young and happy. The other was Eden and the cubs: Dion the oldest, her sister Megan, and Conan, their little one-year-old brother.

Caden's heart ached knowing she would never experience love, family, and pride like her Alpha. No, her wolf mate didn't exist.

"You're very lucky, Alpha."

Dante clasped her hands and looked at her mating ring. "Oh, I know that, Cade. Everyone who meets Eden tells me that." She sat back in her chair and smiled, as if thinking of her mate. "Oh, she wants you to come to dinner soon, and she promises not to introduce you to any more potential mates."

Eden had long tried to match her up with some eligible wolves but no one had ever tempted her. "Of course I will." She gulped away the sadness she felt and smiled. "It is an honor to be invited to your family den."

"Excellent, now we better get through to the conference room." Dante put on the black suit jacket that had been hanging over the back of her chair and picked up her tablet. "I won't keep you long today—I know you're anxious to get back to the ranch office." Dante led the way out and toward the conference room.

"I am at your service, Alpha, but are you sure bringing more humans in is a good idea? They can't be trusted."

Dante sighed audibly. "Yes, I'm sure. I know how you feel about humans, Caden, but I have made my decision. We've had humans in Wolfgang County since my father was Alpha."

Caden stood and followed Dante through the corridor. "Yes, but only few in number. This human is going to be here with free rein to trample through our business, our territory. And the first human to work in the heart of our business caused great harm."

Dante stopped dead and looked into her eyes. Caden instinctively lowered her own eyes. She had seen a storm of emotion behind her friend's eyes, and she remembered the chaos that surrounded Suzy Mitchell's employment as PR executive. Mitchell's tenure had been brief and turbulent.

After she'd made several brazen attempts to seduce the Alpha in front of other wolves including Dante's daughter, Caden had been summoned to Dante's office to assist in removing her. As Caden had handed Mitchell to security, the human laughed and taunted the Alpha. Caden would never forget that day.

*Maybe your wife has someone of her own to play with. Leroux should be having some fun with her right about now.*

She remembered the fury and pain on her friend's face when they received a call to say the Mater had been attacked. While Suzy Mitchell was taking up their time, the Alpha of the Lupa pack had cornered the Mater at her children's school and effectively declared war on the Wolfgangs by laying her claws on their Mater. The Lupa pack were old adversaries but hadn't launched an attack on Wolfgang land since Dante's grandmother was Alpha.

"I know exactly what harm she caused, Second. She aided and abetted one of the most vicious wolves I have had the displeasure of knowing. Luckily, Leroux is such a pathetic specimen of a dominant wolf, she couldn't subdue a small submissive wolf like Eden."

Dante said that last sentence with evident pride. Eden had fought back and repelled Leroux's attack, and it was only Dion's turning up in the middle of the fight that stopped Dante from finishing the job. Leroux made good her escape and was still at large.

Caden had vowed never to let anything like that ever happen again. The Alpha and Mater were essential to the harmony and well-being of the pack. Without them, the Wolfgangs simply couldn't function.

"I'm sorry for mentioning it, Alpha, but it's my job as Second to keep you and the Mater safe. Having a human among us is asking for trouble."

Dante sighed. "We can't hold them all responsible for the act of one person, just as we can't judge every wolf by another's actions."

She couldn't help the soft growl that escaped her mouth. "They are all like that, Alpha. They have no rules, no code by which they live. I know personally what kind of destruction they can bring."

Dante stopped at the conference room door and put a comforting hand on the back of her neck. "I know you do, Cade, but not every human is bent on hurting us. Trust me?"

"Of course. You need never doubt it." Caden gave a brief nod and followed her Alpha into the conference room. But she could not let go of the anger deep inside. *Humans are always a threat.*

Selena sat on her bed in her new apartment, overwhelmed by the mess and boxes all around her. The movers had left not long ago, and now she was alone, and the full enormity of her new life hit her. She was truly out on her own now.

She had nearly turned back a few times on her way here, but as the city streets and roads turned to country farming communities and forested backdrops, she began to calm slightly.

Wolfgang County and the surrounding areas were beautiful, and as she passed through the ancient natural environment, it seemed like she was entering a different world. Maybe in this new world she could be a different person, not the anxiety-ridden woman she was at home. She'd approached the county line and slowed down to look at the sign. It read *Welcome to Wolfgang County* and pictured two wolves with smaller wolf cubs standing beside them howling at a moon in the night sky. It was then that she thought of what her uncle had told her: *Follow your heart and follow the moon.* Maybe this new job was meant to be?

Her cell phone beeped with a series of text messages and her stomach churned when she saw they were from her mother.

*Let me know how your first day goes, and remember to wear something that flatters.*

*You insisted on taking this job, Selena, so you better make sure you don't embarrass the family as you are prone to.*

*You've made your bed, Selena, now lie in it.*

Selena threw the cell phone on her bed, her positive mood now vanished. She looked at the mirror on the closet and was, as ever, displeased with what she saw.

"Fat and clumsy," she heard her mother's voice say.

The mess and chaos around her further agitated her anxiety. She grabbed for her purse on the bed and took out a long tin case that held her collection of pens. She counted them out. "One, two, three, four, five," handling each one, putting it in its place again.

Selena repeated the ritual twice before closing the tin and holding it to her chest, breathing in the calming effect. She knew it might be an odd habit, but it worked to quell her anxiety, and that's what mattered most.

Okay, it was time to get this apartment in some sort of order.

## Chapter Two

Caden walked up the long driveway that led to the Alpha's den. As she got closer she noticed Dante standing beside her car, watching Eden through the family room window with a huge smile on her face. Eden was dancing around the room with Conan, their youngest, in her arms.

"Alpha?"

No response. Dante was lost in her happiness. It wasn't for nothing their kind used the phrase *drunk on love* to describe the complete adoration two mated wolves felt for each other—half a joke, Caden thought, since wolves couldn't tolerate alcohol and never touched the stuff. But if someone who didn't know observed Dante right now, *drunk* was exactly how they'd describe the look on the Alpha's face.

She walked closer and Dante finally scented her friend standing beside her. "Sorry, Cade, I was lost in my thoughts."

"No apology necessary, Alpha. I would be too if I had such a beautiful family."

Dante smiled. "I was just thinking about the day of our mating ceremony. Do you remember?"

"Of course I do, you were a nervous wreck." Caden laughed.

"Can you blame me? I'd been counting down the days till I was eighteen and permitted to take Eden as my mate. It was the longest wait of my life." Eden waved at them with a smile as big as Dante's.

Caden took off her Stetson and lowered her eyes respectfully. "At least you had the den to build—that kept you busy."

Caden, Dante, and their friends had spent a year building on the large piece of land Dante's father had given her, in order to present Eden with the traditional mating gift.

"True." Dante shut the car door and picked up her briefcase. "I remember standing on the dais at our mating ceremony and thinking nothing could make me happier than this moment, but then Dion came along, a blessing from our first night together, and it just keeps getting better."

Caden looked down at her boots, hoping that she could hide the emotions that were always bubbling beneath the surface.

Dante said nothing for a minute and then, thankfully, changed the subject. "I hope you don't mind me calling you over early. I thought we could take Dion out for a run before dinner. I've had enough shouting at idiots over the phone for one day. My wolf's been clawing to get home to see Eden and the cubs."

"Of course not, Alpha. I was finished up at the ranch office for the day."

Eden appeared at the door with Conan in her arms. "Are you two coming in, or are you going to gossip like a pair of old hens all day?"

Dante gave a soft rumbling growl and hurried to her mate.

Caden chuckled behind her when she heard Eden say, "Those growls don't work on me, so just kiss me."

It always amazed her that the most dominant wolf in the pack, a wolf who could tear you limb from limb—and had just about done so to the Lupa pack Alpha—could be tamed by a gentle wolf like Eden.

Eden beckoned her to follow into the den, and she walked to the front door. *No one will ever tame me.*

❖

Selena walked into the large glass-fronted building owned by Venator. She saw the reception desk ahead, and the well-dressed, pretty girl who tended it. She dreaded talking to new people, and today would be one introduction after the other. Best to get started.

She looked down at her letter of introduction from her old job, ready to hand to the receptionist, and her hand shook with nerves. Selena observed the large foyer filled with smart professionals, coming and going to offices and the elevators, and wondered how she could ever fit in a busy place like this. She never would.

Selena turned to make her escape—now, before she had a total meltdown. The security guard gave her a strange look, seeing as she had only just come through the door.

The look stopped her in her tracks. *They don't know anything about me. I can do this.* She rummaged in her purse for her pen case, and counted them out, one by one. She closed her eyes and took a breath. This was her chance.

She adjusted her glasses and made herself turn and walk back to the desk, before she could change her mind.

"Good afternoon, ma'am. Welcome to Venator. I'm Kyra—how can I help you?"

Selena stood rigidly still and forced herself to talk. "I start here next week…and I was told to come in at"—she mentally calmed her racing heart and prayed she wouldn't hyperventilate and embarrass herself further—"at four thirty, to get my security passes and things." Selena thrust the letter forward, hoping no more explanation would be necessary.

Kyra looked over the letter and said, "Of course, Ms. Miller." She smiled and pointed to a reception area with comfortable-looking couches. "We've been expecting you. Please take a seat and I'll get someone from Human Resources to help you with that."

As Selena sat down, glad to have that part over with, she heard shouting and commotion coming from the front door. The security guards were trying to stop a glamorous-looking auburn-haired woman from forcing her way onto the premises.

"Get your hands off me," the woman shouted.

The female security guard kept a tight hold on her arm and strong-armed her back out of the entrance. Everyone in the busy reception area stopped to watch the commotion.

"What are you looking at?" the woman shouted.

"Leave now, ma'am, or we will throw you out." The guard continued to herd her away from the entrance.

The fury on the woman's face was clearly evident to Selena. A disgruntled employee?

"I'm going. You haven't seen the last of me. I know your secret. Leroux and I"—Selena caught the worried look that passed over Kyra's face at the mention of that name—"will destroy all you Wolfgangs." The staff whispered frantically to each other.

Secret? What on earth could they be keeping secret?

❖

Dante and Caden were enjoying a quiet chat in Dante's home office when they heard Eden roar at Dion. Ah, teenagers, Caden thought, offering a sympathetic smile to her Alpha.

Dante shook her head. "I think we better go out running before Eden bites the future Alpha's tail off."

Caden got up and laughed. "I remember being that age. You're so full of energy, big trouble just follows you about."

Dante sighed. "Uh-huh, it sure does. When the height of the rush hit me, I was about fourteen, and it felt like every cell in my body was on fire, and nothing could quench it. It was like I wanted to mate, kill things, and rip things apart all at the same time."

"Yeah, I remember." Caden remembered a lot. While her friends were picking out mates and exploring their sexuality, she had been alone with no girlfriend to make sense of these new feelings. "I'm glad I'm through that phase." In some ways, though, she never really had gotten through it. Her friends had been able to hush the thundering needs of their bodies by finally mate-biting and becoming one with their chosen partner, but she still felt that fire that only a mate could quiet.

She followed Dante up to the kitchen and found an enraged Eden sweeping up the remnants of a casserole dish. "Dante," Eden said, "take her out before the whole dinner is ruined, and talk to her about doing what her mother tells her."

As much as this chaotic family scene might put some off, Caden enjoyed being around it. The responsibility of being a parent and passing on knowledge and wisdom to the youngsters of the pack was something she envied, and she liked being able to take part in it vicariously through her friends.

They made their way from the kitchen to the mudroom, which led out to the large gardens and forest beyond. It functioned as a sort of changing room, with benches around the wall, shelves that Eden kept topped up with fresh clothes, and showers.

Caden and Dante found Dion sitting on the bench, her head down, looking thoroughly admonished. "I know. I'm grounded. You don't have to tell me, Pater."

"You're not grounded." Dante rested her hand on her daughter's shoulder. "You, me, and Caden are going to have a talk, little warrior, that's all."

Dion looked surprised she wasn't in big trouble. Caden sat beside her and gave her a soft punch to the arm. "We'll run some of that energy out of you."

Dante began to unbutton her crisp white shirt. "I'm not mad at you, so don't worry that you're in trouble, okay? I just want to talk to you about how you've been feeling. You're growing up fast, and I should have talked to you more about what you're feeling. Cade reminded me just how much a wolf your age feels."

Dion looked everywhere but her pater's eyes. "I'd like to talk, Pater." She sounded relieved. "I feel weird trying to explain to Mom. It's dommo stuff, you know?"

Caden looked at Dante and murmured, "Dommo?"

"Dominant wolf business." Dante winked at her. "Really, Second, you're going to have to keep up with the modern wolf world."

"Ah, yeah, we'll have a dommo-to-dommo talk, Dion." Caden smiled and started to take off her boots.

Dion rubbed the back of her head bashfully. "For a while now, I've felt weird...different."

"Tell me what you feel."

"I feel so full of energy all the time, but like, I can't get rid of it.

I know I drive Mom insane sometimes, but I can't control it, and…" Dion hid her face in her hands.

Dante rubbed her daughter's back, soothing her as they talked, urging her to continue.

"I feel so aggressive all the time, Pater, like I want to fight for no reason, just to show I'm the best. I want everyone to know I'm the best wolf, and that I'm totally bigger and stronger."

Caden laughed internally but kept her expression serious. Dion's distress was palpable.

She continued, "Then a few weeks ago, I saw Tia playing with one of the cubs from her class. He just held her hand to help her up, but I felt so angry. Before I realized what I'd done, I was in pelt growling over him. I just kept thinking *don't touch her, she's mine*. But Tia is my friend—she's not *mine*."

Dante threw her shirt into the laundry basket beside them and sat down. "Everything you're feeling is perfectly natural."

Caden remembered their school days like they were yesterday. Dante had walked Eden to every class and growled at anyone that looked her way. She had been envious but happy for her friend. It had been clear from when they were cubs that Eden was meant for Dante. They had all three been friends, but there was a special connection between Dante and Eden that always marked them out. When she had asked her grandmother why she didn't feel that connection with someone, her grandmother had foretold that her wolf mate didn't exist.

Caden remembered, and she still felt the sadness deep within her.

"We've talked about the rush before, remember?" Dante said gently.

"Yeah, I guess." The teen's cheeks flushed. "It's getting stronger though, Pater. Making me do stupid stuff."

"There's nothing to be embarrassed about." Dante reassured her cub. "It's a natural part of growing up. It's getting harder because your wolf is getting more mature, and it'll get more intense right through till you're eighteen. Second?"

Caden hung up her shirt and said, "Intense is an understatement.

Boys or girls fill your head twenty-four hours a day. It *is* hard, Dion, and for wolves as dominant as us, even more so."

Dion looked up at them and sighed. "I've always really liked girls, but lately they're all I can think about, and I feel like I'm shaking apart. I've got so much energy."

"Your mom and I always thought you might prefer girls like we do, and Caden and I just want you to know—everything you feel is normal. You feel surges of aggression for no reason. You want to fight and scrap with your friends to prove you're strong."

Caden met Dante's eyes above Dion's head and smiled at her friend. She still bore the scars of their youthful battles.

Dante put her arm around Dion's shoulders. "It's really hard, and the energy…well, that's an urge to mate. But even though you're maturing and starting to have these feelings, you are too young to mate, all right? You need to manage it other ways—play sports, go running until you can't stop."

Dion nodded. "When I heard that Lupa wolf had hurt Mom, I felt so angry. I'm sorry I followed you that day."

Dante hugged her daughter close. "Listen, little warrior, your hormones are telling you that you're an adult, but you need to catch up. You are going to be a fine dominant wolf, Dion, and I want you to know that in my absence I feel better knowing you are here to guard Mom, Meggie, and Conan."

Dion's whole demeanor changed. She raised her head, and her chest puffed out. "Thanks, Pater. I love Meggie and Conan and I'll protect them, I promise."

Dante kissed Dion's head. "You're a good wolf, Dion. And my pater had this same talk with me at your age."

Dion looked surprised. "You? What did you do?"

Caden held her hand to her mouth, trying to stifle a laugh, and Dante gave her a sharp look. "Well, I tackled a boy to the ground and held him down while I snapped and growled at him. We were playing soccer and this guy touched your mom—it turned out to be perfectly innocent, but I just steamrolled in regardless and…well, your mom wasn't speaking to me for a while."

"Make that a week." Caden laughed.

"Mom is real fierce when she's mad."

Dante rolled her eyes. "She sure is."

After a few moments of silence, Dion asked, "You knew Mom was your mate at my age?"

"I'll leave this one to you, Alpha." Caden stood and continued to undress for their run.

"I've always been close to your mom, as far back as I can remember. She was always my friend, and we were always looking out for each other. We were part of the same group all through school. When I was about ten or eleven, I remember hunting for flowers and different things like that to give her as gifts; it just seemed to creep up on me. When I was your age, I started to feel very territorial over your mother, and quite soon after the incident at soccer practice, I told her I liked her, and we started to date." Dante smiled at the memory. "It seems like I was always destined to be with your mother. I have never been interested in anyone but her. Some wolves are like that—then others like lots of different girls or boys, or both, until they find the right one."

Dion leaned forward so her dark shoulder-length hair hid her face. "I've only ever liked Tia, Pater."

Caden wasn't surprised to hear that Dion liked Tia, the sheriff's daughter and Megan's best friend. Whenever she saw the cubs together, they reminded her of a young Dante and Eden.

"I bring her gifts like you said, and she's just so beautiful," Dion said. "She makes me feel calm when I feel out of control too. I can't imagine ever liking anyone else. Do you think we'll be like you and Mom?"

"Does she like you back?" Dante asked.

Dion squirmed. "I'm not sure. She's kind of shy, and she blushes a lot when we're together, but she tries to never miss any of my games. She watches me and cheers, you know?"

"Tia's a beautiful girl, Dion," Caden told her. "You'd be one lucky wolf to have her as a girlfriend."

"Yeah, I know. Meggie said today that Tia worries I'll like some of the older girls better than her."

"Tia *is* younger than you, so you must respect that," Dante said seriously. "Tia's family will expect absolute respect from you for their daughter, especially since you are the future Alpha. Do you give me your word, Dion?"

"Of course, Pater, I would never—"

"I mean it, Dion. Think how you would feel if a dominant your age was interested in dating Meggie."

Dion's face turned angry. "I would bite them if they did anything like…you know."

"Well, that's exactly what Tia's pater will do to you if you push her too far. Got it?"

"Got it, Pater."

"Go to the movies, go running, have fun, and spend time together. If you build a strong friendship, then you're halfway there. Make her smile, and make her feel special." Dante smiled at her daughter and ruffled her hair.

"I will, Pater. I've been saving my money, and I thought I could maybe take her out for Valentine's Day, you know? I should have just enough by then."

Dante said, "That sounds great. Just remember to ask Tia's pater, okay?"

Dion nodded. "I will, Pater. I promise."

Caden hung up her clothes and said, "I can give you more work down at the ranch if you like, Dion." Dion had been working after school with Caden since she was ten. Dante and Eden brought up their cubs to realize the value of money, and of hard work.

"Good plan." Dante nodded in agreement. "Okay, let's get going. We've got some hunting to do. Lead the way, Second."

Dion pulled off her clothes quickly and dumped them in a pile. "Come on, you two. The chase is on."

Caden shifted immediately and bounded out the mudroom door.

Selena was exhausted. After returning from Venator with all her employment paperwork done and staff passes acquired, she'd set to work on putting her apartment in order. She emptied boxes and put away her things for the better part of two hours. She took a long drink of her bottled water and looked at the last large box sitting in the middle of the room.

She had unwisely packed all her books into the one big box, and realized she wouldn't have the space to shelve them. Lots of the books were old hardback textbooks, mostly on mathematics and its history. It had taken three men to carry the box upstairs, where they unceremoniously dumped it in the middle of the room.

Selena gave the box a push, and it didn't move an inch. "Looks like I'm going to have this here for the duration."

She lifted out one of the books from the top; it was one of her favorites, *A History of Greek Mathematics*. As she flicked through the old pages, she felt the warm reassurance that she always felt from her books and her numbers. Numbers were clean and predictable, and most of all, beautiful.

The tiredness she felt grew into a big yawn. It would be an early night for her.

Just as she was about to head for her bedroom, the telephone rang. She froze in the middle of the room. There was only one person who would be calling her here, and she just couldn't face her tonight after such a long, anxiety-filled day.

The voice mail kicked in and her fears were realized. "Selena? It's your mother. You never called. Since you're not there, I assume you're out jogging. Remember, don't eat too much just because you're away from home. Baby elephants don't find good men. I expect results. No slacking off because I can't check up on you. I'll call back tomorrow."

As her mother hung up, the ever-familiar dread seeped in. Obeying it as she always did, Lena went to change into her exercise gear.

## Chapter Three

Dante, Caden, and Dion ran back toward the Alpha's den as fast as they could. While they'd hunted, Dante felt something was wrong with Eden. They shifted and pulled on sweatpants, then entered the kitchen and saw Eden waiting, worry evident in her expression.

When she saw Dante she held her hands up in a calming gesture. "It's okay—I'm safe, and the cubs are safe."

"Then what is it? I can feel your tension and worry inside me."

To an outsider, Dante would have been a terrifying sight. Sweat from the hunt was rippling down her muscled shoulders and chest, her teeth were bared ready to bite and snarl, her fingers shifted to claws, and her bright blue eyes now glowed yellow.

"Blaze called from the sheriff's office. Suzy Mitchell tried to force her way into Venator this afternoon. When she was ejected she was heard to shout that Leroux was alive, and waiting to take her revenge with the Lupa pack."

Dante, barely restraining a snarl, said, "Second, take Dion and Megan to Stella's den and meet me back here. I'll call for my elite wolves. We're going out on a patrol."

"Of course, Alpha." Caden brought her arm to her chest in salute. She would escort Dion and Megan over to the sheriff's house, where they would be looked after by the sheriff's mate, Stella.

Dion hurried to Dante's side. "Pater, let me come. I can help. I'm old enough to fight."

"An adult wolf would tear you apart, Dion—do as I ask. Your job is to protect your sister. Now, go."

Dion didn't need to be told twice when her pater was in this kind of mood, and she followed Caden out of the kitchen.

As they left, Caden heard Eden say, "Calm yourself, Alpha. Leroux will never get near me again." She could feel the Alpha's rage in her blood and in that moment promised herself that they would kill Leroux even if she had to die trying. Caden would allow no one to threaten the Alpha and Mater ever again.

❖

Leroux lay in the dark of a motel bedroom. She felt every part of her body in pain. The injuries she'd sustained in her fight with Dante had been so severe that she had not yet healed, but she would soon, and she would then be able to take her revenge.

The one thing that her slow-healing injuries had given her was time. Time to think and to plan her next move. Dante was strong, to be sure, much stronger than her, but she had a weakness: Dante loved her family and pack with ferocity.

If Dante's daughter hadn't turned up during their fight, Leroux knew she would not have been able to make her escape.

Her own heart was hard, and that was the one advantage she had over her nemesis. She picked up her cell phone and called her pack Second. "Ovid, it's me."

"Alpha, thank the Great Mother. We feared the worst."

Leroux swung her legs over the side of the bed and sat up, carefully supporting her broken ribs. "I'm safe. Injured but safe."

"What happened, Alpha?"

She ran her hand through her hair. What had happened was Eden Wolfgang. Suzy had done her part of distracting Dante, and Leroux had Eden cornered. The taste of Eden's blood was like nothing she had ever experienced. Leroux felt such hunger at the mere memory of it, and her sex burned demanding relief.

"Alpha? Are you still there?"

She had nearly forgotten she was talking on the phone. "I'm

here, Ovid. I have a new plan. We are not going to only take the Wolfgang riches—we are going to destroy the heart of the pack."

"What do you need from me, Alpha?"

"I need you to contact someone on the inside. A Wolfgang who has been waiting a long time for justice."

❖

Dante's elite wolves made their way around pack land, scent-marking the border to the neighboring county. They found no trace of Leroux's scent anywhere. If there was a threat as Suzy Mitchell suggested, it wasn't imminent. Since it was getting dark, Dante ordered the wolves back to their dens but asked Caden to make sure daily patrols were stepped up for the time being.

After organizing the patrols, Caden headed home. As she ran back through the forest, she was glad of her solitude. Seeing the strength of the Alpha's love for her mate and family brought home to her all she was missing out on. She had no family to protect, and never would. The thought made her feel sad and alone, although to her pack mates she gave the pretense of loving the solitary wolf life.

Even the Alpha's cub, Dion, was starting to enter the world of mating. Her grandmother's words echoed in her brain. *Don't look for your wolf mate, Caden, because she doesn't exist. I have seen the future and your life will take a different path.*

What was her path? Did she have to be alone? She shook her head, trying to get rid of the memories, and ran fast through the trees trying to feel the energy and smells of the woodland.

As she was running a new scent brought her to a stop. She raised her snout into the air and took a huge lungful of air. The scent was strong—it smelled of sweat, but sweet, warm, and comforting, somehow. It couldn't be Leroux. *Human.*

She heard the telltale noise of twigs being broken up underfoot and hid behind a large tree to see who came by. A human female came into view, jogging through the woods, which was unusual as the sun was beginning to set.

She studied the female intently: she had light brown hair pulled back into a ponytail and was wearing sneakers, yoga pants, and a T-shirt. Her breathing was heavy, and she appeared to be struggling with the terrain.

Then everything changed. The human tripped over a branch and fell, hitting her head against a fallen log. Without thinking, Caden ran to her. Only when she got closer did she wonder what on earth she was doing by going to her aid. If the human saw her it could be disastrous.

She was out cold, and Caden licked her forehead, trying to rouse her. The taste of the human's sweat and the blood from her head injury was an explosion of sensation on her tongue. Before Caden had a chance to think what that meant, the human started to moan, and her eyes flickered open. They stared at each other silently for what seemed like an eternity before the female fell into unconsciousness again.

Caden nudged her with her snout, used her teeth to pull her T-shirt, trying to shake her awake, but nothing worked. She had to get her to a doctor.

The impulse to help a human surprised her. A memory gripped her and twisted her guts. *I'm sorry, Caden, they didn't have a chance. The human driver was drunk...*

She turned to walk away from the human, but her paws wouldn't budge. Her head said leave, but her heart and sense of decency overrode her long-standing hatred of humans. She couldn't drag the injured woman all the way to her den, so she shifted back to skin, lifted the unconscious woman, who fit well in her arms, and walked as quickly as she could through the forest.

Not how she'd expected to spend the evening.

❖

Leroux heard a car door slam outside the motel room. She stood behind the bedroom door and waited for the person's scent to filter through to her.

*Suzy.* Perhaps she could distract herself with her while her blood ran hot with thoughts of Eden Wolfgang.

When she had come across Suzy Mitchell in a bar here in Rutherford County, it had been a brilliant piece of luck. The few humans who worked in Wolfgang County all came across the county line to get a drink, since there was no alcohol in wolf communities. Suzy had piqued her interest when she heard her talking about Dante to another woman, and then Leroux began to buy her more and more drinks until she had all the information she needed. Finally, Suzy had agreed to distract Dante.

Suzy had been useful since the confrontation with Dante, taking care of her while she healed, but her usefulness would soon be coming to an end.

The door creaked as it opened and Leroux pulled Suzy into the room. "Suzy? I missed you."

Suzy gulped nervously. "You did?"

"Of course, a wolf always misses its mate." Suzy backed up to the wall as Leroux walked toward her. She might have been horribly injured, but she still towered over the human. Leroux lifted her hand to stroke Suzy's cheek, and smiled when she flinched. "That's what you want, isn't it, Suzy? A werewolf for your own? That's why you helped me get close to the Wolfgang Mater, so you could have Dante all to yourself."

Suzy's breathing became more rapid as her fear increased. "Yes, but…"

Leroux stroked her hair softly and brought her lips close to Suzy's ear. "Shh…I know. Dante wasn't wolf enough for you. She is nothing but her mate's bitch, but you have a real Alpha wolf now."

Suzy's hand began to shake. "Of course I want you. How are you feeling?"

"I'm feeling almost healed and then I'll be whole for you." Leroux sniffed and nuzzled into her neck. "Did you get the information I wanted?"

"No, I couldn't. I was escorted off pack land by security guards. They wouldn't let me near the town hall."

"Why?" Leroux snarled. "Town hall security has never seen

you before. You were to slip in, get the records I wanted, and get out."

"I went to Venator first. I wanted to speak to Dante for just a few minutes. She humiliated me. I had to speak to her."

Leroux grabbed her by her hair and spat, "You stupid bitch." Leroux's teeth and hands lengthened to sharp points. "You've just outlived your usefulness."

❖

Caden paced the hospital corridor relentlessly. She hadn't felt anxiety for anyone but her pack mates before, but even though she despised humans, she didn't want this one to be badly injured. The female had looked so fragile lying on the forest floor, and she wanted to make sure she was okay before they went their separate ways.

A white-haired doctor came out of the hospital room and saluted Caden. His name tag identified him as Dr. Jaycen.

"How is she, Doctor?"

Dr. Jaycen smiled. "She is very interesting. It's fascinating how human physiology works. They are so fragile."

"But how is she?"

"Oh, she'll be fine, but she is suffering from a slight concussion."

Caden breathed an internal sigh of relief. "Does she remember?"

"No, she says she has no memory of the accident. She just remembers running."

"Good, so what happens to her now?"

"If she had relatives or friends, I would release her to their care, but she says she's just moved to the county and has no one. She needs to be wakened throughout the night. Unless you—?"

Caden's indifference slipped back into place. She put her Stetson on and said gruffly, "I have important pack matters to take care of, Doctor."

Dr. Jaycen lowered his head, taking on a submissive posture. "Of course, Second. I'm sorry for mentioning it. I suppose I feel a little sorry for her. She seems to be a nervous creature, like a deer always on the lookout for predators."

Caden felt bad for walking out on this human, and that made no sense. "Let me know how she is tomorrow, Doctor, and please don't tell her who brought her here."

"Of course, Second."

Caden walked out of the hospital into the night and had no idea why she felt guilty. She'd done more than enough for the human. Yet her comforting scent lingered.

## Chapter Four

A week later there had been no sign of Leroux, but the Wolfgang territory was large, and the Alpha still had her wolves searching and patrolling the area. Caden had stationed guards around the Alpha's den to protect her family, but so far everything had been quiet.

Caden hadn't been in the best of moods lately. The threat from the Lupas lay heavily on her shoulders, and the arrival of a new human had stirred up a lot of old emotions—and today she was called to the conference room to meet her. Dante walked into the Venator conference room for the twice-weekly board meeting. Her PA Marcy followed behind.

Caden rose at the Alpha's entrance, and everyone followed her lead.

The Alpha took her place and said, "You may sit." One chair remained notably empty. "Marcy? Where is our new employee?"

"She must be running late, Alpha. I emailed her the meeting details, so she does know."

"Hmm." Dante shook her head. "Well, it gives us a chance to speak in private." She turned to Caden. "Thank you for joining us, Second. I want to introduce you all to our new member of staff, if she ever gets here. As you are all aware, we have recently changed accounting firms, and they have sent one of their best people to audit our business, so they can give us a clear picture of how we're doing. Caden, I asked you to join us because she's going to be starting with the ranch."

Caden felt anger bubble in her stomach. She knew this was a mistake but would never question her Alpha in front of the other wolves. She had very little tolerance for pen pushers and paperwork, and even less for humans, but she would do as she asked, without question.

"I know it's not ideal, Caden, but you're my Second, and you know every inch of our business, so if you could, make sure she has everything she needs and doesn't see or hear anything we wouldn't like discussed outside the pack."

"Of course, Alpha. I'll see to it."

Dante looked at her watch and growled. "I hope this isn't an indication of Ms. Miller's timekeeping."

At that moment, everyone's attention was drawn to the glass conference room doors as a woman hurried toward them, carrying files and a laptop case. Several wolves snorted with laughter as she struggled with the glass doors, expecting them to open inward, but Dante just raised a quizzical eyebrow.

"It looks like Ms. Miller has arrived."

Selena's first morning at Venator had been a complete disaster so far, but that was nothing unusual in her life.

She could hear her father's voice as if he was right next to her. *Selena, you're a clumsy fool. Stand up straight, shoulders back.*

Walking into a packed conference room was her worst nightmare, especially after making a fool of herself, but there was no turning back now.

Selena eventually managed to navigate the apparently difficult doors and rushed into the room like a whirlwind. "I'm really sorry I'm late. I was going to be early, but then I couldn't find the room, and then…" She hesitated when she realized the rest of the room was looking at her in stunned silence. "Well…anyway, I'm sorry I'm late." She felt a burning heat flash up her neck and face.

The commanding woman at the head of the table, her new boss, Dante Wolfgang, gave her a smile and indicated the empty chair waiting for her. "I think we can forgive you this first morning, Ms. Miller. Please sit down."

Her head down, Lena hurried toward the safety of the empty chair, grateful as ever that her long, wavy hair covered her face like a blanket of protection. Her foot caught the leg of the chair and then everything seemed to happen in slow motion. The files she was carrying and the laptop went up into the air.

She waited for the pain of hitting the floor, but it never came. Instead, she fell into a pair of strong, reassuring arms. When she looked up into the eyes of her rescuer, she saw a flash of gray and yellow in her mind, but the memories were gone as soon as they arrived.

"Are you okay, Ms. Miller?"

"It's Selena…um, Lena."

"I'm Caden." The way this woman said her name made her shiver.

She looked silently into Caden's eyes. *I know her.*

Lena's heart raced, and she reached out her fingers to touch Caden's face with curiosity but was interrupted by Dante clearing her throat.

"Is everything all right? Are you hurt, Ms. Miller?"

"I'm okay, Ms. Wolfgang, thank you." As she realized the room was watching them, she saw Caden become conscious of their predicament. Caden pulled her back to her feet and gathered up the files for her.

"Thank you, Caden."

"No problem," Caden said gruffly and quickly handed the files back to Lena and hurried off back to her seat.

When Lena realized her rescuer's chair was way over on the other side of the table, she couldn't imagine how she had gotten to her in time.

Her boss interrupted her thoughts. "If everyone is okay, perhaps we could get on?"

Lena took her seat but still had her eyes locked on Caden. There was something about her that seemed familiar, and she stood out because she wasn't dressed for the office like everyone else in the meeting—she had on jeans, a checked shirt, and cowboy boots, and a Stetson sat on the table in front of her.

She felt a nudge from someone beside her. The woman next to her whispered, "Hi, I caught your laptop. It's good as new."

"Thank you."

"Now if we could get to business," Dante Wolfgang boomed.

❖

Caden drove Lena over to the farm office in silence. She had been shaken up by her reaction to seeing the woman she rescued again.

She had just acted on instinct when she'd seen the woman falling and couldn't understand it. She could have risked the pack's secrets by showing how fast she could move and remembered the hard stare Dante gave her.

When she had taken her to the county hospital, she never imagined she would see the woman again. Then this morning, the same woman had fallen into her arms. She looked a little different though. Her long hair was not tied up—it hung long, wavy—and she wore a pair of black-framed glasses.

It had thrown her completely when she looked into her eyes. She had felt something, a stirring recognition within her, that she didn't understand. She concluded it was a mixture of annoyance and anger.

Caden stopped her truck outside her office, which was a timber-framed building overlooking the livestock fields. Around the office was a busy barn and stable area, where all the horses and equipment were kept and lots of pack members went about their business, mucking out stalls, looking after the equipment, and tending the animals.

She opened the truck door and saw Lena trying to gather her things together. "Leave your things and I'll lift you out." She didn't hesitate to reach in and lift Lena up in one movement.

"What do you think you're doing? Put me down," Lena snapped.

Caden was taken aback at the quiet young woman's sudden anger. "What? I'm trying to help you." Lena wriggled in her arms and Caden couldn't help but notice how her short business skirt rode up, revealing a fleshy thigh. She ran her tongue over her fangs as she was hit with an image of her biting into that thigh.

"Put me down," Lena repeated, rousing Caden from her lustful thoughts.

"Huh?"

"You can't just pick someone up that you barely know and lift them out of a truck like a child. Put me down this minute."

Caden was not used to being spoken to like that. All but Dante and Eden followed her instructions. This was the type of insubordination and anarchy humans brought to the pack, and she didn't like it one bit.

"If that's what you want, Ms. Miller." Caden let Lena's legs and feet drop into the muddy puddle beneath them with a splash.

Lena let out a shriek as her shoes submerged in the cold muddy water. "What did you do that for?"

Caden gave Lena a serious look. "If we are going to work together, you'll need to learn that when I give a command, it is always for a purpose, and advisable for you to follow it."

Lena was clearly fuming. "Of all the arrogant—"

Caden adjusted her Stetson. "Oh, and wear more suitable footwear from now on." With that, she marched off toward the farm office, leaving a mucky and furious Lena behind her.

When Lena made it to the office, Caden informed her that the spare desk and computer across from her own would be hers, before walking out with no further explanation. After setting out her pens and equipment exactly how she wanted them, Lena should have started to work, but she couldn't get rid of the anger swirling around inside her.

What had she done?

She had given up the safety of her former apartment to start a new independent life, away from the suffocating scrutiny of her parents, all to come and work with the most domineering and arrogant person she had ever met.

When she had fallen into her arms, she had felt safe there. They had looked at each other and connected somehow, but Caden had changed completely on the drive over to the farm.

Lena felt a sense of steely determination rise inside her. She might not be able to stand up to her family, but there was no way she was going to let someone she didn't even know subjugate her. Lena determined that her new life in Wolfgang County would be different. It had to be different.

❖

Caden found her thoughts troubled for the rest of the day. At night her dreams were filled with old memories and hurts that she tried to keep buried, deep down where no one else could see.

*"No, no! They can't be gone," Caden screamed.*

*Dante's father kneeled and pulled her into his arms. "I'm sorry, Caden. No matter how strong your parents were, they had no chance when the car was engulfed in flames. The pack will take care of you. Pack always takes care of its own."*

*Caden pushed the Alpha away angrily. "I want that human's throat. Please, Alpha? Take a hunting party and make the human pay. Kill him."*

*Dante's mother, Iris, walked closer and said, "The human police have arrested him, and he's most likely going to jail. We can't interfere now. Come with us, cub. We will take care of you." Iris opened her arms expecting Caden to fall into them.*

*Caden howled and kicked the table and some chairs over. "I swear I will make humans pay for what they have done. They are evil creatures who deserve to die."*

The dream suddenly changed, and now she was in pelt, a full-grown adult. She was standing over the unconscious form of Lena, in the forest. Blood dripped from her fangs, and Lena lay dead with her throat ripped out. What had she done?

Caden awoke from her sleep, gasping. "It's just a dream," she repeated over and over like a mantra. "You could never hurt her." Could she?

❖

The next day, Lena was just finding her feet in the office and going through the computer system for the files she would need. After their altercation yesterday, she was glad that Caden was barely in the office today. When she did come in, she was even more dismissive and arrogant than the previous day.

Lena watched her look manically through the paper files on her desk, and grumble and growl when she couldn't find what she was looking for. Caden thumped her fist on her desk and cursed. "Damn order sheet."

*Uh-oh*, Lena said to herself. She had that document right in front of her. She had picked it up by accident, with some of the other files she needed for her work this morning, and had forgotten to put it back.

Her heart thudded with anxiety as she plucked up the courage to say something. "Um, Caden?"

"What?" Caden barked.

She held out the order form and said, "Is this what you were looking for?"

Caden took one look at the document and snatched it from her hands. "Why do you have this? Have you been snooping around my desk? You are to ask permission for anything you need here."

After years of her father's temper, Lena felt shell-shocked. An angry Caden was the most fearsome thing she had ever seen, but strangely she didn't bury her own feelings deep down inside and say nothing as she usually did.

She felt an unusual burst of confidence as she sprang from her chair with fury. "Don't you dare talk to me like that. I am not one of your farmhands who you bark orders at all day—I am a professional doing a professional job. I have the perfect right to look at any documents I feel are applicable to my job." Lena was shocked at herself. She never talked back to anyone.

Caden took a step toward her and snarled, "You don't just walk into my territory and take my things."

They were so close to each other and pulling closer. She watched as Caden ran her tongue over her teeth and exhaled a low breath. Lena's heart hammered hard in her chest.

This was the first time in her life that she'd had the courage to stand up for herself and she wasn't stopping now. "This isn't about a stupid document. You have had a problem with me ever since I arrived yesterday. Do I offend you so much?"

"Yes, humans like you, from outside the county, and your way of life offend me. If you want to come into my territory, then you play by my rules. Just like everyone else."

Lena's righteous anger was fading fast, and in its place was a sadness that again she was being dictated to. In a small, sad voice she asked, "Why do I make you so angry?"

The tone of Lena's voice seemed to stop Caden in her tracks. She was silent for what seemed like forever. Her breathing was heavy, and Lena noticed her eyes fixed on her neck. The look in Caden's eyes made her shiver.

Caden turned away and stomped out of the office, slamming the door after her. Lena sat back down at her desk and tried to calm herself and her shaking hands.

## Chapter Five

For the first two weeks of working alongside Lena, Caden tried to keep out of the office as much as possible. She wasn't used to sharing her personal space with someone—especially a human someone, who did not take her instructions.

She thought back to the fight they had in her office. She had been so angry at the human encroaching on her territory, but when Lena had stood up to her, all she could think of was sinking her fangs into her elegant neck and sucking on its throbbing pulse point. She had felt the saliva fill her mouth in preparation, and her sex burned for her.

She had never found a human attractive before and she was furious with herself every time the memory of it popped into her head. She had tried to console herself with the fact it was probably just a need for sex, but the feverish need she had felt was more than she had ever felt for an attractive wolf.

After those tense few weeks, she found herself spending a bit more time each day in the office with Lena. She told herself it was simply so she could keep a close eye on this potential threat to the pack, but deep down there was more. They never mentioned the argument and hardly ever spoke to one another unless it was a question about work, and even those questions were frosty. For some reason it troubled her that the human didn't like her, and she couldn't work out why.

This morning, Caden actually whistled as she arrived for work, something her wolves didn't often see from the serious lone wolf.

She walked into the ranch office and threw her Stetson onto the coat hook without even looking and sat at her desk.

She turned her gaze over to Lena, who was looking at her in a somewhat surprised and impressed manner.

"Hi, that flip took years of practice," Caden said, trying to cover for her physical abilities.

Lena gave her a shy smile and put her head back down again. That one shy smile caused a thaw in the atmosphere and in Caden's heart. She sat at her desk and watched the quiet young woman with fascination. Although they had spoken rarely to each other over the weeks, Caden had spent the past several days studying Lena, and in that time she noticed a lot of her idiosyncrasies.

It was the little things that had struck her, little things that a wolf could see that maybe a human wouldn't notice. Caden had purposely not spent a lot of time with humans before, but she didn't think Lena was typical of their type. She saw that Lena was obsessed with order and neatness. Her pens, pencils, and stationery were set out on the desk in order of size and color, and she seemed insistent about keeping them in the prescribed order and took time to make sure they were as she wanted them. She noticed the way Lena would push her hair behind her ear and bite her lip when she was thinking hard, but would pull her hair down to cover her face if anyone came in the office. And the way she would tap her nails on the desktop for five minutes before asking Caden a question, as if she had to build up her courage to do it. The scent of anxiety poured off Lena and it made her sad that another creature felt like that, even if it was a human.

One thing that was strange: no matter how quiet things were in the office, she didn't feel the silence was awkward between them. In fact, she felt very comfortable just sitting quietly.

Her contemplation was interrupted by one of the staff from the ranch cookhouse coming in for her lunch order. He came to a stop in front of her desk and started to salute, but Caden quickly shook her head.

"Caden, what can I get you for lunch?"

"I think I'll have the T-bone steak with an extra-large portion of fries on the side, and a large slice of apple pie with ice cream. Thanks, Avery."

Avery smiled. He pulled out his notebook to write the order down and grabbed a pen from Lena's neat lineup of pens and pencils, knocking the rest out of order. Caden saw the look of panic and horror on Lena's face and immediately felt bad for her.

"I think we should ask before we borrow, shouldn't we, Avery?"

The wolf looked confused until Caden indicated with her eyes to her office mate, feverishly realigning her things.

"Oh? Yes, sorry, ma'am. I should have asked—here you are."

Lena gave Caden a grateful smile and said, "Thank you, you can use it."

"Would you like anything to eat from our cookhouse, Lena?" Caden offered. "Our food is very good." She had noticed that all Lena seemed to eat every workday was a small salad she had brought from home.

"Thank you, but no, I've brought mine with me."

*You eat like a little bird, Miss Miller. Why?*

"That will be all then, Avery." He gave the pen back, and Lena immediately put it back into its ordered place.

"Lena, please feel free to use the cookhouse facilities while you're working here. The food is free and provided by the company."

Lena started to tap her fingernails on the desk nervously. "Thank you, but I'm on a diet, and so I really have to stick to the salad I bring from home."

Caden was quite taken aback and immediately said in all innocence, "A diet? Why?"

Lena blushed, clearly uncomfortable with the conversation. "That's a very personal question. You shouldn't ask a woman that."

"Why shouldn't I?" She thought she would never understand humans—pack shared everything. There was no embarrassment, no secrets, and she wasn't going to let Lena off the hook. "Tell me," Caden said flatly.

Lena furrowed her brow in annoyance. "If you must know, I need to lose a lot of weight, and if I ate something like a steak and fries I'd need to run three times a day, and once is enough for me."

She couldn't imagine why Lena would want to lose that sort of weight. Lena had a soft, curvaceous figure just like any submissive wolf should have.

"Oh? You run every day?" Caden asked. She had assumed after the accident that she wouldn't have gone back out running in the evening. With Leroux's threat hanging over their heads, she didn't want a lone female like Lena out there on her own.

"Yes, every night. It's not my favorite thing to do, but it helps. At least it's a lot more picturesque to run in Wolfgang County than the city."

Caden was grateful that Lena brought up the subject. It gave her the opportunity to warn her about setting off into the woods alone. "You have to be very careful where you run around here, Lena. There are wolves and other wild animals in the forest."

Lena's eyes went wide. "Wolves?"

She got up and walked over to sit on the chair beside Lena's desk, feeling the need to get closer. "Yeah, you're not in the city now. The animals are drawn down from the hills by the cattle and deer herds we keep."

Lena's nervousness and anxiety were obvious as her fingers began to tap the desk in front of her. "I had no idea. The first day I moved here, I went for a run in the forest. I got lost, and I don't remember much, but I slipped and knocked myself out. I woke up in the hospital. The doctor said someone left me in the emergency room. If they hadn't come along—"

On instinct, Caden leaned forward and placed her hand over Lena's much smaller one. "Don't worry about what might have been. Someone found you, and that's all that matters." She thanked the Great Mother she had found her. Her chest tightened at the thought of Lena lying on the forest floor, unconscious and helpless.

"I wish I knew who found me, so I could speak to them."

She looked directly into Lena's dark green eyes and said, "What would you say to them?"

Lena's breath caught as she met Caden's gaze. "I would say thank you for saving me. Thank you for protecting me."

She squeezed Lena's hand and said, "I'm sure whoever it was knows that." Caden leaned back in her seat, releasing Lena's hand.

"I still have to run though. I have to exercise."

"Why?" Caden asked.

"To lose weight. I hate it, but I have to do it."

Caden cocked her head to the side trying to work out why a female with such a womanly figure would have to lose weight. "Stick to running around town—if you stick to the populated areas, you'll be okay."

"I will, from now on."

Caden nodded and got up to go over to the cookhouse for her lunch. She picked up her Stetson from the hook and turned back to Lena. She was itching to say the words that kept running around her head. "Lena? I know it's none of my business what you do with your life, but can I say something to you?"

"Yes, if you like," Lena said.

Caden walked closer to Lena's desk, holding her hat to her chest. "I'm just a simple farmer, Ms. Miller. I don't know how you city people see it, but from my experience the skinny, underweight, weak female will not attract a mate and breed."

Lena looked up from her seated position and forced herself to hold Caden's determined gaze. "No?" She found Caden's unique way of relating people to animals endearing, if not a little blunt.

Caden leaned over the desk, coming well within her personal space. Lena instinctively lowered her eyes, as her heart raced in her chest. These were not her usual symptoms of anxiety. The feeling was different, exciting even.

"The well-fed, stronger animal is more able to attract a mate, produce young to carry on their genes. When I look at you I see…a healthy young woman. You are perfect as you are, but I'm telling you that you must eat."

There was a calm, authoritative tone to Caden's voice. She was obviously someone who was used to having her orders followed. Lena would normally cave to someone as commanding as this, but strangely she felt an unusual confidence when she was in Caden's company. It gave her the strength to voice her true feelings.

She watched Caden walk toward the office door and asked, "What about you?"

Caden looked confused. "What about me?"

She looked up and down Caden's body, as she had done many times since meeting her. "You're not like me. You're tall, lean, and muscular. Why is it okay for you to be slim?"

Caden appeared to consider her answer carefully before saying, "I am a hunter and protector. My body fits my purpose. Every animal in nature has a purpose."

Lena could feel energy between them. An energy that drew her to this stubborn, domineering individual—and it scared her. "What's my purpose, Caden?"

Caden put her Stetson on carefully and smiled at Lena's question. "That's up to you to work out, Lena. Be careful though—the answer might not be what you expect."

Lena and Caden's truce didn't last long. When Caden returned from the cookhouse, she brought with her a huge delicious-looking beef sandwich and a piece of apple pie. She placed them on Lena's desk and said, "Eat it."

Without further explanation, Caden walked out of the office, leaving Lena enraged. "What kind of person orders someone to eat? How dare she." Lena picked up the food and threw it straight in the trash.

When Caden arrived back later and saw the food in the trash beside her desk, she growled and stomped off out of the office. Lena's heart thudded hard in her chest. It took a lot to stand up for herself, but it felt good not to do as someone told her for a change.

She could stand up for herself.

## Chapter Six

That evening the Alpha and Mater hosted some of their friends at their den for a very special celebration. Caden was walking up toward the gates that stood tall in front of the Alpha's den. She spotted Stella and Tia ahead of her, each trying to carry some big bakery boxes.

"Hey, Stella. Wait up." Caden sprinted over and took the boxes from them.

"Oh, thanks, Cade, you don't realize it's that far from our den, but that's quite a hill with heavy boxes."

"Where's Blaze?" Caden asked, shouldering the gate open as she asked. Blaze was Stella's mate, one of the Alpha's elite wolves and the county sheriff.

"He called to say he would be late and he would meet us here. He did tell me I should drive, but I thought it was a nice night and we would just walk." Stella sighed.

"So you got something tasty in here, Tia?" Caden asked Tia.

"We've got a great cake for the new cub."

She smiled at the shy young girl. The whole pack was buzzing after the announcement that the Mater was expecting a cub. There was nothing wolves loved more than new cubs. Cubs meant health, fertility, strength of the Alpha pair and the pack, and a great cause for celebration.

"That's great, Tia." She turned to Stella and smiled. "Another one for the Alpha, Stella? I think she's trying for a whole soccer team."

As they approached the den door, Stella nudged her and said, "You've got a lot of catching up to do, Second—you better find a nice little wolf soon."

Caden smiled and shook her head. "Don't start on the mating thing again, please."

Stella laughed, but Caden's heart gave a silent pang. She never stopped hearing about settling down with a nice little wolf. Although she played along, projecting the committed lone-wolf image, her friends didn't know how much she wanted what the rest of them had, but she knew with certainty that was something not meant for her.

The large oak double doors opened, and Eden flashed a smile to her friends.

"There she is," Stella declared, "the most fertile wolf in Wolfgang County." Stella engulfed her in a hug.

Eden gave Tia a hug and told her all the other cubs were out back, and she ran off happily. "Hmm," Eden said with mock annoyance, "it seems our Alpha only has to look at me to get me pregnant."

"I bet Dante did more than look at you, Mater," Stella teased.

Caden cleared her throat, feeling uncomfortable at the direction the conversation was taking.

"Sorry, Cade, we're embarrassing you," Eden said.

"Congratulations, Mater. I know the Alpha is over the moon at the news." This Caden knew for certain, for as soon as Eden had told Dante, she had run in the forest, howling with joy, broadcasting to her wolves so that they would join her and share in her joy. Caden, Blaze, Flash, and her other elite wolves had heard, and ran to chase, play, and proclaim the virility of their Alpha.

"Thank you, Cade, and yes, she's full of energy and excitement. Drop those cakes in the kitchen and go and help her play with the cubs. Flash and the rest are already out there."

Caden bowed her head and made her way to the kitchen, gratefully leaving the intimate den talk behind her.

❖

At the back of the Wolfgangs' large timber den, there was a huge landscaped garden. There were no fences or barriers—the yard simply led into the forest, giving the family private access to all the Wolfgang lands.

The backyard was alive with laughter, noise, and wonderful smells. Over on a raised custom-built cooking area, two pack members roasted deer over an open pit, while others, led very ably by Dante's mother Iris, were putting out side dishes, cutlery, and drinks on a row of outdoor tables around the perimeter, where pack mates, family, and friends sat, enjoying drinks and watching the dominant wolves play soccer with some of the cubs, while others ran around squealing and playing their own games. And the Alpha was in the middle of it all, holding Conan in her arms.

Caden walked out in the garden, and Dante greeted her with a wide smile.

Caden thumped her hand to her chest in salute. "Alpha. Congratulations again. The pack grows from strength to strength under your and the Mater's leadership."

Eden and Stella come out and headed over to Iris to help with the food. Dante's gaze followed her mate. "I wouldn't be half the Alpha without Eden."

Conan waved to Caden, and she took the one-year-old from the Alpha, ruffled behind his ears, and tickled his stomach, making the baby laugh. "Come here, little wolf." Caden always loved playing with the Alpha's cubs, and they loved playing with her.

"Where's Blaze? I didn't see him come in with Stella."

Caden threw Conan over her shoulder like he weighed nothing, making the little boy giggle all the more. "He's held up at the station. Stella says he won't be long."

"Good. Come on, you two," Dante said. "We've got games to play."

❖

The meat was finally ready, and the Alpha was called over to the spit to ritually take the first bite. Dante and Eden stood on the platform and said a few words before eating.

"My wolves, thank you for coming to our den to share in our joy. The Mater's pregnancy shows, yet again, what a strong and fertile pack we have. We can take great heart from the fact that the Wolfgang pack will walk on our lands for generations to come."

Dante took Eden's hand and kissed it reverently before lifting it in the air to the acclaim of the pack. She howled in joy and the pack joined in.

One of the pack, who had been cooking the deer, brought a plate full of meat and thumped his chest as he handed it over. Dante took a piece of meat from the plate and ate it before taking another succulent piece and popping it in Eden's mouth.

Caden took her place behind the Alpha's cubs, to join in the ritual. The Alpha was entitled to first bite, and the act of sharing her food with the Mater gave the signal that the two wolves were bonded, and that the Alpha would always provide her mate with food. Dante handed the plate to Dion, and each of the cubs took one bite. Then it was Caden's turn. After taking a bite, she returned the plate to the cooks, and Dante declared, "Eat, my wolves."

As the wolves stood in line for their food, Caden noticed Dion getting an extra-large portion of meat and walking proudly across to where her sister Megan and Tia were sitting. As she watched Dion starting the mating ritual by sharing her food with Tia, it suddenly struck Caden what she had done today: she had brought food for Lena.

She had offered Lena food. What was she doing, giving food to a human? *I just felt sorry for her. It didn't mean anything, and anyway, she threw it away.* Caden felt an unexpected sense of sadness at that thought. She'd offered Lena food, and she'd thrown it away.

❖

Caden joined Dante and her family to eat. "This is good, Mater," she said. She and Dante had finished a huge portion of meat and were now working on some of the delicious side dishes that she and some of the other wolves had brought, but her favorite was the Mater's potato salad. She was eating her own meal with Conan on her knee, feeding him little bites of the meat.

"Thanks, Cade, I'm always happy to see my wolves eating well. You don't eat enough home-cooked food."

Caden thought back to today at the office, and how her offer of food to Lena had been disregarded. Beneath the anger, what she really felt was hurt at the rejection of her offer, and she didn't like that emotion one bit.

"You need to find a nice wolf to share mealtimes with, and stop eating takeout all the time," Eden said.

Caden sighed and played with the food on her plate. She watched the closeness of the Alpha and Mater. Dante always kept a possessive paw on Eden, and she envied it. Wolf couples were normally extremely tactile, but even more so when one of the pair was pregnant. Caden couldn't even imagine the happiness that would bring. To love and protect a pregnant mate was a dream, and all it would ever be, she thought sadly.

"You know I'm not destined for a mate." She was becoming tired of having this conversation. This was the second time tonight—first Stella and now the Mater.

"A wolf mate, yes," Eden said.

Caden looked up sharply. "What do you mean?"

Eden fed Conan a piece of meat and looked to Dante and then back to Caden. "Just like I said. Your grandmother said you weren't meant to have a *wolf* mate."

Caden thought hard. "What other kind of mate is—" Lena's face burst into her mind. A human mate.

She dropped her fork onto her plate, and Eden just smiled at her. Oh no. No, no, no. That was not going to happen.

Dante filled the silence by saying, "If the right one comes along, I'm sure she'll tell you. I know Eden did."

Caden did not like the smug look on Eden's face as she continued to feed Conan.

"That's my good little cub. Eat up all your food, and you can have some cake. Good boy," Eden told the smiling boy.

"Pater?" Megan said.

"What is it, my sweet cub?" Dante answered while munching on more food.

"Why isn't Dion sitting with us to eat? She always eats with us."

Dante gave Eden a desperate look, but Eden just smiled in response. "Well, Dion asked permission to share her food with Tia, and your mommy and I thought that would be okay."

Megan seemed to think about this information very carefully. "So if I find a wolf I like, I can go and share their food?"

Dante's lip curled into a snarl, and Eden immediately jumped in to say, "Well, when you find a nice wolf, we can talk about it, Meggie."

Caden pitied any young wolf that came to the Alpha hoping to start mating rituals with her daughter. They would need to be stupid, brave, or both. Wolves were always worried about a submissive cub's first foray into mating, male or female.

Eden nudged Dante. "What? Oh yes, Meggie, of course. We'll talk about it when…when you're a bit older."

Caden ruffled Megan's blond hair. "And when some wolf that's worthy enough comes along. Eh, Alpha?"

"Exactly. Thank you, Second."

Megan seemed to take this very well and said happily. "Okay. Dommos are yucky anyway—well, except Dion and maybe Nix when she's not being annoying."

Caden laughed softly. Phoenix, another of Dion's friends, had a nose for trouble.

"Yes, they are yucky. Just remember that, my sweet cub," Dante said seriously, and Eden glared at her, but she just smiled in return. "What?"

They were interrupted by Dion and Tia running up to the table.

"Mom, Pater? Some of the other cubs are going running in the forest—can I go too?"

"Me too, Dion?" Megan said excitedly.

"Sure, Meggie," Dion said generously.

Eden looked to Dante and then said, "Have you asked your mom, Tia?"

"Yes, Mater. She says it's okay as long as Dion is there and we don't go too far."

"Well, okay then, but be careful," Eden said.

"Dion, watch out for your sister, all right? She and Tia are your responsibility," Dante told her daughter.

Dion gave her pater an arrogant dominant smile. "Sure, Pater. I always look after the missies."

The cubs all turned to pelt and dragged their clothes to neat piles by the edge of the forest before running off into the trees.

Caden looked confused. "Missies?"

"Submissive wolves," Eden said with a smile. She lifted Dante's arm around her shoulder, so that she and Conan were hugged tight to the Alpha's side. "That's what the cubs call it these days."

Dante laughed. "Sometimes when I listen to the cubs yap away to each other, I feel old too, Second."

Eden rubbed the side of her face into Dante's chest. "How could you be old, Alpha? You are so virile and have just sired another cub."

Dante gave a low growl. "When you say things like that, Mater, it makes me want to howl and—"

Caden cleared her throat. "I think that's my cue to go play with the cubs." It was hard enough to watch the many happy wolf couples without being up close to the Alpha and Mater about to devour each other. "Can I take Conan for you, Mater?" At the offer, Conan struggled to get to her.

"Where's my big cub?" Dante lifted Conan into the air and blew a raspberry on his stomach, making him giggle and laugh, before handing him to Caden. "I'll join you in a few minutes, Cade."

As Caden walked off, she smiled when she heard Dante whisper to her mate, "I'll hold you to that promise you just made, Mater. I want to make you howl."

The festive mood was broken when Blaze arrived. Caden felt the sheriff's tension as he entered the backyard. His mate Stella ran to him. Blaze immediately took her into his arms, as if needing the calming touch of his mate.

Stella sought to soothe him by rubbing her head against the side of his face. "What's wrong, mate?"

"Where's Tia, Stella?"

"She and some of the other cubs went running. Tell me what's wrong?"

Caden and Dante strode quickly over to them.

Blaze thumped his chest in salute to both the Alpha and her Second. "Alpha, Second, I have news. We must convene your elite wolves."

All the wolves stopped what they were doing. The Elite wolves started to gather around their leader.

"Wolves, we must go to the war room."

"Alpha, I think you should call the cubs back as a precaution," Blaze told her.

"Andor, Victor," Dante shouted. Two of her younger dominant wolves hurried over. "Andor, go into the woods and bring the cubs back here, and Victor, protect the Mater."

Eden hurried over and Dante took her into her arms. "Stay close to Victor. As soon as I know what's wrong, I'll tell you, okay?"

Eden nodded, and Caden and the elite wolves followed Dante into the den.

All thirteen members of Dante's elite wolf squad sat around the large conference room table, situated in the basement of the Alpha's den. At the head of the table sat Dante, and Caden next to her. "Blaze? What have you found?"

Blaze tapped the laptop in front of him, and the large war room screen showed the police computer system. "Just before I left the station, a police officer called from Rutherford County. A woman was found dead in a motel room, not far from the highway. That may not be unusual in itself, but when you see crime scene photographs, I think you'll understand why I was immediately concerned."

Blaze clicked open the crime scene folder and set the pictures to play in sequence. Dante growled and broke the pen she held in her hand at the sight.

The pictures showed an auburn-haired female lying in a pool of blood and, crucially, badly mutilated.

"Is that Suzy Mitchell?" Dante asked.

"I think so, Alpha. Her face is badly injured, but her physical description fits and she had her ID badge in her purse."

"What did the police say about the murder, Blaze?" Caden asked.

"The forensic pathologist reports that the injuries indicate some kind of animal attack. The police don't even know where to start with it, as you can imagine."

"It fits, doesn't it?" Flash said. "Suzy boasted that she had helped distract you, allowing Leroux to attack the Mater. Leroux was so badly injured after your fight, she would have needed help to survive."

Dante nodded. "Second? What's your opinion?"

"It's been a month, Alpha. Leroux may not have been strong enough to shift until now. She would have needed help, and if Suzy has been helping her, then she found out our secret. She probably thought she could use Leroux to get her revenge on us."

Dante walked up to the screen showing the bloody pictures. "And when Leroux was nursed back to health, she bit the hand that fed her." Literally.

"A detective will be coming to interview you tomorrow, Alpha," Blaze said.

The Alpha smashed her fist down on the conference table, and her eyes flashed yellow. "I want her found. I don't need to remind you that she attacked the Mater. She declared war on the pack when she laid a paw on my mate. Now she's bringing humans into our territory with questions and suspicions. Caden, I want you to step up patrols around our territory. Blaze, I want officers around the school, and my den."

"Yes, Alpha," they replied.

"Flash, I want you and Robin to head to this motel. See if the scent matches Leroux, and if it does, find out where it's headed."

"Right away, Alpha," Flash said.

Robin was a recent appointment to the elite wolves and jumped up eagerly, ready to go straight away, but Flash indicated for her to sit. No one was to move until the Alpha dismissed them.

"Oh, and Flash, please apologize to Vance for my taking you away from your den at this time, but rest assured I will station two wolves to protect your family while you're gone."

"Thank you, Alpha."

Dante walked back up to her place beside Caden. "The rest of you will join Caden's patrols."

She indicated for them to stand and said, "Good hunting, my wolves."

"Good hunting, Alpha," they replied with a salute.

All the wolves filed out of the war room except for Caden, who hung back to talk to Dante. "Alpha?"

"Yes, Cade?"

"You could send me to track Leroux's scent at the motel. That would leave Flash free to protect his mate and cub. I have no such concerns," Caden said sadly.

"I need you here, by my side, Second. If Leroux is anywhere near here, I don't want you outside the county. I want you here, ready to hunt with me."

Caden nodded. She understood why the Alpha wanted her here, but Flash had a den to protect, so she should be on the hunt. "Yes, Alpha. I understand."

It was then that she thought of Lena, in her apartment all alone. Would she be safe? She felt an urge to go to her and stand guard. Why was she thinking this way?

"Cade, can I say something to you?"

"Of course, Alpha. We've been best friends all our lives."

Dante sat on the table beside Caden and looked down at her. "I know you don't like talking about your private life, and I didn't want to say too much in front of Eden. I know she, Stella, and Vance can be a bit overbearing in trying to match you up with mates—"

"It's just because they care, and I appreciate that," Caden said.

"Yes, but it's my duty as your friend and as your Alpha to make sure my Second is healthy and happy. You shouldn't be on your own, Cade. You should have a mate and cubs to protect."

Caden sighed and said with frustration, "I don't need a family—I have the pack."

"We all have the pack, Cade, but we need the close bond of a mate to keep us healthy and strong, for the pack. What your grandmother told you…"

Caden jumped up and walked toward the screen still showing the pictures of Suzy Mitchell. "You know she had powers, Dante. She was right before." She had lived with her grandmother, Rhea, from the time her parents had died. Rhea had always styled herself as a mystic. Most of the pack thought she was an eccentric old wolf, but Caden knew better.

"That was just coincidence, Cade."

"What? She had a premonition that my parents would be in great danger from a human if they left Wolfgang County on a business trip, and they died, by the hand of a drunk driver. That's a coincidence?"

Dante walked up to her and put her hand on the back of her neck, connecting with her, and trying to soothe her. "I remember the pain the pack felt when your parents died, and I remember your pain. We'll never know if it was a coincidence or not, but that doesn't mean she was right about you. She shouldn't have told a young wolf, like you were, something like that. You've been alone all this time because of that. It's not natural."

"It's not as if I've stopped myself, Alpha. There has been no wolf that I've felt that way about, and by my age, I should have—I mean, I feel the urge to have sex, but not mate. My grandmother said my wolf mate doesn't exist, and I'm sure it must be true, or I would have met her already."

Dante patted her on the back and said, "If that's how you feel, okay. I just want you to happy, Second. You're my closest friend."

"I know that, Alpha. I look at you with Eden and the cubs, and how happy they make you, and I ache to have the same, but it's impossible." An image of Lena lying on the forest floor popped into her head. She took a breath and said honestly, "My wolf isn't out there."

"I won't bring it up again. I'll join you to organize the patrols once I've spoken to the Mater about the situation. Leroux touched my mate, and I want her throat."

A verdant green apple and a bottle of water sat atop Lena's kitchen counter. She leaned on the counter and stared at them. She had never seen something so utterly depressing. After a day of hard work and not much to eat, her pre-jogging snack looked joyless. It was strange that she'd had thoughts like these a lot since moving to Wolfgang County.

Back home it had been easier to stick to her strict regime of diet and exercise. Her mother always survived on cups of coffee and meds from her doctor, as did most of the women in her family, but here, people were more relaxed. The pace of life was slower, the countryside greener, and the fruits and vegetables brighter, the meat juicer.

She thought back to what Caden had said to her: *the skinny, underweight, weak female will not attract a mate and breed.*

Weak was exactly how she felt at the moment. The prospect of a run after the energy boost of one solitary apple was horrifying. Then she thought about the delicious-looking beef sandwich and apple pie Caden had brought her. "Oh God. Why didn't I eat it?"

She laid her forehead down on the counter. It had been so hard not to eat it, so hard when it was sitting on her desk tempting her. It wasn't the only thing that tempted her. Caden might be arrogant and domineering, but she was absolutely gorgeous, even more delicious looking than the beef sandwich.

Lena had never met a woman like her before, someone so athletic and powerfully built. She exuded such extreme confidence, her staff would obey even the slightest look from her, but it wasn't out of fear. She sensed it was out of deep respect. *I'd love to eat a beef sandwich with her, naked—but she can leave the cowboy hat on.*

She pushed herself up from counter. She was going mad from lack of nourishment. There was nothing else to do. She picked up the apple and took a big bite. A memory of Caden running her tongue over her teeth popped into her brain and shot lower. *Don't even think that now, Lena.* Caden was brash and arrogant. Not nice.

The strange thing was when Caden looked at her, as aggravating as she was, she didn't look at her with disappointment as her family did. In fact, she couldn't remember anyone she had passed in Wolfgang County who looked at her with contempt or pity like her family and former work acquaintances did.

Lena jumped when she heard a banging at her door. She didn't know who it could be since she didn't know anyone. She hurried over and looked through the peephole and saw Caden standing there, her Stetson in hand.

"Oh my God, it's her." She quickly untied her ponytail and tousled her hair. What was she doing? She didn't even like Caden.

She took a breath and opened the door. Before she could say anything, Caden said, "I can't stay, I need to get back out on the hunt. Don't go out running tonight. There's a…cougar…yes, a cougar has killed some of our cattle. It's not safe."

Caden looked a little wild, and Lena noticed her shirt wasn't buttoned correctly, as if she'd dressed in haste. As if she'd just gotten out of someone else's bed.

When she didn't reply, Caden said, "I have to go. You'll stay inside tonight?"

"Surely it's safe in the town—"

"No," Caden said firmly. "Look, I don't have time. I can't be out doing what I have to do and worrying about you. Stay inside and lock the door, understand?"

Again Caden's orders infuriated her, and she crossed her arms in defiance.

"Do you understand, Lena? This is for your own safety."

"Yes, all right." No sooner had she conceded than Caden shot off without saying a single word.

Lena stepped back inside and slammed the door shut. Who did Caden think she was? Then what Caden had actually said hit her. *I can't be out doing what I have to do and worrying about you.*

Caden was worried about her.

With that thought, she turned around and locked the door, making sure to put the chain on too.

## Chapter Seven

The next day Caden was out riding with some of her farmhands checking on the Black Angus herd. They raised two different types of grass-fed herd, the Angus steers and the Murray Grey. One of the reasons the Wolfgangs were so successful in the meat business was because they had been organic farmers before it ever become fashionable. This was the part of her job that she loved the most, working hands-on with the animals in the fresh air, and with Flash away, she needed to take on some of his responsibilities.

She closed her eyes and took a moment of calm in her busy day. The only sounds were the wind and the mooing of the cows, but as she listened to the sounds of nature she felt a yearning deep inside, a yearning to go back to the ranch office and sit with Lena.

After breakfast, she had been glad to get out of the office. She had again returned from the cookhouse with food for Lena and placed it on the desk beside her. Lena had looked up at her, sighed, and then continued with her work, ignoring the lunch by her side. The food remained untouched until one of the farmworkers had come in to talk to Caden, and Lena had taken the opportunity to put the food in the trash. Caden had been furious.

"Why do you do that?" she'd demanded. "I'm telling you to eat for the good of your health. Why can't you just do as I ask? It's for your own good."

"Why do you keep giving me orders, just like last night?" Lena snapped back. "Why do you care about what I do?"

Caden hadn't known what to say to that. She didn't know herself. "I don't. Starve yourself, for all I care."

It had turned into a battle of wills, and Caden didn't like to lose, especially to a human. She'd grabbed her Stetson and stomped out of the office in a furious mood, but her time out riding had brought some calm perspective. Lena was such a conundrum. She made her feel annoyed, frustrated, and agitated but yet she still hungered for her company. Every time she thought how much she missed her, she despised herself for it.

She looked over to one of her men and said, "Everything looks good, Gregor. I'm going to head back to the ranch."

As she started off, her cell phone rang. It was the Alpha, so she slowed up and took the call. "Alpha, how may I serve?"

"Flash called to report in. They found Leroux's scent all over the motel and grounds."

"Did he say where the scent led?" Caden asked.

"They followed it to the next county. She's heading north, back to Lupa pack lands, they think."

"To lick her wounds, no doubt."

She heard Dante sigh. "I'm not sure. Something doesn't feel right. I can't explain it, but I think there's more going on here. In any event, I've asked Flash and Robin to keep following her scent and see where it leads."

Caden stroked her horse's neck to calm it. It could obviously feel her tension. "At your command, Alpha. I'll keep guards on both Flash's and Robin's dens while they're gone."

"Thank you, Second. Report in if you find out anything. Good hunting."

Caden rode back toward the office, jumped off her horse, and let one of the farmhands lead it off. Her attention was drawn to the noise of spinning tires far up the dirt track road leading to the farm. Her exceptional hearing picked out Lena's hot-pink Porsche struggling against the mud.

She set off at a run and within seconds was standing silently behind Lena looking at her tires. "Having trouble?"

Lena let out a yell and clasped her hand to her chest. "Oh God! Where did you spring from? You'll give me a heart attack."

"I'm a hunter, Lena. I'm supposed to be able to sneak up on my prey." Lena blushed slightly and Caden's heart sped up at the thought that she had caused it.

"So I'm prey now, am I?" Lena asked.

She stroked her chin, considering the question, and again the image of that succulent, fleshy thigh popped into her mind. "I haven't decided yet. So, what happened, and where are you going?"

"I thought I saw an animal in the bushes, and as I tried to get close enough to see it, I veered off onto this grassy shoulder and got stuck. I've got a checkup with Dr. Jaycen at noon, and I'm running late now."

Caden walked around the car, checking the state of the tires. She crouched by the back wheel that was most embedded and said, "Yeah, you're stuck all right. Did you ever think a pink Porsche maybe isn't the best vehicle for farm country?"

"Look, it wasn't my choice, *nothing* is my choice, so I just have to get on with it. If you could just get me one of your guys with a truck to pull me out, I'll be on my way," Lena said angrily.

*You're a feisty human, aren't you?* She saw Lena look in her bag frantically and then count to five twice before letting out a breath. She had noticed Lena doing that frequently with her pens in the office and could only guess she was doing the same thing now. Dr. Jaycen was right. She was a frightened little deer.

Caden stood and took off her hat. "We don't need a truck. Just go and sit in your car, and I'll push you out."

Lena crossed her arms and said in a sarcastic tone, "You'll push me out?"

Caden pulled herself up to her full height and said, "Yeah, we're made of stronger stuff out here, city girl. Maybe if you ate some more, you would be stronger too."

She had meant it as a joke, but she felt awful when Lena's face crumpled before her and tears welled in her eyes. "Lena, listen, I'm—"

Before she got the chance to finish her apology, Lena jumped into her car and slammed the door shut.

"Good going, Wolf."

Lena started the engine, so there was nothing more to do than push the car out. Caden could have done it easily with one hand, but she had to make more of a show to cover up her unusual strength. As she pushed the car out of its trap, the wheels splattered mud back onto her face. Lena didn't stop as her car sped away down the farm road, leaving Caden to wipe the thick mud from her face.

Which she guessed she deserved.

❖

Caden made her way down Main Street to the New Moon Bar and Grill. After being drenched from head to foot in mud, she had headed home to her den for a shower and to change. The loneliness of her den made her head back into town to eat. She craved the company of the other wolves.

As she entered, the bar customers stood in respect of her position as Second, but she waved them to sit down. She took off her hat and threw it onto the bar.

Judy, a waitress, greeted her with a smile. "Second, good to see you. What can I get you?"

"A large chocolate shake with caramel syrup—oh, and could you put a lot of syrup in it, Judy?"

"Your fangs are going to rot one of these days, Caden," she joked.

"Yeah, yeah. You sound like my grandmother."

"So? You want something to eat?"

Caden picked up the menu and looked down at the options. "You know it. Um…"

At that moment all the chatter in the bar fell away to silence. Judy looked toward the door and said, "Human?" with surprise. The few humans who did live and work in Wolfgang County seldom patronized the local bars because they were non-alcohol establishments, and they tended to live in neighborhoods close to the Rutherford County line.

The strange thing was, Caden didn't scent human. She scented warmth and excitement, but also, strangely, anxiety. She turned around quickly, worried that she hadn't scented the human the other wolves had, and saw Lena, hanging back by the door, looking around at the bar patrons watching her closely.

Some wolves who were not sympathetic to humans looked at her with disdain, and a few of the dominant ones—there were some wolves who enjoyed the novelty of sex with humans—looked at her lustfully.

Caden was on her feet in seconds and over by her new workmate. "Lena? Are you okay?"

Despite how they had parted earlier, Lena looked relieved to see Caden beside her. "Yes—I was looking for the store, and I got lost. I don't have any groceries in my apartment, you see. I've been shopping in the supermarket in Rutherford County until now, but it's closed for remodeling, and I wasn't sure…"

Caden smiled at her. She was beginning to learn that when Lena was nervous or anxious, she tended to ramble. "Hey, slow down. Come and sit with me by the bar and tell me all about it, okay?"

Lena smiled and showed visible relief that she now had Caden by her side. Caden put her hand on Lena's shoulder and guided her toward the bar.

Caden looked around the bar. The chatter and atmosphere had returned now that the pack's Second was escorting the human, but those few dominants interested in the human for base sexual reasons continued to appraise her, until Caden met their eyes and subtly bared her teeth, without letting Lena see.

Their eyes immediately fell away from the human. No wolf would disrespect the second most dominant wolf in the pack, especially when she had placed a possessive hand on the female to claim her.

"Take a seat, Lena."

"Thanks." She sat up on the bar stool and Caden joined her. "Listen, I'm sorry you got muddy earlier, I—"

"Hey, don't worry about it. I deserved it. I know we haven't gotten off to the best start, but how about we call a truce?" Caden couldn't believe she was even saying this to a human, but when she was with Lena she forgot she was human, and her enemy. There was something so vulnerable about her that made Caden want to protect her.

Lena smiled shyly. "I'd like that, thanks."

Caden felt Judy watching her closely, and probably wondering why she was being so friendly to this female. Her hatred of humans was well known. "Judy, this is Selena. She's working with me at the ranch."

Judy gave her a warm smile. "Selena? Goddess of the moon, eh?"

Lena blushed. "Yes, I guess so, but call me Lena. It's nice to meet you."

"Pleased to meet you, Lena. Can I get you something?"

"No, thank you."

"Okay, here's your shake, Caden."

Lena looked down at the drink and smiled at her. "Milkshake?"

"Well, I have a very sweet tooth, and there's no alcohol in Wolfgang County."

"Really? I mean, not that I drink very often, the odd glass of wine, but why isn't there any alcohol?"

Caden thought carefully about how to answer that. "We find alcohol doesn't suit our community very well." She tried to change the subject quickly. "So…you said you were lost?"

"Oh. Yes, I'm looking for the grocery store. I thought I could come in and ask at the bar." Lena looked up and gave her a smile. "I wasn't expecting everyone to look at me like I'm the new cowboy in town."

Caden laughed. "I guess we're not used to a lot of new faces, but it's okay now? Yeah?"

"Yes," Lena agreed. "Now that you're here, I feel better."

"Great." Caden felt an unexpected surge of joy, that her presence could make Lena feel better.

Judy came back over and said, "So, Caden? You were just about to order?"

"Change of plan, Judy." Caden grabbed her Stetson and took Lena's hand. "I'm going shopping with Lena. Come on."

Lena allowed herself to be pulled up from the bar stool, but held her hand up in front of Caden. "Wait. You don't have to do that—you were just going to eat. If you could point me in the right direction, I'll be fine."

"No, it'll be fun, and I need some…um…" She looked at Judy, searching for something to say, but Judy just smiled back at her floundering. "Milk. I need milk and cookies."

Lena looked skeptical. "Milk and cookies?"

"Yeah, sweet tooth, remember?"

"Well, if you're sure."

Caden took out her wallet and handed Judy a couple of bills for her drink. "I'm sure. See you later, Judy."

Lena continued to be surprised by Caden's behavior. One minute Caden was dismissing her and being downright arrogant, and then at other times she would be so kind to her, like last night, and today going shopping. But despite everything, she had to admit she felt so much happier walking down Main Street with Caden by her side.

As they walked, she noticed that those they passed in the street all lowered their eyes and gave Caden what she was sure was a bow of the head. And she'd noticed that when Caden had escorted her to the bar, everyone immediately stopped staring at her and looked away. Caden seemed to be a very important figure in this insular little community.

"Here it is." Caden ushered them into the town supermarket and pulled a cart from the line at the front of the store. "Now, I don't go food shopping too often, so why don't I push this thing, and you point me where you want to go, okay?"

Lena found herself looking in Caden's icy blue eyes and felt her heart thud rapidly. "That would be great. Thank you for doing this."

"No problem."

Lena directed them to the fruit and vegetable section first, and Caden followed eagerly, watching the cart pile up with healthy items. "Lena, do you eat meat at all?"

"Oh yes. Mostly I eat chicken and fish, because it's so healthy. I do love red meat, but when I eat it, it just lands right here." Lena smacked her hand against her hip.

Caden immediately imagined sinking her teeth into that curvaceous hip and making Lena moan. Lust rushed through her and forced a growl from her throat.

Lena looked back from the head of the cart and said, "Did you say something, Caden? You're not going to give me a lecture about eating again, are you?"

Caden felt out of control around this human. Lena bypassed her logical mind and made her angry, frustrated, attracted, and lustful, but above all, Lena made her feel, something she hadn't done for a long, long time. "No lecture. I was just going to say that I couldn't live without getting my teeth into a juicy piece of red meat every day."

She saw Lena blush at her words and wondered what she was thinking.

They walked around the store in quiet companionship, Lena collecting different bits and pieces she needed for her new apartment. Caden was surprised at how comfortable she felt, taking part in such a domestic task. She was happy to follow Lena around the store like a little cub.

The only time they split up was when Caden went in search of syrup for her milkshake. They were far enough apart for Lena to think she couldn't see her, but her superior vision spotted Lena quickly put a large steak into the cart, hiding it under the other items.

Strange. If Lena wouldn't eat that, why was she hiding it?

Then it hit her. Lena had bought it to cook for her. The happiness that she immediately felt inside was overwhelming, and she hurried back to her new friend.

"Did you get what you needed, Caden?"

"Sure. Where to next?" A small part of Caden chastised herself for sounding like an excited cub.

"Just some bottled water to get now," Lena said with a smile.

They set off to find the drinks, and as they rounded the corner, came face-to-face with Eden, Stella, and Vance, Flash's mate. The three friends looked surprised at seeing Caden in the store, and even more pushing a shopping cart with an unknown human.

"Caden?" Eden said.

*Oh God. I'm going to be the hot topic in den talk now.*

"Eden, hi. This is Selena. She's doing an audit of all the Wolfgang accounts, and she's started with the ranch accounts first." Caden knew her discomfort must be obvious.

Vance and Stella giggled at Caden's embarrassment, but Eden just kept smiling warmly.

"Lena, this is Dante's wife, Eden."

"Pleased to meet you, Mrs. Wolfgang," Lena said.

"It's lovely to meet you, Selena. This is Stella, and Vance."

After they all shook hands, Eden said, "I hope you're settling into our little community."

Lena pushed her glasses up on her nose, nervously. "Oh yes, it's a beautiful place. I'm still getting my apartment all set up, you know, and Caden kindly offered to show me to the store. It's a sweet little town—I'm sure I'm going to love it. My apartment's kind of a mess at the moment, but…"

Caden could scent the anxiety and tension Lena felt at meeting these new people. She wished she could put her arm around her and make her feel secure, but she knew her three friends would tease her mercilessly as it was.

"Yes, it's a great town," Lena said finally, and then looked down at her feet.

Eden looked at Caden knowingly, and she could feel the blush burnishing her cheeks.

Vance winked at her and gave Lena a big smile. "I hope you'll come over for tea with us one day when you're free."

Caden was now squirming on the spot, and it got worse when

Stella chimed in, "Yes, it'll give us a chance to get to know you better—after all, the only conversation you'll get out of Caden here is about animals and farm machinery."

Vance and Stella giggled again, but Eden brought the interrogation to an end. "Well, we'll leave you to it and let you finish your shopping. Lovely to meet you, Lena, and I hope to see you again soon."

As they walked away, Lena said, "What nice people, Caden."

"Hmm." Caden watched them walk away, whispering to each other, and she knew she wouldn't hear the end of this. "Yeah, lovely."

## Chapter Eight

"Are you sure I can't carry anything?" Lena asked Caden, who was laden down with shopping bags.

"No, I'm fine. Just lead the way to your apartment."

She led Caden up two flights of stairs and they arrived at her apartment door. As she unlocked the door, Lena looked at Caden, who was holding five bags in her arms as if they weighed nothing. She had never seen anyone, man or woman, who had such strength and confidence in their body, and it was so attractive.

"Thanks for helping me."

"No problem."

They walked into the apartment and Lena heard a growl from behind her. "Is everything okay, Caden?"

"Of course. Where do you want these bags?" Caden replied unconvincingly.

She pointed Caden over toward the kitchen side of her open-plan living space. "You can put them anywhere in there." She followed Caden in and immediately put away the ice cream she had bought.

"It's a nice place," Caden said.

"It's okay, I suppose. There's still so much to do." She gestured at the huge box sitting in the center of the room that held her collection of books. "Excuse the mess. I did ask the movers to put it in the spare bedroom, but they just left it there. It's so heavy."

Lena watched open-mouthed as Caden walked over and picked up the box as easily as she had hefted the groceries.

"Where's the spare room?"

How could she? "That door there," she stuttered, pointing to a doorway on the other side of the room.

Caden entered the room, put the box on the floor, and was overwhelmed by the scent of Lena, just as she had been when she walked into the apartment. She growled low in her throat, and her heart thudded. She took deep calming breaths, trying to regain control of her wolf. She was both shocked and angry that she had a reaction like this to a human. This had never happened before, not even with another wolf.

Just as she was about to leave, she saw a silk scarf hanging on the back of the door. The scent that emanated from it drew Caden like a beacon. She picked it up, held it to her nose, and inhaled Lena's scent. She closed her eyes and felt the same dizzying sensation that she'd felt when she entered the apartment.

"Are you okay in there, Caden?" Lena shouted from the other room.

"Yeah, be right there." In a panic, and on impulse, Caden stuffed the scarf in her jeans pocket. She headed back into the main room and wondered why Lena was just staring at her. "What is it?"

"It took three men to carry that box from the moving van."

Oh, shit. Caden was unused to mixing with humans and hiding her supernatural abilities. The only thing she could do was brazen it out.

"Well…they must have been in really bad shape because it wasn't that heavy at all. I mean, I'm wrangling animals every day, so I've got to be strong."

"I suppose. Thanks, anyway."

"No problem. Is there anything else you need done?" Caden asked.

Lena walked over to her and gave her a shy smile. "No, no, you've done plenty. I'm really grateful for your help."

The smile made Caden's heart beat double time. No matter whether Lena directed anger or a smile at her, each elicited a response from her heart and her body. "Okay, well…" She found herself stepping closer to her, wanting to pull Lena into her arms.

"Would you like to stay for some dinner? Just to thank you for your help?"

Caden watched Lena nervously fiddle with her glasses and push her hair behind her ears. When she had seen Lena secretly put steak and a large tub of ice cream into her cart, she knew it was for her and felt a sense of excitement at the thought of sharing a meal with Lena. It felt far too good. *She's a human. Get out of here.*

"That's really nice of you, but I already have plans." Caden felt like an absolute bastard as she saw Lena's face fall in sadness, before she forced an obviously pretend smile on her face.

"Oh, that's okay. It was just an idea. You probably wouldn't enjoy a big salad anyway. I don't have any meat or anything you would like, so it's probably best."

What made it worse was that Caden knew that was a lie. She could see through the false smile, feel the disappointment and hurt Lena was feeling. "Maybe another time?"

"Yes, sure." All of a sudden Lena was hurrying her out the door. "See you tomorrow, Caden. Have a good night."

"Yeah, bye." Caden found herself out in the hallway, and the door shut behind her. She heard muffled sobs coming from the other side of the door. Fuck. She'd handled that brilliantly. She was the only person Lena knew in the whole county and she'd made her cry. Oh yeah, she had big plans for tonight. Big plans to go back to her den on her own.

Her frustrations were so fierce that she wanted to bite something really badly. She leaped over the banister and dropped two flights of stairs before running out of the building and heading to the forest. There was only one path that could soothe her wolf, and that was to run, hunt, and howl her frustrations away.

❖

Leroux stood in the shadows of a junkyard waiting for her Wolfgang contact. Before her father died, he told them about one family in Wolfgang County who was not loyal to the leadership.

A lone male jumped the tall junkyard gate and landed with ease. He was definitely a wolf. A dominant wolf at that, but not as powerfully built as she. Kurtis, her contact.

He had long dark hair that was held in a ponytail, and he wore a long leather coat. She watched him survey the area, all the time sniffing the air and trying to work out where she was. As he got closer, she prepared to strike, and within moments she leaped out at him and pinned him to the floor.

Leroux held him in the dominant position, daring him not to submit. Her face and claws were partially shifted, and she lowered her face to within inches of his, and the saliva dripped off her fangs onto his face.

He looked terrified, and it sent a thrill through her, especially when he offered his neck.

"Stand up, Wolf."

He stood and brushed himself down. "Leroux, I'm honored to meet you."

"I imagine you are, Kurtis." She walked around him assessing his reactions. She could smell his fear.

"Are you well?" he asked her, and she smiled when she saw his hands tremor.

"I grow stronger every day. My father told me about your family. You were once ranked highly in the Wolfgang pack."

"My grandfather was pack Second to Dante's grandmother. He hated the way she was leading the pack, not expanding pack land, working with humans so closely and giving them respect when we should have been conquering them. He switched sides to fight with the Lupas when your grandmother attacked, but when she was killed, he was made to beg for his life. I hate Dante as much as you. My family has been reduced to nothing in the Wolfgang pack—they do not have my loyalty."

Leroux felt his hatred. It ran deep, and he could certainly be useful in her plans. "My father made me vow on his deathbed to avenge his mother and take the Wolfgang riches. If you and your family help me, you will be returned to your rightful place."

Kurtis immediately dropped to his knees and bowed his head. "I swear my allegiance to you, Alpha."

She made him stand, clasped the back of his neck, and pulled him in close. "Welcome to the Lupa pack, Wolf. If you ever cross me, I will rip out the throats of everyone you love, understand?"

"Yes, Alpha."

Leroux released him and asked, "What news from your pack?"

"Dante has sent two wolves to track you, and the Mater..."

Leroux walked up close to Kurtis. "What about the Mater?"

Kurtis was still visibly shaking with the enormity of what he had done here. "She is pregnant again."

Leroux began to laugh maniacally. "Perfect. Dante is going to be distracted. This will make her defeat all the more glorious. I may even keep Dante barely alive, so she can see me take her Mater as my own, with her cub in her belly. It will destroy her."

Caden was restless. Since leaving Lena's apartment, she hadn't known what to do with herself. She felt bad for hurting her. There was nothing on earth that would have made her happier than to share food with Lena, and that's what had scared her so much.

She paced up and down the living room of her small cabin, which sat on the edge of the forest. It wasn't big but suited her needs, since she had no mate to provide for.

She walked over to a picture of her grandmother sitting on a side table, and picked it up.

"What's wrong with me, Grandma? Why do I feel like my blood is on fire? Like I want to scratch and bite...I want to bite down on something so badly. I've never felt like this before, why? Humans are destructive, they can't be trusted, but this one..."

She held the photo to her chest and closed her eyes. In her mind, all she could see was the silk scarf that she had hastily stuffed in her pocket at Lena's apartment. It seemed to be speaking to her like a siren song, and she could no longer resist. She pulled it out and held it to her nose. The scent told the story of her new human workmate. As with everything that held Lena's scent, there was first a sense of anxiety and nervousness, but after she got past that layer, the scent opened up into a myriad of dizzying elements: flesh, sex, hunger, love, and den.

Caden could not resist the urge to bite and taste any longer, snapping her jaws into the scarf with a growl. The taste was so overwhelming that she shook it in her mouth like a cub with its favorite toy. Her blood thrummed with energy and became so hot, her wolf couldn't be held back. Her canines bulged, and her face contorted and began to shift. She ripped off her clothing with a roar, and her wolf burst forth. She sprinted out of the cabin and headed into the deep, dense forest, leaving Lena's scarf sitting on top of her pile of ripped clothes.

## Chapter Nine

Caden spent the next morning out working, and not much time in Lena's company. After having lunch in the cookhouse she walked back toward the ranch office. Unusually, she hadn't enjoyed the companionship of the other wolves today, preferring to sit alone with her thoughts. After the events of yesterday, she felt disturbed. Disturbed that she couldn't keep this human woman out of her head, and that she had spent most of last night trying to run off the feelings that Lena's scent had produced in her.

She also felt terrible that she had made Lena cry yesterday. She never wanted to cause her pain, but she had been so frightened at how much she made her feel. She'd just had to get away from her.

To Caden, Lena was beautiful, and her very scent made her ache for things she hadn't before. She had, of course, had sexual feelings before, but this was different—it was an urge to mate, to join as one, to protect, and to make a den.

Several of her staff nodded and spoke to her as she passed, but Caden was too lost in her own thoughts to acknowledge them.

She jumped up the outer office steps and found the inner door closed. She could hear Lena's voice filled with anxiety, and a more muffled voice on the other end of a cell phone conversation. She knew she should walk in and make herself known, but something inside told her she needed to learn more. She stood close to the door and tried to pick out the conversation.

The other voice said, in imperious tones, "Selena, I hope you are making a good impression with Ms. Wolfgang. Your father says they may be a little strange in Wolfgang County, but the Wolfgangs are extremely powerful and influential in the business community, and this could be the leg up you need in your career. You're already five years behind where your brothers were at your age, and since you're not pretty enough to attract yourself an advantageous marriage, you're going to have to excel in your career. You know what your father expects from his children."

"Yes, Mother," Lena replied meekly. "I'm doing my best. They're really nice people to work with."

Caden had to stop herself from bursting into the room, reaching down the phone, and throttling Lena's mother.

"Hmm. Just make sure Ms. Wolfgang notices that you're doing a good job. Remember, this is what *you* wanted. How much weight have you lost this week?"

"I…I…"

"Don't tell me that you didn't lose anything this week, again, Selena."

Caden could scent how anxious and stressed Lena was and just wanted to go in there and take Lena in her arms. So this was who made her feel so bad about herself. *I would bite her for you if I could.*

"I'm sorry, Mother, I'm really trying. I took a few weeks off from my running because I had a fall, but I'm back on it, and I've cut down my calorie intake again."

"Well, I expect to see better results, Selena. Remember, no one wants to see you with that flabby stomach and those chunky thighs of yours."

"I know, Mother. I'll do better next week. I promise."

"See that you do. Remember, your father and I will expect you home to attend his birthday celebration. Try and find a dress that flatters."

"Okay, speak to you soon, Mother. Good-bye."

And with that, the call ended.

Caden took a deep breath to calm herself. If she went in there like this, with the anger rolling off her, Lena would know she'd been listening.

These people were the ones who made her into this nervous, anxious creature who wouldn't eat. How dared they?

Caden could spend forever worshipping Lena's thighs.

She slapped herself in the head. Why was she thinking that way about Lena?

But still, Lena's mother's criticism was an entirely foreign way of being to Caden. In Wolfgang County, family and pack lifted you up to help you achieve more than you ever thought you could—they didn't beat you down constantly, trying to mold you into something they found acceptable.

Lena needed someone to show her what a beautiful, wonderful, pretty girl she was.

Her brain told her she shouldn't, but her heart and her wolf told her she should be that someone. Determined, she made plenty of noise to pretend she had just walked into the outer office and made her way to Lena.

She could see instantly Lena's eyes were red from unshed tears, but she didn't make any mention of it. "How are my accounts looking?" she said cheerfully.

Lena wiped her eyes and tried to put a brave face on. "Great. You keep very good records."

Caden sat down at Lena's desk and said, "I hate it. It's the worst part of my job. I'd rather be out there, on my horse, riding over our land."

Lena smiled. "Why don't you get an assistant or a secretary or something?"

"No way, I wouldn't like to share my office with someone else."

"I'm sorry, would you like me to work somewhere else? I could—"

*Well done, Wolf.* Caden leaned forward and covered Lena's hand with her own. "Not you, Lena. I like your company."

The corners of Lena's mouth turned upward to a smile. "Really? It doesn't seem like it. We've argued since I arrived."

"Nah. I'm just not used to having friends who don't follow our structured way of life. I didn't like to see you not eating, and I wanted to help. Normally my instructions are followed."

"Caden, I came to start an independent life here. Not to follow instructions."

"Of course, I'm sorry. It's just my nature. But I'd like to be your friend. You're smart, kind, and beautiful." Caden only half noticed she had been stroking her thumb over the back of Lena's hand the whole time she was talking.

"Now I know you're just being nice." Lena looked down at her desk as if trying to cover her insecurities.

"Hey?" Caden raised her chin with a fingertip. "I never say things I don't mean." She lost herself in Lena's big hazel eyes, until Lena smiled bashfully and looked away.

*How can a human make me feel like this?* Feeling scared, Caden stood and went back to her own desk to get some distance between them. "So, did you get some lunch, Lena?"

"Yes, my usual salad, thanks."

She had no right to question Lena, but she cared. "What kind of salad? Chicken?"

Lena turned away and suddenly found the figures onscreen very interesting. "Just a salad."

"I know it's none of my business, Lena, but why wouldn't you eat the food I brought for you?" Lena seemed about to reply when there was a knock at the office door. "Come," Caden called.

She smiled when Dion strode in confidently. "I've finished for the day, Second—" Dion just then scented there was a human in the office. "I mean, Caden."

"Great. You've done some good work this week, Dion. Give me a second and I'll get your pay. Oh, Dion, this is Selena. Lena, this is Dion, Dante and Eden's oldest."

"Pleased to meet you, ma'am," Dion said politely.

"You too, Dion."

Caden counted out some bills from the petty-cash drawer and put them in an envelope. "Here you go."

"Thanks, Caden." Dion smiled gratefully and pushed the money into her jeans pocket.

"So? You got enough saved up for your big date?"

Dion blushed. "Yeah, I should have."

She turned to Lena and said, "Young Dion's been saving up to take her girlfriend out for Valentine's on Saturday."

"Oh, that's so sweet," Lena replied with a big smile.

Caden smiled as she watched Dion squirm, highly embarrassed about talking about this in front of two adults.

"She's not my girlfriend, yet. It's just a date. Dinner and a movie. I wanted to get some flowers, but I don't know if she'd like that."

"Let's ask Lena. Would a teenage girl like flowers on Valentine's, Lena?"

She smiled almost sadly. "I haven't gotten flowers before, but I'm sure your girlfriend would love that, Dion. It would make her feel special."

Caden was very surprised. *No one's ever treated you like they should, have they, beautiful one?*

"Well...Dion, Tia is a special girl. You're very lucky, so treat her nice, okay?"

"I sure will, Caden. I better run or Mom will bite my butt for being late."

Caden saw Lena look at them both, as if puzzled by Dion's choice of words. Best to end this little meeting quickly. "Well, off you go then, and thank you."

Dion ran off like a shot, happy to be out of the spotlight. Caden sat at her desk and hoped Lena wouldn't question her about Dion's slip.

"She's a lovely girl, Caden. There aren't many kids of rich parents that would work for extra money."

"She's a good person, just like her parents, and one day this will all be hers, but everyone in Wolfgang County has to fulfill their role and work hard."

Lena thought for a second and said, "Wolfgang County is a remarkable place."

Caden and every wolf thought this was the case, but she was intrigued to know how a human would view it. "How so?"

"Well, I've never known anyplace to be so gay friendly. Someone as young as Dion can be out and open about it."

"It's just natural to us. Some animals are born to be hunters and protectors, and some are born to be caregivers and nurture their loved ones. It makes no difference if a couple is formed of two males, two females, or a male and a female in Wolfgang County."

"Wow. It certainly doesn't work that way where I come from." Lena looked down and began to tap her nails on the desk. "Certainly not in my family."

The more Caden heard about Lena's pack, the more she disliked them.

❖

Caden returned to her desk and, from where Lena sat, appeared to be working on her computer. Lena took the opportunity to subtly study her.

She was becoming more and more intrigued with Wolfgang County. It was both a strange and beautiful natural wonderland, and Caden was a strange and wonderful mixture too.

From the first moment she'd laid eyes on Caden, there was *something* about her. Some recognition, a connection between them, that she couldn't explain to herself. When she touched Caden or was simply in her company, she experienced feelings and sensations that she hadn't before.

Physically, Caden was stunning. She was everything Lena wasn't. Tall, fit, powerful, and muscular, she lifted items as if they weighed nothing and was unusually quick. Lena could only imagine what her mother and father would think of a woman like Caden.

But she was a strange character to work out. At first, she'd felt Caden disliked her, and then she was trying to dominate her and make her eat. Now Caden was what Lena could only describe as *sweet*. The time she had spent with her yesterday had been wonderful and exciting, but it had hurt when Caden hadn't taken up her offer of dinner. When Caden had left, she felt bad for the rest of the night. In her mind, it reinforced the many failings she had as a human being. Mother and Father were right about her. She wasn't good enough.

She turned her eyes back to the predicable, reliable numbers on her computer screen.

At that moment Caden called out suddenly, "Oh, Lena, I almost forgot." Caden got up and walked over to her, and pulled a stone from her jeans pocket. She put it down on the desk in front of Lena. "It's a rainbow moonstone. I saw it when I was out running last night, and I thought you'd like it."

What Caden didn't tell Lena was that she had run to her grandmother's burial stone, and there, sitting on the plinth, found the gemstone. It hadn't been there before, and she instinctively felt her grandmother was trying to tell her something.

Moonstone had a special place in wolf society. Its connection to nature and the moon were obvious, but it also stood for prophecy and lifting the veil to the Great Mother and the heavens, her grandmother's particular gift. There had always been moonstones littered around her den, in all varieties.

Lena picked it up and gasped at the rainbow shimmer from the gemstone. "It's beautiful, Caden. Are you sure it doesn't belong to someone?"

"I'm sure. We have an old mine on county land that has these stones. I'm sure it came from there."

"Then thank you. No one's ever given me something like this before. It was kind of you to think of me." Lena looked up to Caden and smiled, and Caden hoped her mother's phone call was temporarily forgotten.

Caden sat on the corner of her desk and said, "You were the first one I thought of when I saw it. Your name means Goddess of the Moon, after all."

They gazed at each other for a few seconds before Caden broke away and cleared her throat. "The moonstone is very special in our community. The different colors and types share some characteristics but can mean different things too. My grandmother always had gray moonstones all over the house. She was interested in mysticism and the other worlds beyond. The gray moonstone is believed to help lift the veil between our world and the next."

Lena turned the stone over in her hands, tracing the stone's contours with her fingernail. "What does this rainbow one mean?"

"It's associated with the Moon Goddess. It's said that it provides protection, deflects negative energy and emotional distress. If you keep it with you, it will help you feel calmer." Caden smiled softly and took her hand.

"Caden? How do you know—"

The office door opened, and in walked Dante, catching them in the tender moment. They sprang apart quickly.

"Dante," Caden said, "I didn't think you were coming till later."

Dante raised a questioning eyebrow, clearly surprised her Second couldn't sense her approach and that she was extremely flustered. "I finished up at the office early. I hoped we could talk while we rode out."

Caden grabbed her Stetson from the hook. "Of course. Lena—I'm going to be out for most of the afternoon. If you need anything, just ask one of my staff."

Lena smiled and nodded. "I will."

"Selena, I hope my second-in-command is looking after you," Dante said.

Lena found the dark and powerful CEO of Venator quite intimidating. Dante wasn't in her suit today, but dressed in jeans, shirt, and boots. Even with this more casual look, Lena's heart sped as she forced herself to croak an answer. "Yes, thank you, Ms. Wolfgang."

Dante gave her a smile. "We shall leave you to your work, then. Let's go, Cade."

Lena watched them leave and held the moonstone tightly in her hand, trying to calm her heart.

❖

Dante and Caden rode their horses over the large expanse of grazing land, inspecting the animals and how they were developing.

The Black Angus steer herd didn't flinch as they rode by, too concerned with grazing to be alert to potential predators.

Caden knew this was the kind of work Dante most enjoyed. Before Dante's pater had died, she and Dante, along with Flash, had spent a lot of time working with the animals. She should bring Lena out for a ride. She'd probably like to see the animals.

"Cade? Caden," Dante shouted.

Caden looked up sharply. "Wha—? Did you say something, Alpha?"

"Everything looks good, Second. The prey are healthy and the changes to the breeding program are excellent."

"I'm glad you approve, Alpha. The changes should increase our output tenfold in about five years," Caden said in a monotone.

Dante maneuvered her large black horse closer to her. "Cade, is there something troubling you? Something I can help you with?"

Caden gave her a questioning look. "Troubling? No, nothing at all. Why do you ask?"

"You seem distracted, as if something is weighing on your mind."

"No, I'm okay, Alpha."

"You appear to be very friendly with our new employee."

Caden shifted uncomfortably in her saddle. "Lena? She's a nice girl."

"Hmm. Yes, she is nice. Beautiful too. A nice, beautiful *human* girl," Dante corrected her.

Caden pulled the reins and stopped her horse. "If there's something you want to say to me, Alpha, please say it."

Dante's horse whinnied, and she patted its neck. "No, I just wondered if there was anything you wanted to tell me. Eden told me she met you in the grocery store, shopping with Selena."

"Since when do you have a problem with humans?" Caden snapped.

Dante gave a warning growl. "You know very well, Second, that my pater and I have always been in favor of allowing humans to be part of our business, and to live here. The very fact that I gave a human company the job of taking care of our accounts should tell you that. It's you who have constantly counseled me against their integration into our world."

Caden lowered her eyes. "I know that, Alpha. I'm sorry. A human killed my parents, and I've always hated them, but my grandmother always tried to tell me they were not all the same. I never believed that, until now. It's just that she's such a nice girl and she...well..." Caden sighed. "She's wounded somehow"—Caden thumped her chest—"inside here. Her pack does not treat her well, and I think she needs someone to be kind to her, to watch out for her. I would like to be her friend."

"Are you sure there's nothing more? When I came in, she was holding a piece of moonstone. Did you give her that?"

Caden started to feel very exposed. "It was just a friendly gift. I was out running and I found it sitting on my grandmother's gravestone. Lena gets really anxious and stressed, and I thought it would help her."

Dante patted her friend on the shoulder. "I just don't want to see you hurt, Cade. Being casual friends with a human is okay, but anything more presents problems that need to be carefully considered. We must keep the existence of our pack secret. You know what dangers would arise for us if the human world found out about us."

Caden flashed what she feared was an unconvincing smile. "Hey, don't worry. I'm not going to fall in love or anything. I'm not destined to have a mate, remember?"

"As Eden said, your grandmother prophesied you wouldn't have a wolf mate. That's an entirely different thing."

"I guess." Caden's mind whirled, imagining Lena as a mate. *I couldn't love a human.*

Dante changed the subject, perhaps sensing Caden's discomfort. "So, Flash will present his evidence to us this evening. I've called a meeting of my elite wolves at seven o'clock."

"Of course. I'll be there, Alpha."

"Why don't you take me to the slaughterhouse now, Second?"

"Sure. Production is..." Caden's words trailed off as her heart begin to beat rapidly, and she felt a deep feeling of doom. Lena was in pain.

"What's wrong?" Dante asked.

"Lena! Ya!" Caden shouted and galloped off at top speed, without a backward glance to her Alpha.

## Chapter Ten

Caden's heart beat out of her chest and her hair stood on end. The only time she had felt a sensation like this was when her parents had been killed. As she got closer to the farm buildings, she saw a group of her farmworkers gathered around a figure lying in the dirt just outside the field perimeter. She could feel it was Lena.

She jumped off her horse and, as she approached, roared for the other wolves to move. Fear and aggression surged in her body. "Move."

The crowd parted and Caden dropped to her knees beside an unconscious Lena. She scanned her body for obvious injuries and found her arm badly misshapen. There didn't seem to be any cuts or bangs to her head, so Caden couldn't work out why Lena was unconscious.

She looked up at the surrounding workers and said with a growl, "What happened?"

They all looked at one wolf, who all of a sudden became very anxious at being under scrutiny from the pack Second.

"I was walking back with the horse across the field. I saw her walking toward the fence, smiling at me—I think she wanted to come and talk to the horse. Then I saw her go down and hit her arm on the stone wall there, and I ran to help her."

"Did she hit her head and lose consciousness? It's really important—she's already had a head injury since coming to the county."

"No, Second. When I got to her, she was crying in pain, but

conscious and asking for help. I think she just landed awkwardly on her arm, and the pain got too much so she lost consciousness."

Caden lifted Lena's head into her lap and began to stroke her hair. "Has someone called for an ambulance?"

"Yes, Second," he replied.

*What has happened to you, beautiful one?*

One of the farmworkers reached out to touch Lena's cheek. Caden lifted her head, showed her teeth, and roared, "Don't touch."

The wolves around them gasped and took a step back in shock, and some submissive wolves clung to the dominants beside them. Through the red mist of her fear and anger, Caden couldn't tell at first who was touching Lena, but when the wolf reared up on her hands and knees to snarl and bare her teeth in response, she realized it was the Alpha.

"Stand down, Wolf. Stand down now," Dante ordered.

No wolf in the pack had ever challenged the Alpha before, and for the second most dominant to do it was unthinkable.

An instinctive defense of the woman Caden considered to be hers slowly faded, and when she realized who she had challenged, she immediately lowered herself and turned her head to the side in submission. "Alpha, forgive me. I didn't know it was you. I don't know what—"

"We will address this issue later, Second. First we have to help Selena. So get your wolf under control before she wakes up and sees you."

Below them Lena began to moan as she fought to wake up.

"Yes, Alpha."

Lena opened her eyes just as the sirens came down the farm road. "Cade…it hurts…"

Caden tenderly stroked her brow and said, "Shh, I know. There's help coming. I'll take care of you, okay?"

"Selena, we think you may have broken your arm. Just stay still, help is on its way," Dante told her.

"Thank you, Ms. Wolfgang. I'm sorry for being so clumsy. I slipped on some horse muck."

"Not at all. Just try to relax." The EMTs made their way over, and Dante turned to Caden. "You'll have to let the EMTs do their work. Do you understand me?"

She understood that the Alpha was trying to warn her in a subtle way. After her earlier aggressive response, she must be prepared to let Lena be cared for and touched. "Yes, Dante." She looked down to Lena and said, "I'm just going to move out of the way, so the EMTs can do their work, but I'll just be right over there."

Caden wanted to lean down and kiss Lena. It felt like the most natural thing in the world, but she knew it would be wrong in so many ways.

She got up and walked toward Dante, to let the EMTs do their job. "Alpha, I'm sorry. I don't know what came over me."

Dante placed a hand on Caden's neck and pulled her in close. "I forgive you, Caden, but we need to talk. Come by my den tonight. Are you going to the hospital with Selena?"

"Yes, I'd like to go with her."

Dante nodded in agreement. "Very well. I'll drive your truck to the emergency room."

Lena was wheeled past them and Caden said, "Thank you, Alpha. I'd better go."

When they reached the county hospital, Lena was quickly x-rayed, and it was found that she had a compound forearm fracture that would need to be pinned.

Caden sat with Lena in the ER cubicle as they waited for her to be taken to surgery. She wasn't feeling any pain after the pre-op medicines had been administered, and Caden found her giggles and odd comments adorable.

"Caden?"

"Yes, Lena?" She moved her chair closer to the bed and took her hand.

"I left my pens all by themselves at the ranch. Will they be okay?"

Caden smiled indulgently. "Of course they will be. The office is locked up tight. They'll be quite safe."

Lena looked as though she was thinking seriously. "But they're just lying there on my desk, and I never leave them out. It makes me feel panicked."

Caden had observed firsthand how obsessive Lena was over her pens and other belongings, and the drugs that were now coursing through her body were giving her an uninhibited view into Lena's anxious mind.

"Well, I'll tell you what. Why don't I go by the office later and put them away in your pen case, where they'll be safe. I have to go and pick up your purse anyway, remember?"

Lena had asked Caden to pick up her spare pair of glasses from her apartment, to replace the ones broken in the fall. So she had to get her purse with Lena's apartment keys from the office.

"That would be nice. You're so good to me, Caden," Lena said in a voice thick with emotion.

Looking at Lena now reminded Caden of the fragile creature she'd found on the forest floor. She felt guilty at the way she had talked to her about her eating habits. *You talked to her like she was a wolf, and she's not.*

"I haven't. I've been too hard on you. It's none of my business what you do with your body."

Lena shook her head from side to side. "No, you're the only person who has ever looked at me and not found anything wrong with me. I'm sorry I was a clumsy idiot. This was my fault."

Caden rubbed her thumb over the back of Lena's hand. She was trying so hard to be calm, but seeing Lena in distress and pain made her wolf claw at her insides. "Don't be silly, it was an accident. It's no one's fault."

"No, you don't understand. These things always happen to me. I'm clumsy. Mother calls me a baby elephant."

Caden couldn't stop a growl coming from deep in her throat. Once again, she had the overwhelming desire to lash out at Lena's mother. "You are nothing like a baby elephant. I think you're the most beautiful female I've ever met. You're warmhearted and extremely elegant in what you wear and how you behave." She suspected Lena wouldn't remember a word of this conversation, so she felt free to be totally honest.

"But I know I was stupid. I left my moonstone on the desk and went out for a breath of air, and when I saw the man with the horse, I wanted to stroke its coat. It was so cute, but you told me my moonstone would protect me, and I left it inside. That's why this happened."

Caden stood up and leaned over Lena. "I want you to stop that kind of talk. The moonstone will protect you here"—she pointed to Lena's head, then to her heart—"and here. Accidents can still happen. How about I bring it here, for when you wake up?"

Lena smiled and giggled. "Yes, I'd like that. You gave it to me, so it makes me feel safe, because you make me feel safe."

Even though Caden realized Lena wouldn't be saying these things without the drugs lowering her inhibitions, it made her feel wonderful that Lena could feel safe, just from her presence.

"Oh, I wanted to check before they take you to surgery—do you want me to contact your parents and let them know what's happened?"

Lena's eyes went wide with panic. "No. Don't tell them, please. I'm going to be fine."

Caden saw the look of horror on Lena's face, and it made her angry. No one should ever feel distressed about what their family would think about an accident.

"Okay, okay. I won't. I promise."

At that moment the orderlies came into the cubicle and nodded their heads to Caden. "Second, may we take her up now? The OR is ready."

"Of course, just one minute." Caden leaned down and kissed Lena on the forehead. "May the Great Mother protect you. I'll see you soon, okay?"

Lena looked intently into Caden's eyes and said, "I remember you had yellow eyes. They were so beautiful."

The two orderlies looked uncomfortably at the Second, clearly worried that the human had indeed noticed they were not who they appeared to be.

Caden didn't confirm or deny it. She just smiled and assured Lena that she would see her when she woke.

Then Lena was wheeled away, and it was so hard to let her go.

❖

The nurses at the county hospital assured Caden that she would have at least a couple of hours before Lena woke up from the anesthetic. It wasn't her place, but she felt in her gut that she should be there when Lena awoke. There was just enough time for her to pick up Lena's purse—and her precious pens—from the office and head to Lena's apartment to pick up some things before heading back to the hospital.

Caden walked up to the apartment door and hesitated as she put the key in the lock. Today had turned her world upside down. She could never have imagined a circumstance that would cause her to challenge her Alpha, and her closest friend, but a human woman, whom she barely knew, had done just that.

Dante had assured her at the hospital that they would talk about what happened when Caden came to her den later, but she felt she had let down the Alpha badly.

Why was she doing this? Lena had a family. Let them take care of her. She tried to tell herself this, but when she'd found Lena lying helpless and in pain, her wolf had one thought, and one thought alone: Protect your mate.

Caden shook the thought away and said out loud, "Just go in there, get what you came for, and get out."

She entered the apartment and was hit with the same intoxicating scent that she had experienced the first time there.

The scent made her burn inside, and her mouth began to water. Get in, get out, Caden reminded herself. Lena had given Caden a list of items to bring, and where to find them. So she quickly retrieved the list and headed, with the gym bag she had brought along, into the bedroom.

On a bookcase just outside the bedroom door, Caden saw what looked like a family picture. She picked it up and studied it. "So, this is your pack, Lena?"

The picture clearly revealed the Millers' pack dynamics. The tall, imposing father was in the middle, with his wife and two sons on both sides, and Lena a pace to the side on her own, looking as if she didn't belong in the group. She deserved so much more, Caden thought sadly.

Caden moved into the bedroom and groaned. Lena's scent was so much stronger here. Her gaze went immediately to the bed, and a growl escaped when she saw a collection of four stuffed toys set atop the pillows. She imagined Lena hugging them close to her at night as she sought comfort from them.

Caden's wolf wanted to leap on the bed and taste those toys that scented of her.

She gulped hard and forced herself over to the closet. She needed to get this over with. She pulled open the doors and in almost frenzied fashion stuffed a couple of wool sweaters and pairs of jeans that she saw there into her bag.

After that she pulled a few items of underwear from the drawers without looking too closely, but the feel of the silk on her fingers made her imagine the way they would look and feel on Lena's curvaceous body.

This was torture.

Her breathing heavy, she looked over to the mirror on top of the dresser and observed her wolf features. Caden ran her tongue along the length of her fangs, which she had been unable to hold back.

She took a long breath, trying to control her shift, and then looked down at what remained on Lena's list.

"Last thing. Spare glasses, in the bedside cabinet. Okay."

She knelt down to open the drawer and grabbed the glasses in their case and threw them in the bag. Her close proximity to Lena's heavily scented bed made the call of her wolf all the more hard to resist.

Caden's vision had gone fully wolf, and saliva dripped from her fangs. In her mind, she saw Lena lying on her side, under the covers, snuggled into her pillow with one of the soft toys, the cover riding up, and showing a naked leg and curvy buttock that she just ached to bite.

The sensations were too much for her. She dropped the gym bag as her heart thudded faster and faster. Her blood thrummed around her body, carrying transmutation molecules to every cell. She stood quickly and tore off her clothes, before the cracking bones moved and reshaped her body to her wolf form. Caden's groans grew to loud roars as her shift was complete. She leaped onto the bed and buried her snout in Lena's pillow.

Lena's scent was heady, and Caden closed her eyes and let her senses reel. Her sex burned and throbbed to the beat of her heart.

*Lena...Lena...mine.*

She licked the pillow, allowing Lena's taste to explode on her tongue, and let out a long, loud howl. A warning to any nearby wolves that this human was hers.

One of Lena's stuffed toys caught her eye, a scruffy-looking bear, and Caden took it in her mouth and shook it hard from side to side. After her initial burst of energy, she calmed and began to enjoy chewing on the bear and rolling around the bed, spreading her own scent across Lena's most private space.

As her energy calmed, contentment came upon her, and that was when she started to realize what she had done.

She looked up at the mirror on the dresser and saw her reflection staring back at her. A wolf who covered the entire expanse of Lena's king-size bed, blankets all ruffled up and half on the floor, and pillows strewn around the room. Worst of all, though, was the bear sitting next to her, its head and ear hanging off, and the stuffing bleeding from its belly.

She shifted to skin in an instant and held her head in her hands. "No. No, no, I didn't do this, no."

Never in her life had she lost control of her wolf like this. She had always been in control of herself, always cool and levelheaded, but this human woman made her lose control like a cub.

She held the bear's head in one hand and the body in another. How could she fix this? How would she explain?

Caden jumped up and threw the injured bear into her gym bag, then hurriedly made the bed as best she could, brushing the stray wolf hairs off the bedding.

She looked up at the clock on the bedside table. "Great Mother, I'm going to be late." She ran from the apartment and down to her truck, where she changed into her spare clothing.

Caden thought back to the ripped bear in her bag. She had to make this right. If she hurried, she could squeeze in one last stop before heading back to the hospital.

Her engine roared as she zoomed off on her mission.

## CHAPTER ELEVEN

Lena's muscles and lungs burned as she tried to stay ahead of her pursuer. Dressed only in her nightdress, her bare feet snagged every sharp twig and branch in her path. She looked behind her and saw that the huge dark wolf was gaining on her with every step.

Its hungry yellow eyes shone brightly in the clear night. Lena didn't know why she was running here in this forest, but she did know that the wolf wanted her, and wanted her badly. She could feel it in the air and every fiber of her body. This wolf would not give up till it had her.

The wolf was now only a few feet away, and about to catch her, when Lena tripped over and fell to the dirt. She threw her hands over her head, waiting for the wolf's jaws to bite, and claws to slash.

When the expected pain of attack didn't come, Lena lifted her head and peeked behind her. Standing there was not the fierce wolf that chased her, but her friend Caden.

She leaped up into Caden's arms, shouting, "Caden. Thank God. I thought…I thought…"

Tears overwhelmed her, and Caden pulled her in tighter. "Shh, shh, now. I've got you. I'll always protect you."

Lena's perspective suddenly changed, and she was now floating above the scene, watching as Caden held her body tightly. Caden slowly looked upward, as if she knew Lena could see her. She smiled and her eyes changed to flashing yellow in an instant.

❖

Caden hurried down the corridor with Lena's things and a couple of gifts she had brought. She only hoped she wasn't too late to be there when Lena woke up.

The nurse she was following said, "We moved her to the rooms we use for any humans who are admitted, Second. It's a quiet part of the hospital, where we hope they won't see anything they aren't meant to." They finally came to Lena's room. "Here we are. The doctor is just checking on her at the moment."

Caden walked in and was given a salute by the friendly silver-haired doctor. Thankfully Lena was still asleep. "Dr. Jaycen, how is she?" Caden put the gym bag down by the side of the bed and ran her hand along the newly applied cast and down to Lena's fingers at the end, feeling the overwhelming need to touch her.

"She's done well. Ms. Miller is a strong young woman. I must say, it's a pleasure to treat a human from time to time. It tests your medical skills much more than our kind do."

"What will happen next? I mean, she can't shift to accelerate the healing process."

Jaycen checked the levels of drugs and fluids being fed from the drip. "Ah, yes. That's what makes humans fascinating creatures. Instead of shifting to heal, they wait."

She gave the doctor a questioning look. "Wait? What does *wait* mean?"

Jaycen walked over and put a comforting arm on Caden's shoulders. "Their bodies require time and care to heal, unlike ours, Second. Young Ms. Miller will take her time to heal. We have pinned the bones together and placed her arm in a cast. In six weeks, I'll check the position of the bones and perhaps change it to a lighter cast. But it could take up to three months to fully heal."

Caden was shocked. "Three months?"

"Yes, followed by a great deal of physical therapy. Humans are delicate creatures, Second." Lena began to murmur in her sleep, drawing the doctor's attention down to her. "She'll awaken soon."

As Caden looked down at her, she realized just how fragile human life was. She wanted to gather Lena up, take her back to her den, and protect her from every harm that could come to her, but it was impossible. "When can she go home, Doctor?"

Jaycen stroked his white goatee beard as he thought. "Hmm... tomorrow morning probably. As long as there's no sign of infection overnight. I'll leave you to it, Second."

"Thank you for taking care of her, Jaycen."

He thumped his chest with his fist. "It's my privilege to serve, Second."

Now alone, Caden sat down by the side of Lena's bed. Her mumbles had continued, and her eyes flitted back and forth under the lids.

Caden stroked the hair on Lena's forehead tenderly. "Are you dreaming, beautiful one?"

Lena began breathing heavily, her head moving side to side as if she was struggling. Caden placed a kiss on her forehead and whispered, "Don't be scared or anxious. I will protect you."

Lena's eyes sprang open. "Caden. You...saved me." She tried to grab Caden but fell back when she realized her arm was in a cast.

Caden cupped Lena's cheek and looked her directly in the eye. "Hey, hey. Calm down. You're safe, I promise."

Lena's breathing got deeper and calmed. "I had a nightmare. I was running through the forest, and this huge wolf was chasing me. Much bigger than an ordinary wolf, you know?"

Caden's heart started to beat double time, and she wondered what was coming next. "A wolf, huh?"

"Yes. I was running as fast as I could, but it kept getting closer and closer, and somehow I knew inside that the wolf wanted me, badly. A voice kept repeating in my head, *The wolf wants you.*"

*The wolf does want you, Lena, but can't have you*, thought Caden sadly. "What happened next?"

"I tripped on a branch or something, and I remember being so terrified. I knew this was it, and I just waited for the bite that would kill me, but it never came. I looked around and *you* were standing there, instead of the wolf. I've never been happier to see another human being in my life. You held me, said I would be safe, and just as I was waking, your eyes flashed yellow like the wolf's."

Caden tried not to show any emotion on her face, but she was certain Lena's subconscious was trying to tell her who Caden was. Somewhere in Lena's mind, she knew Caden was the wolf that rescued her the first time in the forest. "That's quite a dream."

"What do you think it means?"

Caden hesitated. She hated lying to Lena like this. "I know it seemed like a frightening dream, but my instinct tells me it wasn't meant to be a nightmare."

"How could you think that?" Lena asked.

"The wolf is a great omen in Wolfgang County. They are greatly revered. Wolves help us manage the deer population spread over our vast territory. We live in harmony with them. So I think the fact that you saw one in your dream is a good thing."

"Really? Do you think so?"

Caden nodded her head. "I do. You have nothing to fear."

"Why did you have yellow eyes in my dream? I'm sure I've seen those eyes before, somewhere…"

Caden needed to change the subject and fast. "Hey, I got your things. Here's your purse, and some clothes."

"Oh, thanks. Could you give me my glasses, please?"

"Sure, hang on." Caden fished around in the gym bag for the glasses, but instead of handing them over, she put them on Lena herself, her fingers grazing Lena's face tenderly.

Lena's gaze caught hers, but when Lena raised her good arm to touch her, she pulled back. Lena's cheeks went red with embarrassment at what she'd been about to do, so Caden decided to lighten the mood. She pulled Lena's pen box out of the gym bag. "Here are your pens, so you don't have to worry about them."

Lena held on to the box tightly with her good arm, instantly seeming calmer for having them in her possession. "Thank you so much. I know I must seem strange."

She placed a finger over Lena's lips. "Shh…you don't need to explain. I understand you, and that's all you need to know."

❖

Lena had been overwhelmed with feelings and emotions since opening her eyes. The dream had been so vivid, and the meaning was in her mind somewhere, just out of reach.

The pain in her arm was just about bearable with the drugs, but everything was made better when Caden looked at her or touched her. She felt safe and protected. No one in her life before had been able to quiet the constant anxiety that turned over in her mind, and no one had made her want to be touched like Caden did. Her body came alive with needs and wants which she had never experienced before. Everything seemed connected to Caden, and she just had to work out why.

"Are you in pain, Lena?" Caden asked.

"It's not too bad. I was just thinking, that's all." Thinking was an understatement. Everything around her seemed to be a puzzle waiting to be worked out.

"If I can interrupt your thinking," Caden said with a big grin, "I almost forgot. I got you some presents—hope you like them."

"You didn't have to…Oh!" Lena was surprised when a big bunch of flowers was placed in her lap along with a rectangular wrapped box and a gift bag. "Oh, these are beautiful. I've never gotten flowers before."

"I know. I remembered. That's why I wanted to be the first," Caden said proudly.

Caden looked at her with a huge smile and wide eyes, and to Lena she looked like a little puppy trying to please its owner, so unlike the serious and tough person she normally was.

Lena was unused to this kind of kindness. It became too much for her, and the tears started to fall.

"What's wrong? Don't you like them?" Caden asked, looking stricken.

"I'm sorry. I love them—it's just no one's ever been so kind to me, and I don't understand why you would be." She took off her glasses and wiped away her tears.

"I like you, what more reason is there?"

Lena was stumped by this question. Caden was stunningly good looking, like a tall, rugged cowboy from the movies. She could imagine a five-foot-eight, super-skinny blonde waiting at home for her. So why was Caden spending so much time with her?

"Open your presents." Caden was just about bouncing with excitement.

She smiled and looked down at her arm in the cast. "Could you help me out?"

"Oh, sure. Sorry, I didn't think of that." Caden started to unwrap the rectangular box. "I got the girl in the store to wrap these for me, or else you would have gotten them in a paper bag."

Lena giggled. She was seeing a different side to Caden, a more lighthearted, playful side to her personality.

"I hope the dream you had hasn't turned you against wolves altogether." Caden opened the box and revealed a beautiful silver pen with a wolf engraved on it.

Lena gasped.

"I know you love your pens, so I hoped…"

"It's wonderful. Thank you so much." Caden was like no one she'd ever met.

Caden rubbed the back of her neck bashfully. "It's something to remember Wolfgang County by, wherever life takes you."

Lena didn't want to think about that. Think about when her assignment came to an end and she had to go home, back under the scrutiny of her parents. "Thank you. Truly." Lena's eyes went to the gift bag. "What's in there?"

"Ah…it's just a bit of fun. I noticed when I was getting your things, you had a few stuffed animals, and I thought you might like this noble animal to sit with them."

Lena laughed when Caden pulled a stuffed wolf out of the gift bag. "Aww. It's so cute." She took it in her good hand and brought it to her chest in a hug.

"Cute?" Caden raised an eyebrow in mock annoyance. "A wolf is not cute, Ms. Miller. A wolf is a hunter, a protector, a passionate mate, but never cute."

"Well, I think it's cute, and I love it. It'll keep me company tonight. Did you see the scruffy-looking bear on my bed?" Caden nodded, trying not to look worried.

Lena gave the wolf a kiss on the snout, and Caden wished she was receiving that affection. "My uncle gave it to me. He died a few months before I moved here. I know it may seem a little childish, but it always makes me think of him."

Caden changed the subject quickly. "Dr. Jaycen said you could leave tomorrow morning, as long as there was no sign of infection overnight. So I'll come pick you up."

Lena stroked the wolf in her hand. "You don't have to."

"I do, and I will. I'm only sorry I can't stay any longer tonight, but I have to attend a meeting with Dante."

"If you insist, then that's very kind."

Caden stood and lifted the bunch of flowers. "Great, I'll just go and see if I can get someone to put these in water." She turned to leave. "Oh, and before I forget, I found your moonstone." Caden got it from her pocket and placed it on the bedside table.

"Thank you. I'll make sure to always keep it safe."

❖

The door opened before Caden had knocked twice. "Hi, Caden. Come in." Eden ushered her into her den.

"Thanks, Mater." She took off her Stetson and saluted.

"How's Lena doing?" How typical of the Mater, Caden thought, to ask after Lena's well-being, even though she was a human. "Dante said she had an accident."

"Yeah, she has a bad break in her arm, but Dr. Jaycen pinned it. He thinks she should get out tomorrow, lunchtime."

"I'm glad to hear it. I thought Stella and I would go to the hospital in the morning and visit her. As Mater I should make her feel welcome and let her know we're here if she needs any help at all."

Caden felt nervous all of sudden and clenched her hat tightly to her chest. "That would be kind, Mater. Lena is a very nervous, anxious creature—like a deer. She's constantly worrying and is very self-conscious with other people. I—"

Eden held up her hand to stop Caden and smiled. "Don't worry, Cade. We'll be very gentle, I promise."

"Thank you, Mater."

"Dante is waiting for you in the war room. Go on down."

Just as Eden turned to return to the family room, Caden said, "Mater? Could I ask a favor?"

"Anything, Second. You know that," Eden said.

Caden opened the bag she had with her and lifted out Lena's stuffed bear. "Um…I wondered if you would be able to fix this for me."

Eden took the ripped bear and its decapitated head from her and said, "This has been in the wars. It looks like Conan's stuffed animals after he shifts and plays with them. What happened?"

Caden rubbed her forehead in resignation. She knew that she would be the main topic of den talk for months to come. "I was at Lena's apartment picking up some of her things, and I had…an accident with it. Can you fix it? Lena's uncle gave it to her and he died recently, so it means a lot to her."

Eden smiled and shook her head as if she knew exactly what had happened, but there was no way Caden was going to admit she had lost control of her wolf while being intoxicated with Lena's scent. *Drunk on love.* She remembered how Dante looked at Eden sometimes. Was that what was wrong with her?

"I can fix it," Eden said. "With three wolf cubs, I've had to do plenty of this type of thing. Go on down to Dante, and I'll have it ready before you leave."

"Thank you, Mater."

Caden entered the war room and found the Alpha sitting on the edge of the conference table, watching the big screen, with Blaze standing beside her.

"Alpha?"

Dante didn't turn around, but said, "Blaze? Could you leave us?"

"Yes, Alpha." Blaze thumped his chest and nodded to Caden as he passed. "Second."

On the large flat screen in front of Dante flashed some gruesome images, similar to the ones they had seen of Suzy Mitchell.

"What is this, Alpha?" Caden asked as she reached Dante's side.

"That, Second, is a wolf out of control. Blaze noticed a pattern of human murders radiating out from Suzy Mitchell's murder scene. He wanted us to see it before my elite wolves got here."

"It looks as if Leroux is mutilating them, not just killing. Why?" Caden said.

Dante folded her arms and continued looking at the screen. "She doesn't value human life, and because she feels weak at the moment, she wants to feel powerful for the few seconds it takes to tear a human apart. She's drawing unwanted attention to our kind, and that worries me."

She knew exactly what Dante was trying to say to her. "Alpha, please forgive me for my behavior today. I would never challenge you, and I would never risk our world by letting a human into my confidence. Today was...*I* was..."

Dante turned and grasped her Second by the shoulders, and looked her straight in the eye. "Today you were reacting to your natural programming, the very essence of your DNA. Protect your mate."

"I wasn't, Alpha. She's not my mate—I barely know her. I promise you I'm telling you the truth," Caden said desperately.

"I know you'd never lie to me, Cade, but your wolf sees her as your mate. I saw it when she tripped into your arms that first day."

Caden shook her head. "No, she can't be. Not a human."

Dante pulled her closer, so their foreheads were touching. "Cade, you are my best friend, my Second, and I love you. I can feel your heart warring with your head when I see you together. How did you feel when you found her injured today?"

Caden thought back to the afternoon and felt pain and the utter panic all over again. "I felt out of control. Like I would tear apart anything that came near her. She makes me feel out of control, Alpha, but she's a human. How can I feel this?"

Dante let her go and walked over to the large screen. "Who knows how and why the Great Mother pairs us up as mates? The only thing I'm certain of is that your wolf is never wrong. As Eden reminded me, there have been humans who have joined the pack before. It is a risk—one that would need to be considered carefully."

Caden felt the pressure building inside her as Dante spoke, until she could hold it in no longer. "No," she shouted.

Dante looked at her sharply. "No?"

"I'm sorry for shouting, Alpha, but no. I won't put the pack at risk, especially now. The pack comes before everything. Lena is my friend and will stay my friend. I can control my feelings."

"If that is your wish."

They could both hear the elite wolves descending the stairs to the war room.

"It is, Alpha. I will always remain unmated."

Dante walked toward her and placed a hand on her shoulder. "If that is your wish, I shall say no more unless you wish to discuss it again, but remember, my door is always open to you, Second."

"Thank you, Alpha."

Dante stood behind her seat at the head of the conference table. "One thing, Second. When a mate comes along, we have little say in how we act and feel. Nature is a formidable foe to battle, but if you are determined to fight it, just be careful one or both of you do not get hurt."

*Lena couldn't love me, and I could never hurt her.*

The elite wolves entered, bringing their discussion to an end.

❖

"We followed Leroux's scent across four counties and lost her in Lennoxtown. We believed she was heading north, but then her scent became erratic," Flash explained to the elite wolves.

"Blaze? What's your opinion?" Dante asked.

The sheriff sat forward in his seat and stroked his chin. "It matches the pattern of murders. North, then spreading out beyond Lennoxtown. It makes sense, if she's still recovering from injury, to head back to Lupa pack land and gather her forces."

"Second?"

"She could easily board a bus or train bound for Canada without raising too many eyebrows."

"Hmm..." Dante stood and walked toward the large screen which had a map of the murders and Leroux's movements on it. "Perhaps it fits too perfectly. Leroux is a weaker Alpha, a weaker fighter, but she has cunning in abundance. She is a careful planner and used Suzy Mitchell to get exactly what she wanted. She also has an ego, and running away does not sit easy with those attributes."

"You think there is more going on here, Alpha?" Caden asked.

Dante looked at the picture of Leroux on the screen, and her claws started to extend from her fingertips. She drew a long claw across her face and said, "I may be wrong, but I don't believe Leroux's only plan would be to gather her wolves for an all-out attack. She is more subtle than that."

She turned around to face her wolves. "Until we know more, I want guards to remain around my den, and I want each of you to continue to lead patrols with your own sections, and report to Caden. Blaze and Xander, you're out in the community talking with my wolves. Keep your ears to the ground and listen out for anything unusual. Any strangers around town, anything unusual at all, report back to either Caden or me. That goes for all of you. Understand?"

The elite wolves stood and said, "Yes, Alpha."

"Good hunting, Wolves."

With a salute, they replied, "Good hunting, Alpha."

"Dismissed."

❖

Leroux lugged a heavy trash bag down to the harbor edge, under the cover of darkness. She pushed the bag into the water, and it splashed before quickly sinking to the depths. "Hope you enjoy being fish food, Human."

She walked back up to the small fishing shack she had commandeered. Inside, there was food cooking on the small stove, which the fisherman had been tending to when Leroux attacked him. She pulled the food off the burner and sniffed. "Processed human muck."

Her hunger overcame her revulsion.

Leroux took the food over to a worn armchair and began to shovel it into her mouth. Her phone rang, and she said, "Speak."

"Leroux? It's Kurtis."

"It's *Alpha* to you, Wolf. You only have one Alpha now."

"Of course, Alpha. Have you found a base?"

Leroux looked around the small shack, with the blood of the fisherman splattered across the wall. "Yes, a temporary base. When my wolves arrive they will set up a more permanent position. I need money. Wire me some straight away. This is your chance to prove your loyalty, Kurtis. If you bring any Wolfgang wolves to my door, you and your family's lives are forfeit. Do we understand each other?"

There was a silence on the end of the phone until Kurtis croaked, "Yes, Alpha."

She ended the call and sneered, "Dante and Caden? You won't know what hit you."

## Chapter Twelve

The next morning, Dr. Jaycen made his rounds and was happy enough with her progress to release Lena that day. The nurses helped her get washed and dressed, and she sat in the chair by the bed, ready to be picked up by Caden.

She was just checking the messages on her cell phone when Nurse Skye popped her head round the door and said, "Ms. Miller? You have visitors."

When Eden and Stella walked through the door, Lena jumped up in surprise. "Mrs. Wolfgang?"

Eden smiled warmly. "It's Eden, please. I hope you don't mind Stella and me coming to see you, but Caden told me about your accident at the ranch, and I wanted to see how you were."

"That's kind of you. Please sit down." Stella brought a couple of chairs over for herself and Eden.

Both Eden and Stella were what Lena considered effortlessly beautiful, Eden in a simple dress, with a few pieces of jewelry, and Stella in a beautiful skirt and silk blouse. This was the type of woman Caden would want, Lena thought sadly.

"So, how are you, Ms. Miller?"

She cradled her arm self-consciously. She was embarrassed by it, as it was a testament to her own foolishness. "Please, call me Lena. I'll be fine. If I hadn't been so foolish, it would never have happened. I saw the horse and had to go and talk to it when I should have been working on the books. Caden did warn me before to wear more sensible footwear, but of course I didn't listen, and over I went in the animal muck, and—"

Eden smiled sweetly. "Lena, don't be hard on yourself. I don't know how many times I've ended up on my behind when I've been dropping Dion at the farm, and I refuse to wear those big clunky boots Dante and Caden wear while they're there."

Stella nodded and held her hand by her mouth, stage-whispering, "I try to go there as little as possible."

The three women laughed, and Eden said, "See? Don't feel bad. Our partners may find rolling in mud fun, but we do not."

"Thank you for understanding, but you can assure Ms. Wolfgang that I'll be back at the ranch office tomorrow."

"Oh no, you won't. I won't hear of it. You're to take the rest of the week off and see how things are. Dante told me to make sure you took enough time to get better. Your assignment with us is as long as it takes, so that means take your time. I'll get Caden to make sure you do."

Lena was touched. Everyone she encountered in Wolfgang County had been so kind to her. The feeling of community spirit permeated the town and its people, starting with those at the top.

Stella retrieved a beribboned box from her bag and handed it over to Lena. "Eden and I thought you'd enjoy something sweet to eat while you recuperate."

Chocolates. "That's very kind of you both. Thank you." Lena accepted the gift and imagined how good they would taste. One more thing she would have to deny herself.

"They're from a local chocolate store—they hand-make everything, and these are a favorite of a certain tall, good-looking ranch manager, so I'm told," Eden hinted.

Caden. Lena imagined waking up in her arms yesterday, and feeling so safe and protected. It had only been a night, but she missed Caden terribly.

"I see you have some beautiful flowers there," Eden said.

"Oh yes. Aren't they lovely? Caden got them for me, and this cute plush wolf, and a beautiful wolf pen. She's so kind." Lena beamed.

"Caden bought flowers?" Stella asked.

Lena nodded.

"And a wolf stuffed animal?" Eden added in surprise.

"Well, yes. Is there something wrong with that?" Lena fiddled with her glasses nervously.

Eden leaned forward and placed her hand on Lena's knee. "Oh no, not at all. It's only that our Caden isn't known for doing that kind of thing. She must think you're a very special friend."

Lena's heart started to race. It didn't mean anything. Caden felt sorry for her. Nothing more.

When Eden got so close, Lena noticed a moonstone similar to the one Caden had given her was mounted in Eden's necklace and ring. A quick look over to Stella, and she found the same in her ring.

"Excuse me for asking, but could you tell me about the stone in your jewelry? It's very unusual."

Eden held out her ring finger. "This? Oh, it's moonstone. It's traditionally a stone used for wedding rings, love tokens, things like that. Why do you ask?"

Lena opened her mouth, but nothing came out. She thought of the moonstone, in her purse, that Caden had given her, and wondered what she'd meant by giving her that gift.

"Lena? Why do you ask?"

"I've seen a few people wearing the stone and wondered what it was, that's all. It's beautiful."

Caden arrived at the hospital midmorning, determined to give Lena a ride home, and nothing more. She had promised herself that she would see as little of her as possible in order to try to control her growing feelings.

She tipped her hat to some of the hospital staff she passed, and stopped at the nurses' station. The nurse on duty looked up and smiled. "Second, good morning."

"Morning, Nurse Skye. Is Selena Miller to be released today?"

"Yes, Second. She responded well overnight and shows no sign of infection. She's all ready for you and the doctor has left human medication for her to take."

"Excellent. Thank you." Caden turned to leave the nurses' station when Nurse Skye stopped her.

"Second? There's just one thing I wanted to mention, and perhaps you can help."

"What is it, Nurse?"

"We couldn't get Ms. Miller to eat, and it worried me. An animal in good health should not refuse food, and Dr. Jaycen had left dietary instructions that she was to be given milk and plenty of meat to aid recovery. She refused to eat last night and this morning, saying she would eat at home. We weren't sure what to do."

Caden sighed and scrubbed her face with her hands. *I need to make you see how perfect you are.* "I'll take care of it. Thank you for letting me know, Skye." Caden knew this meant spending time with Lena, and becoming closer, but she had no choice. Lena's welfare was more important than her feelings.

Caden helped Lena up into the passenger seat of her truck and put the seat belt on for her. "Is that all right? Your arm's not too sore?"

"It's okay. I can take my pain meds when I get home."

She knew that meant Lena was sore, so she jumped into the driver's side quickly and started to drive.

Lena pushed her glasses up on her nose. "This is kind of you, Caden. You didn't have to do this."

Caden looked around and smiled. "Of course I did. You were injured on Venator property, and I am Second…in command, so to speak, in our business. Besides, we in Wolfgang County always look after each other. Which reminds me"—she pressed the call button on her center console—"call New Moon."

Lena looked at her questioningly. "What?"

Caden placed a finger to her lips.

"New Moon Bar and Grill, how can I help you?"

"Hi, Judy, it's Caden. Can I make an order and have it delivered to apartment six in the River View building?"

"No problem, Second. What can I get you?"

She looked at Lena and smiled, hoping she wouldn't be asked about that slip. "Could I have two bumper breakfast plates, two orders of pancakes, and hang on a minute…"

Caden muted the call and asked, "Lena? Do you prefer strawberry, banana, chocolate, or vanilla?"

"Strawberry, I guess…but why?"

"Hi, Judy, we'll have two extra-extra-large shakes, one strawberry, one chocolate with caramel syrup."

"No problem, Cade, I'll have it sent in thirty minutes, tops."

"Thanks, Judy."

When she ended the call, Lena said, "Why did you order all that food?"

Caden turned around in her seat to face Lena. "Dr. Jaycen told me how important food and milk are in curing injured…ah, people, and Nurse Skye told me you hadn't eaten the food they offered you."

Lena sighed and lowered her head, allowing her hair to hide her face. "You know I can't eat things like that. I told you I was trying to lose weight. I can't eat fatty meats and full-fat milk."

"I promised Nurse Skye I would get you to eat well, so since I can't cook, and you can't cook with your arm, I thought we'd get some food delivered."

Lena was fuming inside but didn't have the courage to say anything. Food was the one thing in her life she had control over, and she didn't like having what she ate dictated to her. She turned away and stared out the truck window.

"I just want you to get better, Lena. Let's talk about it when I get you home." Caden drove off, both of them in silence.

❖

Lena sat down at her small kitchen table while Caden put her bags in the bedroom. They hadn't spoken, apart from Caden asking and Lena instructing where to put the bags. Lena was annoyed at Caden's dominating commands. It was bad enough that she had to put up with that from her family. She thought her new friendship with Caden could be different.

Maybe it was her. Maybe people saw someone who needed to be controlled.

The doorbell chimed and Caden hurried to answer it. Lena watched carefully and saw the delivery boy put his fist to her chest and say, "Second, here is your food."

She couldn't understand why everyone kept calling Caden *Second*. It was odd. Lena's eyes followed Caden's hand to her back pocket as she took out her wallet to pay for the food. Her eyes lingered over Caden's muscular, solid backside, and she felt a hot flush right to her core. In her mind, she saw an image of that muscular backside undulating and thrusting…

"Lena? Lena, are you okay?" Caden's voice knocked her from her thoughts.

"What? Oh yes, fine." She felt the deep heat climb up her neck to her cheeks.

Caden threw her Stetson onto the table and put the food containers down. She kneeled at Lena's side and said, "Listen, I'm sorry if you felt I was being…controlling." She dropped her head with a sigh, clearly struggling to explain herself. "I'm used to giving out orders and people following them—it's the way things are done here—but I only wanted to help you heal. The nurse and the doctor said you have to eat."

Lena looked down and rubbed her cast, as if that could soothe it. "I know you mean well, but if I eat things like that I'll never lose weight. I have my father's birthday party in two weeks, and if I haven't lost more…" She shrugged. How could she explain?

Caden placed her finger underneath Lena's chin and gently raised her head. "Why do you worry so much about losing weight, and what you eat?"

"Because I'm fat. I have fat hips, fat thighs, and a huge butt. That's why," Lena shouted and ran off crying to her bedroom.

Caden was shocked and had no idea how to handle an upset submissive female. She was totally outside her realm of experience. She paced, not knowing what she should do for the best. This was why she was meant to be a lone wolf. She had no idea what to say and do around submissives.

Caden looked over at the table with the food growing cold and decided she had to do something. She knocked at the bedroom door and walked in to find Lena wiping her eyes, holding on to her bear.

*Thank you, Mater, she hasn't noticed.* She had placed the mended bear back where she'd found it, while putting Lena's bags in her room.

"Lena, I'm sorry I upset you—"

"No, I'm sorry. I should never have had an outburst like that in front of you." Lena put her glasses back on and visibly pulled herself together. "Can we please forget it? I really don't want to talk about it."

Caden put her hands in her jeans pockets and rocked back on her heels. "If that's what you want, but how about this? If you'll eat what I've ordered, I'll take you out on a hike to Whitefang Hill on Saturday to work it off. It's quite a hike and it looks down over the lake. The view is beautiful, truly."

Lena smiled. "Why are you trying so hard to get me to eat?"

Taking the chance that she was winning the argument, Caden walked over to her and said, "Because a wounded animal must eat and take care of itself to heal. If it is unwilling, then the pack must help it heal."

"The pack?"

"Well, you know I always speak in terms of animals. I mean the family, the community, the collective. We'll help someone who is struggling or injured."

Lena raised an eyebrow to her. "And this hike will burn a lot of calories?"

"Oh, millions, I should think. I'm going to push you hard." Lena giggled at that and so Caden held out her hand to her. "What do you say? Will you share my food?"

*What did I say that for?*

Lena grasped her hand and pulled herself up. "I'll share your food, Caden."

Caden felt both extreme elation and terror at the same time.

"Wait a minute." Lena stopped and stared down at the bed. "Is this dog hair?" She picked up some between her thumb and forefinger. "How on earth did that get there?"

Caden panicked. "Maybe it came from my clothing?"

"How?" Lena asked.

Caden tried to think on her feet. "Well…there are a couple of dogs that live at the farm, and I sat on your bed while making up your overnight bag. Yes. That's it. It was on my clothes."

Lena nodded, but looked as if she was a bit suspicious about the explanation. "Oh…okay."

"Let's go eat. I'm starving," she said, hoping to avoid more unanswerable questions.

❖

"I must say, that was delicious." True to her word, Lena had eaten as much as she could, which was about a third of what Caden managed. Lena was amazed at how much Caden ate, and how quickly.

"I'm glad you liked it."

"You sure can eat a lot," Lena blurted. "I'm sorry, that was probably rude, but I don't think I've ever seen anyone eat as much, and be so lean and fit."

"Well, I do a really heavy job, and like I said to you before, my body suits its purpose."

Lena felt a blush rise up her cheeks, but Caden didn't seem to notice and got up to take the plates to the sink.

"Can I get you your medication now?"

"Yes, please. It's aching a lot." She flexed her fingers, trying to ease the pain.

Caden brought over the boxes and began to read the labels.

"Okay...one of these, and two of those red ones." Caden placed them in front of her and said eagerly, "What happens now?"

"What do you mean?" Lena asked, mystified.

"How do you take it? The medicine, I mean."

"You've never taken pills before?" Every time she thought she had heard the strangest thing come out of Caden's mouth, another oddity followed behind it.

"No, I never get sick."

"Not even painkillers for a headache or a pulled muscle?" she asked in disbelief.

"Nope. So, what else do you need?"

Lena stared at Caden, trying to work out this puzzle. "A glass of water would be good. You can find a glass in the right-hand cupboard up there."

Caden filled a glass and brought it back, and watched her with a strange fascination.

Once she swallowed her pills, Lena yawned. "Sorry, I'm really tired. I—"

Without warning Caden lifted her into her arms.

"Caden! What are you doing?"

Caden stopped and looked down at her with confusion. "You said you were tired. Do you want to go to bed or to the couch?"

"It's my arm that's broken, not my legs," Lena snapped.

"I'm sorry, I just jumped in headfirst again. I'll put you down." Caden looked like she'd lost her last friend.

Lena sighed and gave her a small smile. "Hey, it's okay. Why don't you pop me on the couch."

Caden's expression lightened. "Hold on tight, then."

With her good arm Lena held on tight around Caden's neck. Lena's eyes closed and a moan escaped from her lips as she burrowed nose and lips into the crook of Caden's neck.

Caden gently placed her on the couch, then propped her injured arm on some cushions and placed a blanket over her.

"I'll be fine now, Caden. Don't feel you have to stay with me—you've done so much. You have work at the farm to be doing."

Caden smiled and carefully removed Lena's glasses, placing them on the coffee table. "I'm going to stay for a while and make sure you get some rest. I've taken a day off. That is, if you don't mind me staying?"

"Of course not. I don't know what I did to deserve a friend like you," Lena said sleepily.

Caden sat in the armchair opposite. "You deserve someone who cares. Sleep well, Lena."

Lena drifted off and murmured, "Cade..." as sleep overcame her.

❖

Lena was awoken from her sleep by a loud howl, coming from outside. Her heart thudded in her chest, as she jumped up and ran to the window. It took all her courage to pull back the drapes and peek out the glass.

Seeing nothing, she slowly opened the window. The wind rushed in, blowing the drapes in the air. Behind her, she heard a deep growl, which both terrified and excited her.

Her breathing became shallow and rapid as the growl got closer. She forced herself to turn her head to the side, and there, bathed in the shadowy light of the moon, was Caden, naked, muscles taut, with a dark and dangerous look.

"Caden?"

She said nothing in reply, but prowled forward, like an animal stalking its prey. Lena snapped her head forward, too fearful and excited to face who and what was approaching her.

Caden got so close that Lena felt her hot breath on her neck. She throbbed inside and moaned, "Caden..."

She felt Caden's hands travel up and down her silk negligee, feeling her curves, grasping her breasts through the lace material that covered them.

Her eyes closed and she moaned in pleasure. She wanted Caden's touch everywhere, she wanted Caden inside her, taking and possessing her.

Caden's lips ran over her neck, and her body was on fire. Caden's tongue laved a spot on her neck that felt directly connected to her clit.

She heard Caden say one word, "Mine," and with a growl she sank her teeth into Lena's neck. Lena's eyes sprang open in shock, and there, reflected in the windowpane, were the pair of yellow eyes that haunted her.

❖

Caden was enjoying the quiet contentment of watching over and guarding Lena. She had quickly fallen asleep after taking her pain medication and so Caden had taken the opportunity to lie back in the armchair, with her booted feet crossed and her Stetson over her eyes. Her wolf would have much preferred to be lying next to Lena, guarding and snuggling into her, but this was the next best thing.

As Caden dozed, she began to hear murmurs and small moans coming from Lena. Her first thought was that she was in pain, but the moans became deeper, and sounded of longing. Caden replied with a growl.

She jumped from her seat and walked over to Lena. She knew she shouldn't watch, but she could not tear her eyes away from Lena as she moved and squirmed in her sleep, stretching and offering her neck to her dream lover.

"Who are you dreaming about, beautiful one? Who makes you moan desperately?"

"Caden…Cade…bite me," Lena moaned.

Caden scented Lena's arousal. She fell to her knees, and her fangs pierced through her gums, in response to Lena's call.

*She's dreaming about me.*

She allowed herself to inch closer to Lena's neck and inhale her scent. It would have been so easy to bite the exposed area, so easy to make Lena hers. She ran her tongue over her elongated canines, contemplating what it would feel like to sink them deep into her neck.

It took all of Caden's will, but she managed to pull back and stand away from Lena. Her head was swimming with lust and sensation. Her claws were already starting to shift. She had to get Lena to wake and stop calling for her, or she could lose control.

She bent over and shook Lena gently. "Lena? Lena, please wake up. You're dreaming."

Lena gasped, and her eyes shot open in terror. She jumped up so fast her head smashed Caden in the face. "Oh God. Caden, I'm sorry, I was dreaming." She crouched down beside Caden, who had both hands over her nose.

"It's okay," Caden's muffled voice said.

Lena gasped when she saw the blood starting to flow through Caden's fingers. "What have I done? Quick! Get to the sink."

Caden leaned over the sink and let the blood drip down the drain.

Lena hugged her from behind. "What can I do? I'm such an idiot. I'm so sorry."

"Look, don't panic. It'll be okay." Caden spat blood into the sink. "Can you get me a wet towel or something?"

Lena looked around the room in a panic. "A wet towel, a wet towel. Oh yeah. Hang on."

When she ran in the direction of the bathroom, Caden mumbled to herself, "How do I get myself in these situations?" Since meeting Lena, Caden's ordered world had been thrown into flux.

Normally a simple injury like this would cause no problems. It didn't hurt much and would heal as soon as she shifted, but she couldn't shift. Not now, and not later, or Lena would know clearly that there was something different about her.

Lena came running back with the towel. "Here you go."

Caden turned and leaned against the sink, holding the wet towel to her nose.

"Are you okay? Is it broken?" Lena asked.

She waggled the bridge of her nose with her fingers. "No, it seems okay. Don't worry about it. It's just a lot of blood. No harm done."

She watched Lena look down to the ground in sadness and

instantly wanted to make her feel better. "We make a great pair, eh? Me with a busted nose, and you with your busted arm," she joked.

Her words had quite the opposite effect, as she heard Lena start to sniffle and cry. Caden mentally kicked herself. *You have no business talking to a submissive female, Wolf.* Look at the effect she had on them.

"Don't cry, Lena." She threw the bloody towel in the sink. "Look—it's stopped bleeding." Caden caught a glimpse of herself in the living room mirror. Her nose had stopped bleeding but was still a mess.

Lena looked up and cried anew at the sight. "Look what I did to you. Everyone is right about me. I'm a baby elephant that stomps around, breaking everything in its path."

Caden took Lena in her arms without even thinking, and pulled her tightly to her. "You are not clumsy, not a fool, none of those terrible names bullies have called you, and if I hear anyone call you a baby elephant I will bite them. I mean…smack them around."

They held each other quietly for a while, before Lena pulled back and looked into her eyes. "You were in my dream again."

"Was I?" Caden feigned ignorance.

"Yes. Your eyes…your eyes are always yellow." Lena touched Caden's temple with her fingertips.

"Why would my eyes be yellow?" Caden asked, as their faces inched toward each other.

"I have no idea, but I know it's important. Somehow, it's important."

They were a hairsbreadth away from each other, and Lena licked her lips, unknowingly seductive.

Caden's eyes zeroed in on her plump red lower lip and ached to take it between her teeth. *I'll bite it, and suck it and...* What was she doing? She let Lena go like she had been burned.

"I'm sorry. I better go." Caden grabbed her hat and, walking backward toward the door, said, "I have to get going. If you need anything, just call me okay? Bye."

She ran from the apartment like a frightened rabbit, leaving Lena to wonder what had just happened.

## Chapter Thirteen

Caden drove straight to the sheriff's office, where the elite wolves met before leading their squads out on the nightly patrols.

Dante, Flash, Blaze, and Xander were already in the sheriff's office when Caden arrived. She walked out back into the locker room where they were congregated, and all conversation stopped immediately.

Dante gave her a lopsided smile and said, "Second? Did one of our prey kick you in the face?"

The other wolves sniggered. Caden had never felt so embarrassed, and she knew it was about to get worse.

"Please don't ask, Alpha."

The locker room had an exit directly into the forest so they could undress here and lead their wolf squads all over pack land. While the others were in various stages of undress, Caden remained clothed and sat on one of the benches.

"Second, I have to ask myself why you would let yourself remain injured, when you could shift and heal yourself."

Caden held her hands over her face and said, "I can't shift and heal because it was a human who injured me, a human who might work out our secret if I show up the next day with not a scratch on my face."

Caden knew that Dante had an idea who that human was, but her silence allowed Caden to keep the rest of the story to herself.

Xander, the county fire chief, walked over and looked closely at her injured face. "You let a human do that to you?"

Caden's dominant feathers were getting extremely ruffled. "I didn't *let* some human do that to me, Xan, it was an accident."

"So why don't you just shift and stay away from the human in question?" Blaze asked.

Caden looked up at Dante with a pleading look and sighed. "Because I work with the human at the farm, and I promised to take her out on Saturday."

"A human female did this to you?" Xander asked, barely controlling her laughter.

Then Flash realized who it must be. "Not Selena? The little-bitty human girl who acts like a mouse?"

"Don't say that about her," Caden boomed.

"It is." Flash and Xander howled with laughter, and Caden launched herself across the room and tackled Flash, one of her best friends, to the floor.

"Take it back now." She growled and bared her teeth.

A shocked Flash turned his head to the side and offered his throat in submission. "I'm sorry, Cade. I didn't mean anything by it. You know I would never insult you or anyone you liked."

Dante gave a warning growl. "Second, get up now."

Caden pulled back and was helped up by Blaze. When she got to her feet, she seemed dazed and confused. "Wha—?"

Flash, now on his feet walked up to Caden with his eyes cast down. "I'm sorry, Second."

Dante watched closely but allowed her Second to patch up this dispute, like the dominant wolf that she was, for which Caden was grateful.

Caden put her hands around the back of Flash's neck and pulled him close. "I need forgiveness, not you."

Xander then approached with her own apologies and they reconciled in seconds.

Dante stepped forward and said, "Second, go to Blaze's office and wait for me there."

"Yes, Alpha," she said with resignation.

Caden stalked to the office and paced up and down, waiting for Dante. She ripped her shirt off in frustration and threw it across the room.

"Second."

Caden stopped her relentless pacing and looked at her Alpha. "I'm sorry, Alpha. Forgive me. I don't know what's happening to me. I feel like my wolf is clawing at my skin from inside. All I want to do is shift, and I can't."

Dante took a seat at Blaze's desk and indicated for Caden to sit. "This is what we are going to do. You are going to shift and run with me tonight. You cannot deny your wolf, especially while you are experiencing these new emotions. You have to shift."

"But Lena will know something is different about us. She's already dreaming about me having yellow eyes. I'm sure in the back of her mind there's a memory of when I first saved her."

Dante sighed. "That's probably true. Are you sure this day out on Saturday is a good idea?"

"I don't have a choice—I promised her, and I can't let her down. Everyone she knows lets her down, judges her, and finds her wanting. I can't bear to have her think I'm the same."

Dante was silent for a moment. "I can't imagine letting Eden down, and I won't force you to do that, Second. You will have to stay away from her these few days, and on Saturday you'll just have to convince her you're a quick healer."

Caden nodded her head in resignation. "But she's injured. Someone will have to check on her until then. I would just worry."

Dante stood and began to unbutton her shirt. "I'll send someone to check on her." Before Caden had a chance to reply, Dante added, "And no, I won't send a dominant wolf. I'll ask a submissive to go. Stella or Vance, maybe. Is that acceptable?"

"Yes, Alpha. Thank you. Thank you for understanding."

"I understand what drives you to protect your mate. And although you want to suppress it, that's who your wolf thinks Lena is."

Caden just hung her head and didn't reply. Dante, now divested of her clothes, smacked her on the shoulder. "Come, Second, we will run all that aggression and mating energy out of you, and if Leroux's scent is anywhere near pack land, we will put it to good use."

They shifted quickly and Caden ran after her Alpha, her injury already nearly healed.

❖

That night as Lena lay sleeping, Caden, her evening patrol finished, stood guard from the fire escape outside her window. *I will watch over you, beautiful one.* She couldn't stop her wolf seeking out Lena. Lena was addictive.

Caden had been all around the apartment building, scent marking so any wolves in the building would know this was now part of her territory. She had even padded inside and up the stairs to rub her scent on the welcome mat at the door. Any wolf that approached Lena's apartment would scent a big warning sign, lit up in neon. *Caden's. Do not pass.*

Lena murmured in her sleep and Caden slinked away. She was not prepared to risk being seen, but Saturday couldn't come quickly enough for her. She would be able to spend the whole day with Lena, and try to show her how wonderful she was.

❖

Caden sat in her truck outside Lena's apartment waiting for her to come out. She had called Lena the night before to set up a time to pick her up. Lena had sounded surprised that Caden remembered her promised day out, as she hadn't heard from her in two days.

Caden hated the deception, but it was essential to maintain the pack secret. Of course, unbeknownst to Lena, Caden had in fact seen her every night while she slept. She prowled around the building, guarding, scent marking, and climbing the fire escape at the back to gaze upon her as she slept.

She caught a glimpse of herself in the rearview mirror and checked the large aviator sunglasses she had chosen to wear today.

Between the sunglasses and the brim of her Stetson shading her face, her healed injuries should be less obvious.

When Caden saw the apartment building door open and Lena walk through, she felt that thrum of excitement in her blood, a new feeling since meeting Lena. She jumped out and took the picnic basket from Lena's good arm. "Hey, you sure made a lot. Did you manage okay?"

She had offered to pick up some food for them to take with them, since Lena's arm was pretty useless, but Lena had insisted she wanted to provide food for them and that she would cope.

"Yes, I hope you like it all, and don't worry, there's no salad in there for you. Stella and Vance took me to the store and did all the lifting for me. I asked them what you liked."

Caden laughed nervously, wondering what those two troublemakers had said to Lena. "Great. I can't wait to eat." She stowed the basket in the back, then helped Lena into the high truck cab and jumped in. "So, we ready?"

"How's your face? I've felt so bad about it."

"I told you—it's fine. I'm made of tough stuff." Caden looked straight ahead and turned on the engine. *Don't ask anymore. Please.*

"Caden?"

When she turned, Lena reached up and took the sunglasses from her face. Caden didn't stop her.

"I don't understand. You don't have a mark."

She had tried to prepare what she would say, but now in the moment, her mind went blank. "Uh…it wasn't that bad once it was cleaned up. The blood made it look worse than it was."

Lena stared at her openmouthed. "I expected you to have two large panda eyes at least, but it looks like nothing ever happened."

"Well, I'm a fast healer, and the doctor has this special cream. He makes it himself from plants that grow in the forest. It's an old family recipe, and it takes away bruising superfast."

Lena was about to ask another question when Caden spotted Dion across the street, and it seemed the perfect way to change the subject. "Oh, look! It's Dion."

"Where?" Lena looked around.

"Over there, outside the flower store. It's her big date with Tia tonight."

Lena brought her hand to her mouth. "That's so sweet. She's buying her flowers. What excitement she must feel. Her first date."

Caden did know what that felt like—she was feeling it now. "Can we get going now? We have a lot of things to see today. I have it all planned out."

Lena gave her a sweet smile and said, "I can't wait."

❖

Caden marched up the incline holding the picnic basket as if it weighed nothing. Behind her, a struggling Lena tried to keep up.

Lena stopped to catch her breath, and called in desperation, "Caden?"

"What? Oh, are you okay?" Caden hurried back to her. "Is your arm hurting?"

Lena stood cradling her cast and breathing hard. "I can't keep up with you—you're going too fast."

"I'm sorry. I'm forgetting my stride is a lot bigger than yours. The picnic spot is just over the brow of this incline. It's a beautiful spot."

"You're too everything," Lena teased, still gasping for air. "You're carrying that basket like there's nothing in it. How strong are you anyway?" She'd noticed that every time she mentioned something about Caden's physical prowess, Caden's eyes flitted about nervously, as if trying to work out an answer. There was something different about Caden, and she was going to work out what it was.

"Well, I…"

"You're the strongest person I've ever met," Lena said and saw a smile form on Caden's face and her chest puff up at the compliment.

"Thank you. Take my arm for the last part of the climb. I'll get you there."

Caden did indeed help get her over the brow of the hill. It led to a meadow, which looked down over the lake and made for a stunning view.

"Wow. This is beautiful. It's just breathtaking."

"I hoped you'd like it."

She looked over to Caden and smiled. "Like it? That's an understatement. I've never been in a place as beautiful as Wolfgang County. You're very lucky to live here."

"We all think so." Caden laid the blanket she had brought from the truck and said, "So? Can we eat? 'Cause I'm starving."

Lena dropped to her knees on the rug and began to organize the food, which wasn't easy with one arm in a cast. Caden sat and reminded Lena of a puppy waiting for a treat.

She pulled out various containers from the box and placed them on the blanket. "Okay, we have chicken wings, basted with my own spicy sauce, turkey, corned beef, and ham sandwiches, some slaw, potato salad…what would you like?"

"Some of each, just pile it on. I'm ravenous."

Lena started to pile up the plate with a bit of everything with a chuckle. "I think you must have a hollow leg the way you eat."

Caden took off her checked shirt and tossed it to the side, leaving her in a sleeveless T-shirt. Lena was mesmerized by Caden's muscular arms and shoulders.

She took the plate Lena was holding and said, "I need a lot of energy, you know."

Without thinking, Lena replied, "Yes, I can see that."

Caden grinned, and Lena felt the familiar feeling of a blush climbing from her neck. The feeling of embarrassment was different from her usual sort of anxiety—it was a heat rising from inside that made her heart beat fast in a good way. She was ogling Caden like a schoolgirl with a crush, and it was making her look like an idiot.

Before Caden took a bite of her food, she asked Lena, "You *are* going to eat something, aren't you? You did promise if I took you up here to burn calories, you would eat."

"Technically, I promised I would eat the large breakfast you bought the other day, but I will eat some, don't worry."

"Great." Caden attacked her food and was obviously enjoying it so much, Lena was sure she could hear a soft growl. "Mmm, these chicken wings are so good, Lena. You can really cook."

Lena smiled shyly. "Thank you. That's one thing I'm proud that I can do. I spent a lot of my childhood in the kitchen with our cook. She was my best friend and taught me all she knew."

Caden finished her huge plate and watched Lena nibble at her own. "Will you tell me about your family? I'd love to know more about you."

"If you like. We're not very interesting. My father, Luther, is a judge, and my two brothers are partners in one of the top law firms in New York. My mother, Veronica, owns her own fashion magazine company."

"Wow, an accomplished family."

Lena stared downward to her plate and set it aside. "Yes, career success is very important in my family. My brothers—Greg and Tom—graduated top of their class at law school. Father and Mother are very proud."

"So you thought you'd be different and be an accountant. Do you enjoy that?"

Lena smiled. "I love numbers. They're predicable, they never change or let you down. But I didn't want to be an accountant."

Caden raised an eyebrow at this news. "Oh? So what did you want to be when you grew up? A ballerina? An astronaut?"

Lena giggled and nudged Caden with her good arm. "No, silly. Since I was in junior high, I wanted to be a math teacher. I wanted to show kids that numbers didn't have to be scary or boring—numbers can be beautiful and fun."

"Why didn't you do it, then?"

Lena was fascinated watching Caden eat her food. She stripped every last piece of meat off the chicken wings, leaving perfectly clean bones. She sucked at the bones with a low growl until she saw she was being watched, then quickly put them down and inhaled all the side dishes in a minute.

Caden put down her plate and lay back on the blanket, resting up on her elbows. "So?"

Lena shook herself from her thoughts and said, "What? Become a teacher?"

"Yeah, if you loved it like you said you did, why not?"

Lena's breath caught at the sight of Caden lying back, her arm muscles taut and the afternoon sunlight blazing down on her. She was magnificent.

She realized Caden was calling her name and had caught her dreaming. "Huh? Oh, Father would never allow one of his children to be a teacher. He always says, *People who can do, do, and people who can't, teach, Selena. We are a family that do*."

Caden looked annoyed. "He said that? Who does he think teaches the next generation of lawyers, doctors, judges, and accountants? People who teach cu—children are respected in Wolfgang County."

"I know, but that's who Father is, and Mother too. They said if I wanted to work with numbers, I should be an accountant." When she saw Caden shake her head and scowl, she said, "There's no changing them. I just have to accept it. But I love kids—I used to do tutoring all through high school and college. It was the most fun part of my day."

Caden thankfully let the matter drop. Lena was embarrassed trying to explain her dysfunctional family.

"In a way I'm glad you took this career path, because I would never have met you otherwise, and your friendship means the world to me."

"It does?" Lena asked with surprise.

"Sure, I feel like I've known you all my life, like I was meant to know you."

Lena couldn't quite believe somebody as good looking and supremely confident could think she was anything more than a weird, strange oddball, but Caden did, and that had never happened before. She had a connection with Caden that she couldn't explain. Every failing she saw in herself, Caden seemed to possess the opposite quality. Her utterly unashamed confidence in her body and place in the world made her so attractive.

"Me too. I've never been able to talk with someone like this, without them thinking I was weird, anyway."

Caden reached up and brushed her long hair out of her face. "You're not weird. You are perfect."

Lena opened her mouth to speak, but nothing would come out. She was struck dumb by that comment. No one, apart from her uncle, had ever said anything like that to her before, and with such kindness. She didn't know how to respond.

An awkward silence settled between them until Caden said, "Tom and Greg are very everyday names. How did you get a beautiful name like Selena? It doesn't seem like a name your parents would pick."

"It wasn't. Uncle Joel chose my name. He was my mother's brother, and the black sheep of the family. He was a musician, an artistic type. The only one who really connected with me." Lena smiled sadly. "I was an unexpected baby, to say the least, for my parents. My brothers are six and ten years older than I am. Mother often tells me how I came at a very inconvenient time. Her first two magazines were a huge success, and she was just about to launch them overseas when she became pregnant."

"How could a child be inconvenient?" Caden said angrily.

Selena shrugged her shoulders. "It wouldn't be to me, but my parents are life planners, down to the very last detail. A third child and a girl did not fit that plan. Anyway, when I was born, my uncle asked what they had called me. Mother told him they couldn't think of a name, as they had picked out all boys' names. Uncle Joel wasn't like my parents, he was kind and loving, and the only person to ever look at me and find nothing wrong with me." *Until you.*

Caden looked utterly horrified at her description of her family, and she was embarrassed. "Mother and Father told him he could name me. He told me that when he walked over to the hospital window and looked out on the cold, clear night and saw a full moon, he chose Selena. I loved him a great deal."

"He sounds nice, and he couldn't have chosen a better name. Magical things happen on a full moon," Caden said with a smile.

Lena smiled back and started to clear up the picnic things.

"Hey, Lena? Once we've got everything cleared up, how about I take you down to see the lake?"

"That would be really nice. It's beautiful."

Caden stood and began to help gather up the picnic things, and a question popped into Lena's head. She summoned all her courage to ask. "Caden? Will you have dinner with me?" She held her breath for the reply. Caden had turned down dinner once before and it had hurt. She was taking a big chance asking a second time, but she really did not want their day to end.

Caden hesitated for a few seconds before saying, "I'd like that, but only if you let me help you. Your arm's going to be really sore after this afternoon."

She took Caden's offered hand and stood up. "Okay. I'll let you help." *You make me feel so much, Cade.*

## Chapter Fourteen

After their day out, Caden and Lena stopped off at the store so Lena could pick up some things for dinner. Caden had persuaded her that it would be acceptable to eat steak after all the exercise she had done today.

They were now sitting at the table enjoying what they had made, and Lena hummed in contentment at every bite. She had to let Caden cut the steak into bites for her, as she couldn't use a knife, and that was embarrassing, but she couldn't remember the last time she had eaten a steak. It was certainly a long time ago. She looked up and saw Caden grinning and watching her eat. "What?"

"I enjoy watching you eat. Do you realize, the color has come back to your cheeks today. All because you've been eating well."

Every time Caden mentioned her eating habits, a small part of her felt resistant and annoyed. "I can't eat like this all the time—besides, I'm still having a salad." That was the one concession she had persuaded Caden to make. Caden had a baked potato with her steak, but she simply had a side salad.

"Your body is crying out for nourishment, Lena. You don't have to be a doctor to see that."

Lena sighed. "You know I don't want to talk about this." Caden couldn't seem to help trying to dominate her again.

They had nearly fallen out in the store when Caden insisted on buying the food for them, demanding it was her role—whatever that meant—to provide the meat for Lena's table.

Lena had been left fuming. The car ride home had been very quiet, but Caden managed to patch things up with her by laughing and joking as she helped Lena cook dinner.

But now, Caden had gone quiet, and Lena felt the need to make things better. "Cade?"

"Yeah?"

"I have ice cream for you for desert."

Caden's smile returned. "I can't wait."

"Only if you're good, though."

Caden snapped her head up and said, "I can be good."

Her heart started to beat double time. Caden had this way of looking her, which made her blood feel hot, something she had never felt before in her life. The only way she could describe the look was that Caden had predator eyes. Eyes that made Lena feel naked, and ready to give her anything she wanted.

She ached for Caden to touch her, to take possession of her body, and the dreams that she continued to have about her left her frustrated and hungry. It was a strange, foreign sensation to feel hungry for another person, but one that was inescapable when Caden looked at her.

"How do you wish me to be good?" Caden asked.

"Well, I'd like to know about you. I told you about my family earlier, and you never talk about yourself."

"There's not much to tell. I live a very simple, uncomplicated life. What would you like to know?"

Lena pushed her plate to the side, with the knife and fork perfectly positioned at an angle, and rested her chin on her good arm. "I'd like to know about your family."

Caden stabbed her fork into her last piece of meat, and then didn't feel like eating it. She hated to talk about her past. She only ever had spoken about it with Dante or Eden, but she felt safe opening up to Lena. "If you want to know anything, I'll tell you."

"Why don't I take my meds, and we can sit on the couch. It'll be much more comfortable."

"Sure." Caden stood and cleared the table for Lena, then walked across the room to the couch. How would she explain it to a human?

"So? The story of Caden?" Lena sat cross-legged on the couch beside Caden, cradling her cast, and eagerly waiting to hear what made her tick.

"It's hard to know where to start. I'm not much of a talker."

"Neither am I, but I can talk to you. I hope you feel the same."

Caden saw Lena looked unsure and was determined not to let her down. "My pater was…"

"Pater?" Lena asked.

"Yeah, it's kind of a local tradition. Because we don't assign roles based on gender, we say *pater* for what you would know as *father*."

"So a woman could be pater?"

*I'm digging deeper and deeper here.* "Yes, my pater was a woman."

"Really?" Lena was learning a lot more than Caden ever intended. "Wolfgang County just keeps surprising me. It's the most wonderful place I've ever been."

It pleased her so much that Lena liked her home. She was so proud of the Wolfgang pack, and it made her happy to see Lena see what every wolf did. "We think so. I'm glad you do."

"Wait—you said *was*. What…?"

"My parents died when I was twelve. They were on a trip outside the county, when a big rig swerved to miss another car and smashed into them on the freeway. The driver was drunk, and they were killed instantly."

Lena clasped her hand to her mouth in shock, and then took her hand. "I'm so sorry, Cade. I shouldn't have asked about them."

Caden let out a sigh. "It's okay. I don't get to talk about them often. I'd be happy to tell you about them."

"I would love that." Lena never let go of her hand, and Caden welcomed it.

"My pater was called Chase and was Second to Dante's pater."

"Second? I've heard people use that term for you. Is it like second-in-command of the company?"

"Yeah, just like that. Dante is CEO and I am Second, like my pater before me."

"Is it an inherited thing?"

Caden now had to explain wolf hierarchy to a human, which was nearly impossible without giving too much away. "Oh no. Dante's CEO position is, well, as long as she is capable, but Second goes to the strongest candidate. Dante and I have always been close, and it was just natural for me to be her Second."

"And your mother? That is the right term, isn't it?" Caden nodded. "What did she do?"

"My mom was a nurse up until they had me. Then she stayed at home to look after me." She would have loved Lena.

"It must have been nice to have your mom at home with you. I hardly ever saw Mother when I was growing up. I spent a lot of time on my own."

Caden rubbed her thumb across the back of Lena's hand in response. "It was. She was a kind and beautiful woman, and my pater adored her. I can remember them talking and laughing together when they thought I was asleep. They were very happy."

"They must have been a beautiful couple. Who took care of you after…?"

"My grandmother. She was a wonderful woman and kept me going through a lot of dark times. Dante's family took me under their wing too. Everyone takes care of each other in Wolfgang County."

"I'm beginning to see that." Lena was quiet for a long time before asking her next question. "Do you have someone in your life now, Caden? Someone who cares for you?"

Caden gave a hollow laugh. "No, I've never loved anyone before. I watched all my friends at school fall, each in turn, to a mate, but I knew I wasn't destined for love."

"Oh."

Caden was sure she could feel Lena's disappointment and was eager to ask her own question. "What about you? Has there been anyone special for you, Lena?"

As she usually did when faced with a difficult topic, Lena bowed her head, allowing her hair to cover her face like a shield. "I don't mix well with people and I prefer my own company. My mother tells me I need to make more of myself."

As Caden opened her mouth to tell Lena how beautiful she was, the phone rang.

Lena jumped up. "Excuse me a moment, help yourself to a drink."

Caden got up and walked to the fridge to pour the milkshake they had brought in earlier.

"Oh, hello, Mother."

Caden busied herself making the drink, so as not to appear as if she was listening, but she could hear every word.

"Selena? We've just gotten back from our two-day trip to a voice mail from the hospital in Wolfgang County, to say you had been in an accident. Why didn't you call us?"

Caden chastised herself for forgetting to tell Nurse Skye not to notify Lena's parents as she'd asked.

"I'm sorry, Mother. It was just a simple broken arm and I didn't want to bother you."

The anxiety was evident in Lena's voice, and Caden didn't need to turn around to scent the tension, as well as hear her heart rate.

"Your father was extremely annoyed. You got this prestigious account, and within a week, you're out of commission because of your own clumsiness, no doubt. Really, Selena, this is just not good enough. We're getting tired of making excuses for you. I have no idea where your father and I got you—you are nothing like us."

Caden's knuckles were white with the force of stopping herself from turning to rip the phone from Lena's hand.

"I'm sorry, Mother..." Lena's voice began to crack with emotion.

"I only hope this hasn't made Ms. Wolfgang consider using a different company next time."

Lena looked over to Caden. "I'm sure it'll be okay, Mother. Ms. Wolfgang and her wife have been very kind to me."

"Her *wife*? Oh, dear God. Well, it's an important contract for the company, so you will have to put up with it. I wouldn't tell your father, or discuss it at his party."

Lena took the telephone into the bedroom, to get some privacy, Caden guessed, but of course she could still hear everything.

"Yes, Mother."

When Lena went out of sight, Caden threw her glass in the sink and pulled off her shirt in anger. Lena's mother didn't once ask how Lena was? How her pain was? When she would get better? What kind of mutts were those people?

Caden stopped dead when she heard Lena crying. She rushed to the bedroom and found her sitting on the bed with tears rolling down her cheeks.

"Why do you let them treat you like that?" Caden asked.

Lena walked over to the window, trying to hide her tearstained face. "You don't know how they treat me."

"Your mother does nothing but make you feel bad about yourself. She called to criticize you for having an accident, and never once asked how you were. That's all I need to know."

Lena turned around angrily. "How could you possibly know that? Were you listening on the other handset?"

"I have excellent hearing," Caden said in a matter-of-fact fashion.

That seemed to make Selena all the more angry. "Excellent hearing, impossible strength, perfect body? We aren't all that lucky, Caden. My mother is just pointing out the obvious. I'm overweight, clumsy, and a disappointment. She's trying to help me make the most of myself."

Caden strode up to Lena and forcibly turned her around so that she was looking at her own reflection in the closet mirror. "Lena, you need to stop living your life with fear, trying to live up to their impossible expectations. Look at yourself."

Lena struggled and tried to turn away.

"No. Look," Caden demanded.

Her voice softened considerably as her eyes took in Lena's soft curves and full breasts. "I see a perfectly healthy female." Caden ran her hands from Lena's shoulders, down her sides, and finished by grasping her hips.

She heard Lena groan, and the scent of her arousal was beginning to fill Caden's senses. "You are the one who is perfect, beautiful one," she told her. Caden lowered her lips till they were brushing Lena's ear, and her hot breath whispered, "You have curvaceous hips to bear young, full breasts to feed them, and soft flesh for your mate to kiss and adore."

Lena's head fell back, exposing her neck. Her eyes were still tightly shut and she groaned, "Cade…"

Caden was close to becoming lost. She could scent the female's readiness to mate, and her wolf was demanding she respond. She pulled Lena's hips to her center and felt the deep-seated need to thrust into her. She pressed her lips to the expanse of neck offered to her and was overcome with the urge to bite down, deep and fast.

Her teeth started to shift, and her mouth watered at the thought of tasting Lena's blood. "My Goddess of the Moon," she whispered.

Lena squirmed and moaned, seemingly lost in utter lust. Caden opened her mouth in readiness to bite, and her eyes lifted to watch Lena's face in the mirror. She stilled when she was faced with her own yellow eyes, burning bright and hot, and her fangs about to bite into the human before her.

The human. What was she doing? Caden was rudely awakened from her lustful haze. She had to get out of there.

She let go of Lena's hips and pulled away. "I'm sorry, I have to go." Lena's eyes sprang open, and the hurt was evident on her face. "Forgive me, Lena."

"Caden, please?"

Caden turned and ran from the room, and out the apartment door.

❖

Caden ran and hunted the whole night, trying to rid herself of the feelings that were driving her insane. And insane was actually the word she would use to describe her mood that morning. She'd grabbed whatever clothes she had found on the floor and driven straight to the head office to speak to Dante. She waited in her truck until she saw Dante's car arrive, then hurried over and jumped into her front seat.

"Cade? Are you all right?"

Caden felt like she was teetering on the edge of control. "No, I'm not all right, Alpha. I need to go, leave the county. I want you to send me to hunt for Leroux. I need to get away from here."

"Wait, wait, just take a breath, Second. First, we have no leads on Leroux's whereabouts, so how can I send you on the hunt? And I need you by my side, to protect pack lands."

Caden let her head fall forward and clasped her hands behind her head. "I can't control my wolf."

Dante grasped the back of her neck and pulled her to her. "Calm yourself, Wolf. I will help you. Let's go up to my office."

Caden knew that every wolf they passed in the Venator building sensed her confusion and tension. This was the last thing the Alpha needed. For the pack to be strong, her wolves needed to feel secure in the leadership. If Caden's situation continued, the wolves below her in the hierarchy would start to feel frightened and insecure, and insecure wolves brought conflict and fights for dominance.

Marcy stood and saluted as they approached. "Alpha, Second. What…?"

Dante shook her head at Marcy, silencing her. "Marcy, push back my conference call for a few hours. I have pack matters to deal with first."

"Of course, Alpha."

Dante closed the office door and sat at her desk. "Sit, Cade."

Caden obeyed and Dante asked, "What happened? Did you shift in front of her?"

"No, but only because her eyes were closed, and I got away from her." She jumped up and began to pace up and down in front of the Alpha's desk. "She was upset. Her parents…they are not good humans. They judge her, make her feel less. I got angry and forced her to try and see what I do, that she's a beautiful female who the Great Mother has made exactly as she planned."

Dante sat back in her leather armchair and calmly listened to her best friend. "And what happened next?"

"She responded to my wolf, my scent. She called to me, called opened her mouth to speak, Lena cut her off. "What gives you the right to send away my cab? You keep trying to make decisions for me, and I won't have it, Caden, not if you want to continue being friends. I get enough of that back home. I mean, one minute you run off when I think we're becoming close, and then I don't see you for a whole week, and next you show up to drive me to work, as if nothing's happened."

Caden smiled inwardly. The shy, introverted woman she had met had apparently found some teeth. If only she could tell her she hadn't abandoned her and that she had seen her over the week, as she stood watch every night. But Lena's eyes showed her anger and hurt, and that made Caden feel guilty, to know she had caused it.

"I'm sorry. I always seem to jump in and take charge without thinking. I'm not trying to control you. I'm just trying to be a friend and take care of you. About Valentine's night—"

Lena narrowed her eyes and said, "When you were trying to tell me I shouldn't feel bad about myself, and then you ran out on me. That night, yes?"

She felt thoroughly chastised and that wasn't a usual experience. "Lena, I feel bad for running. I'm not used to having a friend, and I suppose I felt…scared, caring for someone."

"You're friends with Dante and some of the others."

She couldn't meet Lena's eyes, so she looked straight ahead and said, "It's not the same. They're fellow hunters."

Lena looked confused. "Hunters? What does—"

Caden had to stop this line of questioning, so she turned and placed her hand on her heart. "Look, I'm truly sorry, and if you let me continue to be your friend I will never run out on you again. I give you my word."

Lena's face softened into a smile. "Of course I want to be your friend. I care about you too, and I missed you a lot. I'm sorry, maybe I said too much. I was just frustrated with my mother and then you ran off, and—"

"Stop." She reached and took Lena's hand. "I deserved what you said. You finally got angry at someone and stood up for yourself. Don't take it back now."

The little shy smile that melted Caden's heart was back. "Okay then. I'm glad we're still friends."

Caden's heart felt so much lighter. "Well? May I drive us to work? You're in charge," she said with a wink.

Lena giggled. "Yes, you may, Caden, but I don't want to be in charge all the time, you know."

That comment, which was probably said in all innocence, went straight to Caden's core. She might be doing the right thing, but it was going to be hard.

## Chapter Fifteen

Caden knew Flash and the other farmworkers raised an eyebrow when they saw the pack Second walk with a spring in her step, whistling across the ranch.

The previous week she had been stomping around, growling at everyone. Today she felt much calmer, now that she had decided running from what she felt wasn't an option. All she had left to do was show Lena how much she cared, and hopefully not scare her off with her wolf ways.

This morning, sitting at her desk, she'd been caught staring at Lena, who'd been concentrating on something on the computer screen while she sucked the end of the wolf pen Caden had gotten her, in a way that made Caden's mouth water.

Caden left the office and went out to work with the animals, hoping the smell of manure and dirt would cool her libido. It worked, only a little.

A few hours later, she strode back into the office and threw her Stetson onto the coat hook. Lena looked up and smiled at her. "I'm back, and I've brought you a present."

Lena put down her new wolf pen and asked excitedly, "What?"

"A blueberry muffin, and before you say anything, it's healthy and I'll even halve it with you, if you don't want to eat it all."

"Okay, we'll halve it." Lena took the muffin and plastic cutlery from the bag and cut the treat in two.

Caden brought a chair over to Lena's desk and began eating her share.

Lena tasted hers. "This is delicious."

"Yep, nothing is ever bought in. Everything from the cookhouse is homemade," Caden told her.

Lena sighed in a contented fashion.

"What is it?" Caden asked.

"I was just thinking what a wonderful but simple place Wolfgang County is. Traditional but at the same time the most modern and open place I've ever lived. I've begun to relax so much since I came here—and met you of course."

"I'm glad you like it so much. Listen, I was thinking, if you didn't have any plans, would you like to come over to my house after work? We could pick up some takeout, talk awhile, what do you think?"

Caden could tell Lena's answer by the breadth of the smile. "I'd love to."

*Yes.* Caden didn't know exactly why, but it was important for her to show Lena her den.

❖

Caden pulled the truck up and said, "Here we go. This is my den."

"It's beautiful." The cabin was set in a small clearing, surrounded by forest, and Lena was captivated by it. "It's like a house in a movie. It must be wonderful to wake up to the sounds of the forest all around you."

"It's not much, but I do plan to build a bigger place one day." Caden lifted the bag of takeout from the truck and led Lena up the steps to the front door.

"I can take the bag till you unlock the door," Lena said.

"It's okay. The door's open." Caden opened the door and allowed her guest to walk in first.

Lena was puzzled at how Caden could leave her property unlocked, but soon forgot that concern when she saw the inside of the cozy cabin. An open-plan, comfortable living room led to a wooden staircase on one side, and on the other a large open fireplace, that had logs piled up on either side.

Everything was rustic—wooden floors, furniture, and rugs. The decoration was sparse and depicted animals of the forest, mainly wolves: wolf pictures, statues, ornaments. *They sure do like wolves around here.* She was struck by the warmth she felt, walking into Caden's home. It wasn't physical warmth, but a sense of safety that she associated with Caden.

Caden dropped the takeout bag on the coffee table and quickly started to gather shirts and clothes and magazines that were strewn across the furniture. "I'm sorry, I'm not that tidy. I have someone come in every week to clean and do my laundry, but I should have tidied up this morning before I left for work."

For some insane reason, the thought of someone else coming in and taking care of Caden made Lena feel jealous, which was a totally new emotion for her. She picked up the food and said in a sharp tone, "If you show me to the kitchen, I'll serve the food for us."

"It's just through that door up over there," Caden said, pointing. Lena marched off, leaving Caden holding a pile of clothes and magazines and looking confused.

In the kitchen Lena leaned against the countertop and tried to shake herself free of these new feelings. She tried to work out what was going on in her heart and knew she was falling for Caden in a big way. Lena could only imagine what her mother and father would say about having feelings for a woman like Caden. She had always known she liked women, but her feelings and true nature were not something her parents took into consideration. What looked right to the outside world, that was what they considered important.

When Caden had held her hips and spoken into her ear the other night, she could have melted into her, and she didn't want her to stop.

Would she have stopped Caden, if she had pursued her? If she was honest with herself, she didn't think she would.

❖

Caden paced back and forth with her pile of belongings, not knowing what to do with them. Eventually she walked over to the closet by the front door, where all her muddy farm boots were kept, and unceremoniously dumped the pile inside and shut the door.

She hurried to the kitchen and stopped in the doorway, her mouth curving slowly up her face into a huge smile. The sight of Lena setting the table and dishing out the food gave her a warm glow in her heart, and a rumble of a growl in her throat.

Lena looked up quickly. "Sorry, did you say something?"

"No, just clearing my throat. So, did you find everything okay?"

"Yes. I just looked around the cupboards to find the plates. I hope that was all right?"

It amazed Caden that any little hard-fought bit of confidence Lena gained could be dashed in a moment. "My den is always open to you. You're having a civilizing influence on me. I usually get dinner at the New Moon or bring home takeout, but I never sit at the table with plates and everything."

"Really?"

Caden shrugged. "It doesn't seem worth the effort when you're on your own."

Lena smiled sweetly at her. "You're not alone now, Caden."

The moment was laced with more meaning than Caden was prepared to admit to, but for that moment, she caught a fleeting glimpse of a future that didn't have to be spent alone.

"That was really good," Lena said to Caden. They were relaxing on the couch after dinner, simply enjoying the peace of each other's company.

"I think chicken and broccoli stir-fry must be the healthiest takeout the New Moon has ever made."

Lena sipped her fruit juice and smiled. "You Wolfgang people sure do like your meat."

"It's our livelihood, so we enjoy it, but we also respect it," Caden said.

"I've noticed that while I've been working, Dante seems to run a very ethical business. Going by your accounts, you don't cut corners in the care of the animals."

"Of course not. The Great Mother tasks us to take care of the animals and the habitats she provides for us. If we disrespect that, we disrespect her, and we will suffer for it."

Lena sat closer to Caden, fascinated by what she had said. "The Great Mother? Is that like Mother Nature?"

"Yes, and any hunter who disrespects the Great Mother will not bring home enough meat for her pack."

"You all talk a lot about wolves, and I notice you have a lot of wolf artwork," Lena said.

The best policy was to be as truthful as she could, without telling her everything at once, Caden surmised. "The wolf is symbolic to us. It's the top predator in these parts, but an essential part of the food chain. The way the wolf leads its life, the pack order and hierarchy, the collective purpose of eating, surviving, and raising a family, is what we strive for in Wolfgang County."

Lena looked surprised. "You mean…"

"I mean we all benefit from the kill, just like the wolf. At the top, Dante is our leader and runs the business, then me, and below me there's an elite group of people who act as counsel to both Dante and myself. Everyone benefits from the business and plays their part."

"That's an astonishing way to organize things." Then Lena asked, "So is there any unemployment in Wolfgang County?"

Caden smiled. "There is a job for every one of us here—it's up to us to take it, and we are rewarded by our position. We take care of each other. There are no poor people in Wolfgang County."

"You make me never want to leave."

Caden took her hand and said sincerely, "Then don't. Stay with us."

Lena shook her head. "I'll have to leave when my assignment is finished. My job is in the city, but believe me, there's nothing I would like more than to move away and keep my independence. I'm even dreading going home this weekend."

Caden sat bolt upright. "You're going home?"

"Yes, remember I told you about my father's birthday party?"

Caden nodded sadly. She had planned to ask Lena out again, and she felt an ache at the thought of not seeing her for a whole weekend. She wondered how she would ever cope when Lena reached the end of her assignment.

Lena rubbed her arm cast protectively. "Mother and Father will be appalled at the sight of their baby elephant in an elegant dress with an arm cast on. I think they would have asked me not to come if it wasn't for the fact that James is back in town."

Caden's senses were immediately on alert at this new name. "James? Who is James?"

"James Thornton, my brother's childhood friend. He's a lawyer at the same firm as my brothers, but he's been working in the Paris branch for a year. He just got back."

Caden's wolf didn't like the sound of this one bit. "What does that have to do with you?"

"Oh"—Lena looked down shyly—"my parents have always had the foolish notion that he would make a good husband for me, or more to the point, a good son-in-law for them, but it's never going to happen. James doesn't look at me like that. He spent all of my childhood teasing me, just like my brothers. I keep telling Mother that James likes women who look like models, not women like me."

Caden had to gulp hard to keep down the growl that threatened to come. Her wolf was disturbed by this news and demanded action. Before she could stop herself, she placed a possessive paw on Lena's arm and said, "Why don't I go with you?"

"What?" Lena questioned.

"If you're dreading it so much, why don't I come with you? I can drive you there and back too."

Lena thought about it for a few seconds. "You realize it'll be really boring. A party full of people who value money and position above all else."

"I don't care, Lena. I just want to be there for you." *And mark my territory.*

Lena threw her arms around her. "I'd love you to come."

Caden drank in her scent. "Great. I guess I'll need something to wear. I don't think jeans and boots will be right for this shindig."

"Don't worry, we'll take you shopping. It'll be fun."

Caden held up her hand and said, "One thing though. I'm not wearing girls' stuff. I'm a hun—"

"You're a hunter. Yes, I know." Lena reached forward and cupped Caden's cheek. "I'd never ever want to change that about you."

❖

Lena and Caden had been inside Roman's Suits and Tailoring for a few hours now, trying to find Caden a suit. Lena sat outside the dressing room while the tailor, Roman, fitted Caden. She had already tried on about five suits. Each had something wrong with it in her eyes. Too formal, too uncomfortable, wrong color.

Lena could barely believe this was real. She couldn't believe how much her life had changed in such a short time. Before coming to Wolfgang County a month ago, she had never had a friend and barely spoke to anyone, and now she had Caden and was taking her home to her father's birthday party.

The anxiety she had felt when she'd asked her mother on the phone returned, gnawing away in the stomach.

She opened her purse and pulled out her pen case. She ritually counted them out, making sure they were in the correct order. The process always calmed her nerves, and especially now with the wolf pen that Caden had given her. She felt a new sense of protection in the wolf symbol and the moonstone she always kept in her pocket.

Her mother had been unimpressed with her request until Lena told her Caden was vice president of Venator. The fact Lena had made a friend of such a high-ranking individual had made her mother very happy. The only problem Lena could foresee was she would be expecting an executive woman, like herself, and not a hunter, as Caden put it.

"Lena?" She looked up and saw Eden Wolfgang standing, holding her son.

She quickly put away her pens and stood. "Hi, Mrs. Wolfgang. It's so nice to see you."

"Please, it's Eden, remember?"

Lena held on to the moonstone in her jacket pocket, trying to calm herself enough for normal conversation. "Sorry, Eden. Is this Conan? Caden told me about your children."

Eden smiled and sat in the seat next to Lena. "Yes, this big baby is Conan. Say hi to Lena."

The little boy burrowed closer into his mother. "Hi."

Lena took her seat again, and smiled at the bashful boy. "Hi, Conan. He's so cute, Eden."

"He's a good boy. We're very lucky. I'm just in to collect a few shirts for Dante and heard you were here with Caden."

"Yes." Lena pushed her glasses up the bridge of her nose. "Caden offered to come to my father's birthday party. She's just getting a new suit, and I said I'd help her choose."

Eden's eyes went wide, and she looked totally surprised. "My, my. Caden isn't usually fond of socializing. It'll be good for her to get out someplace different. She must really care about your friendship, Lena."

Lena flushed. "I think she's just trying to be nice. She knows I don't have a lot of friends, and my parents' parties can be intimidating."

Eden placed her hand on Lena's and said, "Believe me, Lena, Caden never does things like this. She likes her solitude—she's a lone wolf, so to speak. I think you can safely say she cares about you. So, when do you leave?"

"Just after we get finished here. We've booked a hotel room not far from my parents'. It should only take us a few hours to get there."

The dressing room door opened and out came Roman. "Ah, Eden. So nice to see you. More shirts for Dante, I would bet?"

Roman was a short submissive wolf with a big personality. He was immaculately dressed in designer pale gray suit trousers and a pink shirt with white collar and cuffs, a measuring tape hanging loose around his shoulders.

"You bet right. I understand you're fitting our Caden for a suit?"

"Indeed, I can't tell you how satisfying it is to get Caden out of shirts and jeans. She'll be out in a moment. It's been hard work, I can tell you. Miss Selena will testify to that."

Lena chose her words very carefully. "I would say…she's been very careful in what she picks."

Roman burst out laughing. "Oh, I can see why she likes you, my dear."

The dressing room door cracked open, and they saw a bit of Caden's face as she peeked round the door.

"Don't be shy, Cade. Come on out," Eden said.

They heard a big sigh and then out walked Caden. Lena rose slowly to her feet and walked toward her. "Caden, you look so good."

Caden looked down at her silver-gray suit and said, "You like it? Really?"

"Of course she likes it. It's the finest Italian handmade suit, with matching vest, black Stetson, and black cowboy boots. It's fabulous."

"Lena?" Caden asked.

Lena adjusted Caden's white shirt and smiled up at her. "I love it, Caden. It suits you so much better than the others. It's perfect, perfect for a hunter."

Caden gazed at Lena adoringly. "If you like it, then we'll get it."

In an abandoned warehouse, a group of wild-looking wolves sat around a large table, waiting for their Alpha. Leroux, scarred but much stronger, walked toward them. They all stood and greeted her with a salute. A dominant female walked to her and said, "Alpha. You are well?"

Leroux pulled her into an embrace. "I am now, Ovid, my loyal Second. Now that my wolves are with me, I am strong."

Leroux sat at the head of the table and said, "My wolves, this plan has been long in duration, but we are nearly at its end. It may look as if I failed at the first hurdle, but now Dante and her dogs are overconfident, and I have information that will lead us to victory."

"What did you find, Alpha?" A dark male wolf and one of Leroux's and Ovid's most trusted lieutenants, asked.

"When I left our pack land to set off on this journey, I promised you I would bring back prosperity and riches to the Lupa pack, and I will deliver. The Wolfgang pack has riches and resources that we could only dream of, and we will take it from them."

"Alpha? They have numbers and a large territory on their side. How do we overcome that?" Ovid said.

Leroux sneered and said, "We have a Lupa wolf on the inside. One that will distract Dante and her Second from Wolfgang land, leaving the back door open for you to lead a small contingent of wolves to the heart of the pack. Once we take out everything they love and hold dear, they will crumble."

## Chapter Sixteen

The next day Caden and Lena traveled to Salt Lake City and checked into a hotel near Lena's family home. She hadn't seen Lena since they had been shown to their rooms earlier and she couldn't wait to be by her side again. It had taken them a few hours to drive here, and as they had gotten closer, Caden had felt Lena's anxiety steadily increase. It made her want to take her mate and run back to her den and keep her safe from harm, because there was no hiding anymore. Lena was her destined mate, and she just had to prove her love to her now.

Caden adjusted her collar and took her Stetson off before knocking on Lena's hotel room door. The door opened and Caden gasped. Lena was wearing a sleeveless ivory and lace evening dress, and her dark hair hung loose in curls. It was strange seeing her without her glasses and with contacts in, but either way, she simply took Caden's breath away.

"Lena…you look—"

"Ridiculous. I don't know why I ever thought I could wear something like this. Especially with this stupid cast on." She turned and ran into the bathroom.

Caden groaned in frustration. "Great Mother, give me strength."

She walked in, stood outside the bathroom door, and knocked. "Lena? You didn't let me finish. I was going to tell you that you look beautiful."

There was no response, so Caden thought it was time to be

honest. She touched the door as if she could connect with her and said, "Lena, I know you struggle with self-confidence, and you feel beaten down by your family, but I can tell you from the bottom of my heart that you are the most beautiful woman I have ever seen."

Caden heard Lena shuffle toward the door and felt the beat of her heart. *Don't stop now, Wolf.*

"Your hazel eyes hold all the colors of the lush forest, your lips and cheeks glow pink with health and vitality, and your smile...your smile would melt a hunter's heart."

The door unlocked and Lena peered around the door. "You're just saying that to make me feel better. You don't really think that."

She reached around the door and pulled Lena out. "Look into my eyes." Lena looked up into Caden's eyes. "A hunter never lies." She stroked Lena's cheek with the back of her hand. "You are everything I find attractive in a female, Selena Miller, Goddess of the Moon. You take my breath away."

Lena's lips parted and Caden inched closer to her, but at the last second she lost her nerve and placed a kiss on her cheek. Caden knew if she had kissed her, there would be no going back. She might lose control and show her wolf. That was something she wasn't ready for, not yet.

"Let's go to your father's party and wow them with your beauty and your pretty new dress. Yes?"

Lena smiled. "A hunter never lies?"

"Absolutely."

She wiped the last of the tears from her eyes and said, "I'll need to remember that. Give me a second, and I'll retouch my makeup. I don't know if I'll wow them at the party, but I'll certainly be proud to go with you, Caden."

*And I'll be proud to be with you, my Goddess.*

Lena's heart started to beat fast as Caden drove her truck up into the large gated property that was her family home.

She opened her purse and ritually checked her pens before holding her moonstone tightly.

Caden looked to the side, saw what she was doing, and placed her hand on top of Lena's and gave it a squeeze. "I'm here. It'll be okay, I promise."

Lena gave her a quick nod, but it didn't calm her completely.

They pulled up at the front of the large house, and Caden said, "That is a beautiful home, Lena."

"It's big and luxurious, but it's not a home. Your den is a home, a simple warm place with nature all around."

Caden was surprised that Lena had picked up her use of the word *den* but was delighted to think Lena thought of it as a home.

"The only good thing about this house is it was so big, we could live pretty much separate lives. I had my own little places to hide out of the way, until I got my own apartment."

Caden didn't know quite what to say. The way Lena was brought up was the complete antithesis of how the wolf pack worked and brought up cubs. She wanted to give her that. "Let's go, then. I hope there's food, by the way. I'm starving."

"You're always hungry, Caden."

They both got out and Caden handed her keys to the parking attendant. She put her hand on the small of Lena's back and guided her up the steps and into the entranceway. "It takes a lot to satisfy a hunter, Goddess of the Moon."

Lena clearly felt the heat and the humor of those words, and she nudged Caden with her hip while she giggled. Caden's plan to distract Lena from her anxiety was working perfectly.

They stepped into the entrance hallway and were greeted by the staff taking coats and directing guests into the reception room. Caden could see what Lena meant by the house not being a home. The furnishings were rich, the ceilings high, and the rooms large, but there was no warm scent of den, of home. Everything was sterile.

"There's my baby elephant."

Caden scented Lena's anxiety start to rise. *So this is the woman who makes you feel bad about yourself?* Veronica Miller was a small woman, both in height and in body. She was so thin she looked angular, and very unhealthy to Caden's eyes.

"Hello, Mother." Lena received two air-kisses from her mother before she looked to Caden and seemed displeased with what she saw.

"Introduce me to your friend, Selena."

Caden could feel the woman's disapproval from where she stood.

"Mother, this is my friend, Caden. She is second-in-command to Ms. Wolfgang at Venator."

"Pleased to meet you, Mrs. Miller."

She shook Caden's hand as if she might catch something. "Yes, I'm sure. Selena, why don't you go in and see your brothers. I know they were looking forward to seeing you."

Lena looked surprised. "They were?"

Lena was squirming with embarrassment. Since introducing Caden to her brothers and their friend, James Thornton, they had done nothing but tell awful stories from her childhood.

Greg laughed, and said, "Even funnier than that, do you remember the time we tricked Boom-boom here into thinking she had been picked for the cheerleading team? Mother made her go along, even though she didn't want to, and the whole football team watched as the head cheerleader said, *I don't think we've got any uniforms in whale size.*"

Lena's hand started to shake with nerves and shame. She heard a growl come from her side and looked up to see Caden's face incandescent with anger.

Her brother Tom seemed to pick up on Caden's fury too. "Caden, why don't we let my sister talk with Greg and James for a while? Since your business is meat, you'd enjoy talking to Lester Grove. He's in catering."

"I will stay with Lena," Caden said flatly.

"Don't be silly, Selena doesn't mind, do you, Boom-boom?" Tom said.

Lena didn't want Caden to go, but she also didn't want her to hear how her family spoke to her. She saw already how angry Caden was. "I'll be fine, Cade. It's okay."

She watched Caden walk off with her brother, and all she could think of was being back in Wolfgang County, away from her family, and safe with Caden.

❖

Caden soon realized why she was maneuvered over to another group, as she listened to what Lena's brother was saying to her.

"Be a good girl. Father and Mother think it's a good idea that you spend some time with James. He's a great guy with a glittering career and would be good for you. It's not as if you have people beating down the door to spend time with you as it is."

"But I'm here with my best friend. I can't just—"

"You can. She can enjoy the rest of the party. I'm sure she doesn't often get to enjoy high-caliber events such as this."

"You don't know anything about her, Greg," Lena said angrily.

Greg moved closer to his sister and said, "I know enough to realize she is not a lady. Now do what you're told, Lena, and don't be a disappointment all your life."

Caden's wolf was furious, and she turned to react when Tom stepped in front to stop her. "Caden? Would you give my sister a minute with my brother alone? They're discussing family business."

Tom handed her a fresh champagne flute with orange juice. She couldn't embarrass Lena. She had to stay calm and be there to support Lena when she needed it.

She walked to the buffet and noticed James Thornton farther up at the bar, chatting to someone. Caden decided to listen in and find out what kind of man he was.

"So, Thornton? Are you back to stay?"

"Yes, it's time to settle down and build the most important part of my career."

"James Thornton settle down? Now, that I'd love to see. Who's the girl?"

James looked across the room to Lena and smiled. His friend did a double take.

"Selena? You're going to marry Selena Miller? The girl who thinks numbers are more interesting than people? You can't be serious. I thought models and actresses were more your type."

James smiled slyly. "Of course they are, and they always will be, but I'm not marrying her, I'm marrying this." James held his hands aloft, indicating their surroundings. "I've had to fight for everything I've got, Aston. I had scholarships to every school I went to, but now it's time to have the family backing of someone like the judge. Her father loves me, and taking their slightly odd, chunky, spinster daughter off their hands gets me the keys to the kingdom."

Caden's fury was nearly at boiling point. *I'm going to kill him, and I will not make it quick. Keep talking, human.*

Aston raised his champagne glass to James and smiled. "You're a better man than me, Thornton. To give up all those beautiful women for a lifetime with that little mouse."

"I won't be giving them up. Now, if you excuse me, Aston, I have a mouse to charm." He walked off in Lena's direction.

Caden's wolf demanded action. She knocked back her glass of orange juice and started to move. But she only got a few steps when she was hit by a wave of dizziness. "What?" Her knees were weakening by the second, and she had no idea what was happening. Caden leaned against the wall, trying to stay on her feet, when Tom came over to her.

"Feeling all right, Caden?" he asked smugly.

"Feel dizzy…"

"Why don't we get you some fresh air. We don't want anyone to see you like this. Do we?" Tom escorted her out onto a decked area beside the pool.

Caden leaned against the wall, breathing heavily and trying to keep control of her wolf, which was rapidly clawing its way toward the surface.

"Stay in the fresh air and I'm sure you'll feel better soon."

He turned to walk away, but Caden grabbed him by his shirtfront. "What was in that orange juice?"

Tom smiled. "Just some vodka to loosen you up…well, maybe a lot of vodka."

Caden fell to her knees. "You have no idea what you've done."

He laughed. "Can't even handle one drink?"

Tom straightened his tie and smoothed down his suit. "Perhaps you'll stay away from my sister now, you disgusting pervert."

He went back to join the party without a second look.

Caden tried to keep calm. The vodka would wear off, in time. It was what the humans would see in that time that worried her. Alcohol would lower her control over her wolf, and even one glass would have a disabling effect on her. But who knew how much vodka Tom had put in her drink.

She crawled over to the side of the pool and splashed water on her face. Her initial dizziness was lessening, but her wolf was at the surface, about to pounce into a shift. She tried to force her wolf back, but when she looked down at her hands, her claws were already lengthening.

Caden was startled by the sound of the doors to the deck area. She managed to get on her feet and hide around the corner of the building. Then she stopped dead when she scented Lena.

Her mate.

❖

"James, I need to find my friend. I don't need air." Lena was pulled out of the house unwillingly by her brother's friend.

"I only want to speak to you alone, Boom-boom."

"Please don't call me that, James. Just let me go and find Caden. My arm is aching and I just want to go home." Lena felt herself backed up against the wall.

James held her hand tightly, not in the gentle, loving way Caden did, but in a forceful aggressive way. "Why? We've always called you that. It's a term of endearment."

Lena felt suffocated. James was smiling, and trying to be

charming, but it felt wrong to Lena. His intentions seemed wrong. "It isn't, James. It never was. It was a name that you, Greg, and Tom used to torment me."

James raised his hand to try and stroke Lena's face, but she pulled her head away. "What do you want with me?"

He gave her an insincere smile and said, "I think we should start spending some time together, get to know each other better."

Lena was astonished. "What? Why would you possibly want to get to know me better, James?"

"Oh, because I think it's time I settled down. Stop playing around and build my career with a loving family behind me. Your family."

Everything about this situation was wrong. She wanted to be at home, with Caden, in Wolfgang County. "I don't—"

He placed a finger to her lips and said in the gentlest voice he could muster, "Shh. You don't have to understand, just take it from me. You will be the perfect little wife for me, Selena. I know you have your strange ideas and ways of doing things, but I can—"

"James, what is wrong with you? I don't want to marry you. I don't love you."

"Marriages are about more than love, Selena, but believe me, once I spend time with you, you *will* love me. Your mother and father think it's a good idea, your brothers think it's a good idea, and you will too."

Lena was horrified. "This was a setup. You all planned this. You want my father and mother's money and influence, and they get their spinster daughter off their hands. Is that how it is?"

"Don't be ridiculous, Selena. I know you're a little…different, but don't get hysterical. Everything will be okay."

He closed the distance between them, and Lena started to breathe heavily in panic. James apparently took this as a sign of excitement and said, "Just relax. I've never had any complaints."

He placed a cold, hard kiss on her lips. Lena froze like stone, but in an instant he was smacked away from her and knocked to the floor.

"What the…?" James shouted from the floor.

When Lena came to her senses, she saw a wild-looking Caden standing over James. Her suit jacket and vest were gone, and her shirt was ripped apart.

"Cade?"

James touched his face and found blood starting to drip from his face. "What have you done to me?" He scrambled to his feet shouting, "You fucking bitch."

His words were brought to an abrupt end when Caden lifted him clean off his feet by his neck.

"Caden? No!" Lena ran to them and realized Caden was unaware of her as she snarled and growled at her opponent. She'd known Caden was strong, but this wasn't human strength. Her eyes went wide when she saw Caden's fingers had changed into claws of some kind. "Caden, what are you?"

James struggled and made choking noises as he dangled two feet in the air. "Do not touch my mate," Caden roared.

All Lena could do was use her instincts. She held on to Caden's free arm and stroked it tenderly. "Caden? Let him go. He's not going to hurt me, not now that you're here."

Caden turned her head to look at Lena, but didn't release James.

"Please, Caden. My arm hurts, I want to go home. Home with you."

Her words seemed to get through, because James fell to the floor like a stone, gasping for air, and rubbing his neck. "You—I'm going to sue you for every dime you've got, you filthy animal."

Caden's face contorted to her wolven features and she let out a roar. Standing behind her, all Lena saw was James fainting in fear.

"Are you all right?" Lena asked.

Caden turned and stalked toward her.

Lena reached out her hand and touched Caden's chest. "What happened to you? You look…"

"I'm better now."

Caden had her in the same spot James had, but this time, she didn't feel panicked or trapped. She felt excited, and a little scared. Caden's raw sensuality and power called to her and had fueled her fantasies since she met her.

Caden rumbled a growl as she rubbed her face all around Lena's neck and cheeks.

Lena wasn't sure what was happening, but all she wanted was for Caden to touch her more. "Cade—"

She was silenced with a kiss. Lena had imagined what it would feel like to be kissed by Caden, but nothing prepared her for the reality of it. Every cell in her body felt alive with electricity and arousal, and she completely forgot she was standing outside her parents' home, with James unconscious with fright.

The kiss became deeper, and just as Lena thought Caden would take her where she stood, she pulled away from Lena, and snarled, "Mine."

Caden looked at her like a wild predator about to strike its prey, and strike she did. She attacked Lena's neck, at first with kisses and nips that made Lena want more, and then it became different.

The alcohol wasn't the only thing that was making it hard for Caden to control her wolf. The taste and scent of Lena's arousal were more powerful than any alcoholic drink. She wanted to take, to possess, to mark Lena as her own. The urge was unstoppable, and she kissed and licked around Lena's neck.

The taste of Lena's neck made her dizzy and she wanted more. Bite, bite, her wolf demanded, and the moans and noises that were coming from Lena were making it all the more difficult to resist.

Saliva filled her mouth, and her fangs shifted. Even though her wolf was in control, somewhere in the back of her mind she knew she shouldn't bite, only mark. Her sharp fangs drew two bloody lines down Lena's neck. The taste of blood swirled around her mouth.

Caden pulled back and howled to the sky, proclaiming Lena hers to the world.

Lena's eyes were closed, and she absorbed the sensations Caden was giving her. She felt the scratching nip to her neck and gasped. It was both painful and pleasurable at the same time.

Her eyes opened slowly, and what she saw chilled her to the bone—Caden howling to the sky, with blood dripping off two wolflike fangs.

Lena immediately touched her neck and found her hand painted with the evidence of her blood. "Caden. What have you done?"

Caden stopped her howl and looked down at Lena with the yellow eyes that haunted her, and all at once, the clues that had been given to her since coming to Wolfgang County fell into place. The inhuman strength and speed, the reverence for the wolf, Caden's way of talking, the animalistic view of life, and all her dreams. They all pointed to one thing.

"You," she shouted. "It's been you all along. Right from the start. You're the wolf from my dreams."

Caden cocked her head to the side, her wolf puzzled by her mate's reaction. "You're mine. My mate."

"No, I'm not your mate. You've deceived me since the moment we met." Lena pushed Caden back by the chest, and she growled. "Get away from me, Caden. What kind of monster are you?"

Those words seemed to hit Caden like a sword to her guts. She began to shrink away from Lena, looking rejected. Lena saw the hurt she had caused and immediately felt bad for what she had said. She reached out to Caden, but she pulled away and ran, leaping the high wall that ran around the grounds of the Miller estate in one jump.

"Caden," she called, before falling to her knees and breaking down in tears. The commotion and noise had drawn some of the partygoers outside, along with Lena's brothers and parents.

"Selena, what happened? What's wrong with James?" her mother asked.

Lena watched Tom and Greg run straight to James, even though they must have seen that their sister had blood on her. This one action hit her hard, and it was an epiphany of sorts. Caden, and the people she had met in Wolfgang County, were the only ones who had ever shown her care and respect. No matter what they were.

What she had to do became crystal clear, and that terrified her.

❖

Leroux and Ovid stood outside an abandoned half-decrepit mansion. "This is a perfect base, Ovid."

"I thought so, Alpha. It has large grounds, and a good perimeter to defend. We should be able to see anyone coming for us."

She watched as her elite wolves carried supplies and weapons from their van parked outside. "Yes, indeed. Now we just have to hope Kurtis is worthy of the Lupa pack."

Leroux took out her cell phone and made a call.

"Kurtis here. How may I serve, Alpha?"

"We have our permanent base. I'll send you details once you complete your part of the plan. Be ready when I call next, and don't let me down."

She hung up and Ovid said, "Can he be trusted, Alpha?"

"His hate and jealousy of Dante runs deep. I think we can trust him, but we always have other options if he needs to be disposed of."

## Chapter Seventeen

"Here you go, miss."

"Thanks." Lena stood up from her seat at the front of the bus and smiled at the bus driver. She tried, with some difficulty, to get her heavy bag down the step to the street.

"I'll get that for you." The driver lifted her case with ease and set it down on the sidewalk. "You take care now, it's late and it's dark. You don't know what's lurking out there."

*Oh, I know what's out there.* "I will, thanks for your help."

After the bus drove off, Lena took a breath of the fresh, clean air that she had missed so much in the city.

She looked up at the sky and saw the bright stars and the shining full moon hanging low in the sky. *Follow the moon*, her Uncle Joel had said—how right he had been. She heard a long, lonely howl in the distance, and the sound reverberated through her body. *Caden.*

Lena knew for certain that it was Caden. The howl called to her in a way she didn't understand, but felt all the same.

She took her cell phone from her purse and called a local cab. "Just enough time to put this case in the apartment, and then it's time to face your fears, Selena. I'm coming, Cade."

❖

Caden pulled on her jeans and a T-shirt after taking a quick shower. She had taken a long late-night run to try to help calm her wolf, and her loneliness. It hadn't worked. Every thought she had was of Lena, and every cell in her body ached for her.

She looked in the mirror and heard the phrase that haunted her. *Get away from me, Caden. What kind of monster are you?*

"A monster that no one could love." She ran from her bedroom and leaped over the banister at the top of stairs.

When she landed, she could have sworn she scented Lena. She shook it off as merely wishful thinking, but then she heard a knock at the door.

Her heart thudded, and her palms became sweaty as the scent grew stronger. It couldn't be her. Lena wouldn't come back.

She took a deep breath and opened the door, and there she was. The female who refused to leave her thoughts.

"Lena? You came back?"

"Yes. I brought the things you left in the city." Lena shrugged, indicating the duffel bag slung across her shoulders. "Could you take it off me? It's quite heavy with one arm."

"Of course, sorry." Caden took the bag and threw it over her shoulder. "Will you come in? It's safe. I promise."

Lena stepped in and said, "I know that."

Caden started throwing clothes and magazines off the couch. "I'm sorry it's a mess. I told my cleaner not to come this week." Lena sat down while Caden paced nervously. "Can I get you something to drink? Water? Fruit tea? Milkshake?"

"No, please sit down. I want to talk."

Caden had never felt so nervous in her life.

"It's hard to know where to start," Lena said.

"I'll answer anything you want. I promise to tell you the truth."

Lena couldn't look at Caden, but she asked, "Are you a werewolf?"

This was a question she had never expected to have to answer to a human, and it was hard to say the words out loud. "Yes, although we prefer to call ourselves wolves."

Lena stood and started to pace around the room. She stopped in front of the wolf painting that hung above the fireplace. "I should have put all the pieces of the puzzle together before now.

The evidence was everywhere, but I just couldn't believe people as fantastical as you could ever exist. It's insane."

Caden walked over to Lena and touched her shoulder. "There are a lot of things in this world that humans can't see because they don't want to see it. Nature is varied and plentiful. We wolves are simply a different kind of person."

Lena turned and Caden saw tears starting to fall from her eyes. "Don't cry, please?" She tried to take Lena in her arms, but she was pushed away.

"No, let me talk. I need to talk."

"Okay. I'm listening." Caden put her hands in her jeans pockets, to stop her reaching out.

"I've spent the last two days going from terrified to hurt to elated. I researched everything I could find on the Internet about werewolves, and it made me doubt my own eyes. It's all myth and legend. I felt like a big joke had been played on me."

"Myth and legend are what we want to look like. If humans knew of our existence, we believe it would be dangerous to our way of life."

"Were you just going to lie to me for as long as we were friends? You were the wolf that saved me, from the beginning. It's been you, and you kept it from me."

Caden couldn't stop herself from touching Lena. She needed the contact desperately. "I didn't lie. I was working toward explaining everything. You have to understand that knowledge of our world is precious. The Alpha and Mater gave me permission to tell you about us."

Lena looked confused. "The Alpha? Who, Dante?"

"Yes, and Eden is the Mater. They are the Alpha pair of the Wolfgang pack."

"And you are...the Second?"

Caden threaded her fingers through Lena's. "The second most dominant wolf in the pack."

Lena took a step back as if she was scared.

"Hey, I won't hurt you. I never could." Caden pulled her closer. "Please, trust me."

"Why did you kiss me and bite me like you did?"

"Come and sit down. I need to explain a few things." Caden ushered her to sit on the couch beside her. "I kissed you because I've dreamed about kissing you since I first laid eyes on you. Only it wasn't supposed to happen like that."

"What do you mean?" Lena asked.

"Your brother spiked my drink with vodka. We can't drink alcohol because we lose control of our wolves. That's what was happening to me."

"I thought Tom had done something of the sort. He kept asking if you had a problem with alcohol, because you wouldn't accept a drink. I'm sorry my family treated you like that, Caden."

Caden took a breath and continued. "You have to understand, to control the wolf within us takes a lifetime of practice. Our wolf reacts to strong emotions—anger, danger, love, sex. Alcohol dulls our control. I saw him, Thornton, kiss you, and my wolf saw someone touching my mate."

"You think I'm your mate?" There was an angry tone to her voice that surprised Caden. "I don't know why. You run away from me every time we get close."

She hung her head. "I know, I'm sorry. I've been frightened. I never thought I would have feelings for someone, never thought I'd have a mate, especially. I wasn't destined for one, and certainly not a human. I've always hated humans, ever since that human drunk driver killed my parents. But as my wolf looked into your eyes on the forest floor, I was yours." She looked up and held Lena's hand tenderly. "I love you, Selena Miller."

Lena's face remained unchanged, but more tears welled in her eyes as she said, "I don't believe you."

"What? You don't believe me? Why?" All the color had drained out of Caden's face.

"This is all one big joke. Why would someone like you love someone like me. You're perfect, you're gorgeous—"

Lena was stopped by Caden's lips softly, but firmly kissing her.

At first she tried to push Caden away, but she very quickly

melted into Caden's soft lips and mouth. Caden's kiss was everything, and so much more than their first kiss. It was less fevered but even more passionate than the first, and through it Lena started to believe.

Caden pulled away from her and said, "You are my Goddess of the Moon, and I will love you till my last breath and beyond."

"I believe you," Lena whispered breathlessly. "I love you too. You make me feel things like I could never have imagined."

Caden rubbed her mouth and cheek over Lena's face and neck, spreading her scent over her, and Lena felt the warmth of her love spread throughout her body.

Caden said, "I know there's so much more we need to talk about, and a lot of hurdles we have to cross, but can we try? Try to, well, we call them mating rituals."

"Date, you mean? Be a couple?"

Caden nodded enthusiastically. "Yes, date, can we? I will prove to you that we can make this work, because you are it for me, Lena. A wolf only gives their heart once."

Lena stroked her love's cheek tenderly. "Will you show me your wolf? I have to see all of you. I have to see the wolf who rescued me that first night. Please?"

Caden stood before her, began to undo her jeans, and kicked off her shoes. "No matter how scary it might look as I shift, I promise my wolf will never, ever hurt you."

"I know. Show me, show me all of you."

She pulled off her jeans and T-shirt, and Lena was mesmerized by her physique. What made Caden all the more attractive was her unashamed confidence in her body, an attitude as foreign to Lena as being a wolf.

"Are you ready?" Caden asked.

"As I'll ever be." Lena rubbed her cast nervously.

Caden deliberately slowed down her shift to pelt, to show Lena it was her and there was nothing to fear.

Lena gasped when she saw Caden's muscles become pronounced and her eyes turn to the yellow she had seen before. She became a bit frightened when Caden's face contorted and her teeth became like fangs. *It's only Caden, it's only Caden,* she repeated mentally, like a mantra.

Caden crouched and her bones began to crack and twist. Lena quickly covered her eyes and dared herself to peek through her fingers, and when she did, she saw the most amazing sight she had ever seen.

"Oh my God, Caden?" The wolf stood panting and looking right at her. It was a lot larger than she expected, about three times the size of an ordinary wolf, much more muscular, and taller. Its gray, brown, and white fur looked thick and soft, and she had the strangest urge to ruffle its ears and give it a hug, even though it looked like the wolf could tear her limb from limb. "I'm standing in the same room as a werewolf. How can this be real?"

Caden took a step toward Lena and whimpered when she backed away. Lena immediately felt bad and, using all her courage, walked to the wolf. She held out her hand, which shook with fear, and received a lick in return. She surprised herself by dropping to her knees and saying, "You are the wolf from my dreams, the one who saved me and protected me."

The wolf gave her a lick on the cheek. Lena giggled and touched Caden's fur, carefully at first, but then, as her confidence grew, scratched behind her ears. Caden whined and rumbled in pleasure and contentment.

"You're not scary, are you? Well, maybe not to me, but I think you could be to your pack, or your friends."

The wolf growled as if to confirm what Lena had said, and with a final lick, ran for the door. Lena followed her outside into the darkness of the night and smiled as Caden leaped in the air, on top her truck, and then onto the roof of the den.

Lena was amazed at how Caden's wolf could move, jump, and twist in the air. This was why she was a perfect physical specimen. She was perfect.

Caden then ran off at speed into the forest and out of sight. What was she up to now?

A few minutes later, the wolf returned with a mouthful of wildflowers and dropped them at Lena's feet.

"Are these for me?"

Caden lifted her paw and placed it on Lena, and howled long and loud to the moon, proclaiming to every wolf that her mate had returned to her.

Caden sat crouched, head down, before Lena, having shifted back to skin. She slowly stood and revealed the erotic image Lena had seen in her dream. She was slick with perspiration, muscles taut, with those yellow predator eyes. Lena felt herself ache, deep inside.

Caden stalked toward her, looking as if she was ready for the kill.

"Cade, you looked like this in my dream. One I never told you about."

Caden said nothing, but gave a soft snarl. She padded around Lena, sniffing her hair and skin. "Tell me."

Lena's heart thudded harder than it had in her life. Caden hadn't even touched her, but the erotic snarls and soft growls made her wet and ready. "You were like this, naked and with wolf eyes. You stood behind me and ran your hands over my hips and buttocks, and finally my breasts."

Caden took the direction and stood behind Lena, her hands running over her hips and beautifully rounded backside. "Tell me more. I can smell your excitement, Goddess."

Lena arched her neck back and to the side, offering herself to Caden. "You bit me with your wolf teeth, and it felt so powerful, I…"

Caden ran her tongue over the teeth marks she had made at the party and said, "It felt so powerful?"

Lena felt like she was going to combust. The marks on her neck felt directly connected to her clitoris, and she throbbed and ached in response. "I woke up having an orgasm," Lena admitted.

Caden growled. "Goddess, that was the first of many. I want to please you and love you until you fall asleep from exhaustion. Stay with me tonight, please?"

Lena didn't even have time to think before her body and her heart made the decision for her. "Yes."

Caden lifted her, and Lena automatically wrapped her legs around her lover's waist. When Caden reached the bottom of the stairs, Lena started to feel self-conscious. "Put me down, Cade. I'm too heavy."

"You weigh nothing—hold tightly around my neck." Caden let her arms drop and walked upstairs, demonstrating how easily she held her.

The strength Caden possessed made Lena feel safe, but she was still nervous about her body.

Caden walked them into her large bedroom and sighed when she saw how messy it was. Clothes in piles on the floor, the bedsheets half hanging off the bed. "I'm sorry it's—"

Lena kissed her silent. "Don't. It's fine. It's a wolf bachelor pad—I don't expect it to be perfectly tidy."

Lena surveyed the bedroom. It had a wood-plank floor and paneled walls, and floor-to-ceiling doors that led out to a balcony overlooking the forest.

"Your room is beautiful, just like your den."

Caden let her down, and looked around. "It's lonely." Her voice held sadness. "I've been lonely for a long time."

Lena lifted one of Caden's hands and kissed it tenderly. "So have I, Caden, except since I've been here with you."

Caden carefully took Lena's glasses off and placed them on the side table. "Maybe we've both been waiting for each other." She caressed Lena's face and pulled her into a kiss, but Lena hesitated. "Is there something wrong?"

Lena's cheeks went hot as her negative thoughts ate away at her mind. "I've never done this before."

"You don't have to do anything you don't want to."

"I want to. I love you—I just don't want you to be disappointed. I'm not like the women you know, like Eden and Stella."

"No, you're not like Eden and Stella."

Lena's shoulders slumped.

"You're Selena, my Goddess of the Moon."

"I don't feel like a goddess. You're so confident in your body, Cade, I—"

Caden unbuttoned Lena's blouse, left it hanging open, and whispered into her ear, "Show me."

"What?"

Caden trailed her fingers between Lena's breasts. "Show me where you have been made to feel bad about your body."

"I don't think—"

Caden put her hand in Lena's and repeated, "Trust me, and show me."

Lena gathered her courage and placed her hand on her stomach.

"Here?" Caden asked.

She nodded and was surprised when Caden dropped to her knees and slowly shrugged the blouse from Lena's body, and ran her hand over the surface of her stomach.

"This sweet, soft belly?" Caden placed her cheek against the warm skin and rubbed her scent over it before worshiping it with kisses and licks.

Lena couldn't help but touch and stroke Caden's hair as she was loved. She wished she didn't have an arm cast on, so she could put both arms around her. "Cade?" she groaned.

"This belly is perfectly female and beautiful. I could spend all night making love to it. Where else makes you feel bad, my Goddess?"

Caden's reassurance was slowly giving her some confidence, and she unzipped her skirt and let it fall to the ground, then placed her lover's hands on her thighs.

She was surprised when Caden growled and looked up at her with her wolf eyes. "The first time I drove you to the farm in my truck, I helped you out and your short skirt rode up on your thighs. I wanted more than anything to sink my teeth into the flesh then and there."

"You did?" Lena was quickly forgetting all her hang-ups, as Caden was making her feel utterly desirable.

"I have been dreaming of sinking my teeth into them ever since."

In response, Caden slowly eased down Lena's pantyhose, giving each bit of flesh a kiss as it was uncovered. When Lena groaned, Caden's canines slightly grazed her inner thigh, and Lena pushed Caden's head toward her center.

Caden used her teeth to rip off Lena's panties in one movement, and she pressed her nose into the patch of hair protecting Lena's sex. "I need your flesh."

"Take me, Cade," Lena moaned. She was lifted and laid on the bed without ceremony. Lena's breathing hitched when she saw Caden crawl up the bed toward her, her predator eyes burning yellow and bright. She should have been frightened, perhaps, but she wasn't. She wanted Caden touching her, making her moan.

Caden stopped by her thighs and looked up at her with hunger. "I will never hurt you, Goddess. I'm going to worship your body and show how much you are loved. Tell me how you feel."

"I'm scared, but in a good way. I just don't want to disappoint you."

"You never could." Caden pushed her onto her side. "I've dreamed of these hips, these thighs." Caden's hands were hot as they kneaded her thigh and buttock. "I want them."

"Please, take what you want, Cade." She couldn't see exactly what Caden was doing, but she gasped when she felt two sharp teeth grazing her thigh. "Oh God, more, please?" The sharp pain shot straight to her clit, and she moaned into her pillow. When she felt Caden bite down harder, she grasped her own breast and squeezed it.

"Tell me what you want, Goddess."

Lena's head was swimming. What did she want? How could she ask for all the base, lusty thoughts that Caden was drawing from her body? "I want to feel your tongue, your teeth, your hands on me, everywhere."

Caden growled, flipped her on her back, and used her tongue to lick all around her sex and inner thighs. "I need to taste you," Caden said before parting her folds and lapping at her sex with a growl.

The feeling of Caden's tongue made her feel desperate, desperate for Caden to give and take whatever she wanted. Whatever her lover wanted, she would gladly give to her.

Lena's hips started to move in time with the wave of pleasure that was building inside her. It was scary, but at the same time there was nothing she wanted more. She looked down to Caden's hand, which was resting on her abdomen, and saw the tips of her sharp claws scratch along her belly. When Caden's hands scratched, or her teeth pierced her skin, the hot pain stimulated her clit, and she knew she was going to become addicted to that feeling.

Lena pulled her head up and said, "Please, come up here. I need you to be close."

Caden crawled up her body. She gently nipped and licked at the soft flesh of breasts before finding her lips and kissing her deep and hard. She sucked at her tongue as she had with her clit, and acting on instinct, Lena took Caden's hand and kissed it with great tenderness.

"Please, Cade. You're my first and will be my only one. Make me yours."

Caden looked down at her silently. Lena could read the uncertainty in her eyes, as if she was trying to keep a handle on her desires.

"Please?" Lena had never known anything in her life to be so right.

"I don't want to hurt you," Caden said with a shaky voice.

Lena cupped Caden's cheek with her good hand and whispered, "You won't. I need to be yours, Caden. I've never needed anything more."

She felt Caden's fingers slip inside and she groaned at the feeling of being filled.

Caden begged. "I want to bite you so much it hurts, Lena. I can't yet, but I want to."

On instinct, Lena laid her head to the side and offered up her neck. "I'm yours."

Caden pounced on her offered neck and pierced the skin she had marked before with her teeth, while her fingers pushed through the final barrier between them. Lena cried out and sank her fingernails into Caden's shoulder, making her howl into the night.

## Chapter Eighteen

The dawn sun shone its light gently through the french windows of Caden's den, onto Lena and Caden, who were wrapped together tightly. Lena was wide awake and studying her contented partner beside her.

She'd fallen asleep, utterly exhausted from Caden's attentions, but was now wide-eyed and ready to take in the scale of what had happened to her. She was lying in bed with a werewolf, she thought, in a surprisingly calm fashion.

A werewolf who had loved her like no one else in her life. She had made Lena's first time unforgettable by making her feel like the goddess Caden called her. But something niggled at the back of her mind. As much as Caden had been passionate and loving, there was something that told her Caden was holding back.

She gave Lena everything unselfishly and took nothing in return. If Lena was to be Caden's mate as she wanted, then Lena was determined to give her what one of her own kind would.

"You're so perfect, Cade," Lena whispered to her sleeping lover.

Lena never thought that someone like Caden could love her, but after last night she was in no doubt. She stroked her lover's hair and gave her a scratch behind the ear, remembering Caden's wolf liked that. Caden made sounds of complete contentment, which encouraged Lena in her explorations.

She was curious to see if werewolves and humans had many differences when in human form, apart from size and strength, so she began exploring.

Lena ran her fingers down the center of Caden's chest and circled her fingers around Caden's well-defined stomach. She giggled when Caden growled softly and tried to bat her hand away like a dog having a dream.

When she went lower, Caden's growls got deeper and sounded much more serious. She ran her fingers through her lover's hair and the lips of her sex. Although Caden was her first, she knew from her own body that her lover's body was slightly different. Her clitoris was set lower and was bigger than her own, and it appeared to be gaining size as Lena stimulated it. And Caden's opening was also smaller than hers.

Caden's moans grew, and she hoped she would get to make Caden come before she would take over. From nowhere, Caden grabbed her good wrist and said, "Be careful teasing a wolf, Lena. You might get bitten."

She leaned over Caden's mouth and kissed her softly. "Maybe I want to be bitten. Did you ever think of that?"

This brought a smile from her lover, who flipped her over onto her back. "There's nothing on this earth that would make me happier, Goddess, but a wolf can't bite until their mating ceremony. It's like a marriage, only more permanent," she joked.

This was the opening Lena needed to ask about the differences between human and werewolf mating. "Caden? Can I ask you something?"

"Of course. I'll answer any question you have." Caden lifted her lover's hand and kissed it.

"Werewolves like you and Dante, and others I've met, are much bigger and stronger than the wolves who are like Eden, Stella, and Vance."

"All wolves are born either dominant or submissive. Dominants like Dante and me are the hunters and protectors. Submissives nurture, produce cubs, and take care of the den."

"Wait a minute." Lena gave Caden a questioning look. "Dante and Eden have kids. I've met Dion and the baby, Conan, and they look exactly like Dante. How…?"

Caden caressed her lover's face. "You're right. And their middle daughter looks like Eden—she's a beautiful blond submissive cub. They have another on the way, I understand it wasn't planned, but a wonderful surprise."

Lena's eyes went wide. "A dominant wolf like you—"

"A dominant wolf, whether male or female, can make any submissive female pregnant."

Lena was shocked to say the least. "That's unbelievable."

"Why? There are many wondrous types of reproduction in the natural world. Some animals change sex, some use asexual reproduction, and some regenerate. Human females can orgasm the way we dominants do, the only difference being that when we do it, our ejaculate contains the genetic material required to impregnate a female wolf. We're just different, like all the other animals on the earth."

After the initial shock, Caden's words did make sense. After all, Lena realized, she was in a whole different world now, a world where werewolves existed. She was desperate to ask how it was done but didn't yet have the courage. "Is that how a dominant gets their pleasure? Mating that way?"

"A dominant wolf gets pleasure from pleasing their mate," Caden said coyly.

Lena was now even more sure that her lover was holding back a part of herself. Maybe she could talk to Eden and get the truth. Then something more important hit her. "Caden, can wolves and humans breed?"

"A dominant male could impregnate a human female in the traditional way, but for a dominant female..." Caden shrugged. "Well, it's never been known, in my experience. I hope you know I would never mate with you without taking the proper precautions, if I thought I could make you pregnant. Don't worry." Caden began to kiss Lena's neck and shoulders, while stroking from her breast to her hip, hoping to have another opportunity to make her mate come.

"I wasn't worried about that, you silly wolf. I'm worried about you."

"Why would you be worried about me?" Caden stilled her hands and seduction for a moment.

Lena had tears forming in her eyes as she said, "I love you with all my heart, Cade, but if you stay with me, you won't have children."

"Don't cry, my Goddess. I never expected to have a mate. I thought I'd go through life on my own because my grandmother told me my wolf mate didn't exist. She was right—the Great Mother didn't have a wolf mate in her plans for me, but she had a human female in mind for my mate. So you are more than I ever expected to have. I don't need to have biological cubs with you to be happy. You alone will make me happy every day of my life."

"Do you mean it?"

"Of course I mean it. Besides, if you ever want to have a family with me, there are always needy cubs who come up for adoption."

"Really?" Lena asked enthusiastically.

"Yes." Caden smiled and lowered her lips to give her lover a kiss, which quickly turned passionate when Lena grasped Caden's neck with her one good hand and pulled her closer.

"Cade," she moaned, "I want you so much. Please, take me the way you would if I was a submissive wolf."

Caden broke away from the kiss and seemed unsure of what to do. Lena watched her lover look up and down her body, gulp hard, and sit up on the side of the bed. "I think you should have a break. It was your first time and you're bound to be sore."

Lena sat on her knees behind Caden and stroked from her neck down her muscular back. "I'm just pleasantly achy, Cade. I want you, all of you."

She felt Caden's back muscles tense as if she was arguing with herself, before she stood and walked away from the bed. "Soon, I promise. Soon. But I promised Dante that I would help her and Dion set up some tables at the park—there's a company picnic tomorrow."

Lena couldn't help but feel rebuffed at this. "Oh? Okay, can you drop me off at my apartment on the way?"

Caden must have realized Lena was hurt because she immediately apologized and said, "I didn't mean it that way, my

Goddess. I want you to come with me. I don't want us to be apart if we can help it. We can have some more time alone tonight if you'll come back with me."

"Yes, of course I will." Somehow she would get Caden to let her wolf out to play.

❖

Eden opened the door to find the pack Second wrapped around Lena Miller. "Lena, you came back to us."

Lena smiled shyly. "Yes, I couldn't stay away."

"And you've found yourself a mate, it would seem." Eden smiled broadly. "Dante and Dion are dismantling the picnic tables out in the garden, if you want to go and help them, Caden. I'll look after Lena for you."

"Oh? Thank you, Mater." Caden pulled her lover close and kissed her. "Will you be okay without me?"

"Of course she'll be fine, won't you, Lena?"

Lena was equally wrapped up in Caden, stroking her hair, and smiling at her adoringly.

"Lena?" Eden repeated, a bit louder.

"What? Oh yes, of course."

They walked through to the kitchen, where Megan was looking after her brother. Megan rolled her eyes when Caden pulled Lena to her and kissed her.

"I'll just be outside. I love you."

Lena was a bit embarrassed at showing affection in front of others. "I love you."

"Off you go, Second," Eden said to Caden.

When they finally got her out the door, Eden pulled a seat out at the kitchen table. "Take a seat, Lena, and I'll make us some fruit tea. This is our daughter, Megan, and you know the big cub over there."

"Yes, hi, Conan. Hi, Megan—nice to meet you."

Megan smiled brightly. "Hi, Miss Lena. It's great to meet you. I've never spoken to a human before."

"Meggie," Eden warned.

Lena laughed. "It's okay, Eden. I'm glad I'm your first human, Megan. I hope I'm not a disappointment."

"Nuh-uh. You seem really nice. What's that on your arm?"

"Oh, this? It's a cast. I broke my arm."

Megan looked fascinated. "Wow. So you don't just heal when you shift?"

Eden brought over two cups of fruit tea and said to her daughter, "Humans don't shift, remember?"

"Cool. So you just wait till it's better?"

Lena smiled and nodded. It was strange explaining something so everyday to someone, but she reminded herself that she was the alien in this land.

"Why don't you go and play with your pater, Caden, and Dion? Den talk time, Meggie."

"Yeah, if you're going to talk about yucky dommos, I'll go outside."

As Megan ran out of the kitchen, Lena asked, "Dommos?"

"Dominant wolves," Eden told her, shaking her head, "in teenager language. So, you came back."

Lena tapped her fingernails nervously on the table, working herself up to talk. "Did Caden tell you what happened?"

"Yes, she lost control of her wolf. I'm sorry you found out about us in this way, Lena. We had counseled Caden to do it gradually, so as not to shock you, but the alcohol brought that plan to an end."

Lena stirred her tea and took a sip. "My idiot brother. My family didn't like me having such a protective friend, so they tried to make a fool of Caden."

"How did you leave it with your family?" Eden asked.

"I don't have a family. They told me if I came back here to be with Caden, I had no family anymore, and that's because she's gay. Can you imagine if they had found out about her being a wolf?"

Eden placed her hand atop Lena's in a comforting gesture. "Lena, I'm sorry about your family, but I hope you know that you're not just gaining a mate in Caden, you're gaining a whole wolf pack as your family, and if I as Mater can do anything to help, I'm here."

"Thank you. That means a great deal to me. Loving Caden has

given me the strength to stand up to my family. I love her, and I won't let anyone come between us."

"That's good to know, because Caden will love you till her last breath. She has been alone too long and deserves the happiness that only a mate can bring."

"I will do everything I can to make her happy." Lena wanted to ask more but couldn't quite work up the nerve.

Her anxiety must have shown on her face, because Eden leaned close and said, "You look concerned. Is there something you want to ask?"

Lena felt her cheeks go hot, and she knew Eden would realize something personal was up.

"Please don't be embarrassed, nothing you tell me will go any further. Has Caden upset you?"

"Oh no, nothing like that. Caden has been so gentle and caring with me. So gentle, in fact, it's as if she's afraid I'll break. When we made love, it was…well, she was passionate, but I felt she was holding back a part of herself. I want to be everything a wolf partner would be for her. I want her to make love to me like—"

"Like the dominant wolf that she is?" Eden asked.

"Exactly. I don't want her to be different with me, Eden."

"She's probably frightened of scaring you off. Sex with a dominant wolf can be rougher than normal, if you are a human," Eden warned her.

"I'm stronger than I look. I want us to be mates in every sense," Lena said forcefully.

"If that's what you want, I can teach you what to say and do to coax the dominant wolf out to play. First, you have to challenge her…"

## Chapter Nineteen

"Pater? Is Caden okay?"

Caden had hardly said a word since she'd gone outside, and constantly looked back to the den where her mate was.

"Second? Are you with us?" Dante asked.

"Sorry, I was…oh, it doesn't matter." She lifted one of the tables and piled it up with the others.

Dante turned to her daughters and said, "Dion, take some chairs and put them beside the truck. Meggie, you go too, but don't lift anything heavy. I want a word with Caden."

"But, Pater, I can talk about adult wolf stuff now. I'm an expert on dommo-missie stuff," Dion said.

Megan laughed. "Oh, yeah, you're an expert in following Tia around like a little cub."

Dion snarled at her sister. "When you get a mate, Meggie, I'm going to tell them what a lame freak you are."

"Enough," Dante said. "Go now."

Dion sighed, picked up one of the piles of chairs, and said, "Keep up."

The cubs finally out of earshot, Dante said, "Sit down, Second." She indicated the garden bench. "So, what's wrong? You should be howling to the trees, you got your mate."

Caden scrubbed her face with her hands. "It's not that simple. It hurts to be apart from her, and I don't know how long I can control my wolf."

Dante raised an eyebrow. "You mean you haven't mated yet?"

"We've been intimate but…ugh." Caden stood and started to pace in frustration.

"Tell me, Cade. You can tell me anything."

She stopped in front of Dante and sighed. "I'm frightened of hurting her. She's a human, and a pretty delicate human at that. We talked about how we mate and she said she wanted that with me, but I looked at her body this morning and saw the marks on her neck, and"—Caden grinned, half pleased, half embarrassed—"other areas, and I panicked. I mean, for two wolves it was nothing, but she's not a wolf."

"I don't think you're giving Selena enough credit."

"What do you mean?" Caden snapped. "I love her, and I want to protect her."

"When I look at Selena, I see a strong young woman who has been beaten down by her family, who've pointed out her faults and decided what's best for her. Don't be like her family, Cade. It must have taken strength to walk away from all she knew to come back to us, and we're not exactly everyday people."

"It took courage," Caden said, proud of her mate.

Dante put her hand on Caden's shoulder and said, "Of course it did. Trust her to know what she wants, and you need to trust that your wolf would never hurt her mate."

"You're right, I know you are. My heart and head feel like they're out of my control. When I'm not with her, I ache to be with her, and I feel like I have no control over what I do or say. Love is scary."

Dante smiled. "It is, Second, but nothing will give you more happiness than going home to your den and finding your mate there. I hope I will be presiding over your mating ceremony soon."

"You and me both, Alpha."

❖

Dante and Eden invited them to stay for dinner. Caden sat with one arm round her mate while she ate, and Lena rewarded her with smiles and blushes.

"This is beautiful, Eden," Lena said. "I don't think I've ever tasted nicer or fresher food before I came to Wolfgang County."

"Thank you. I'm glad you think so," Eden said.

Dante took Eden's hand and told Lena, "We have the best ingredients to choose from here because we take care of our animals and our crops, and they take care of us. A hunter who does not take care of his environment will not hunt for long. Caden is essential to that process."

Lena moved closer to her mate, looking immensely proud of her. "I could see that from my time at the ranch. She works so hard."

Dion had finished her meal in record time. "Mom, can I go out after dinner? A bunch of us are meeting at the park."

"Have you done your homework?" Eden asked, and she nodded enthusiastically. "Okay, then."

Dion hurriedly cleared her plate away into the dishwasher.

"Can I come too?" Megan said.

"As long as you don't take Tia away to play stupid missie games. I'm going to get changed first, so be ready or I'll go without you."

Dante turned to her mate and said, "Do you think this is a good idea, with Leroux out there? I have a bad feeling…"

"They're only going to the park, they'll be in a big group, and they have cell phones. It'll be okay."

"Have you got homework, Meggie?"

Megan frowned at her mom. "No, we've got no homework because we have that stupid math project due next week. I don't understand it. I hate numbers."

That piqued Lena's interest. She hated the fact the kids had a poor opinion of numbers and loved to explain how wonderful they could be.

"I don't mean to interfere, but would you like me to help Megan with her math project? I'm good with numbers." She looked to Caden, who smiled proudly and nodded that she was doing the right thing.

"Oh, yeah, Mommy, Pater? Can Miss Lena help me? I'd love that."

"That would be wonderful, Lena. Are you sure you have time?" Eden asked.

"Of course. Why don't I come over the day after the picnic. We could work on it then, Megan."

"Great."

❖

Caden and Lena stopped by her apartment to pick up some of her belongings.

"Do you want to pick anything up from the store before we go back to the den?" Caden asked.

Lena locked the door, and Eden's words and advice ran around her head. *Be confident, be strong, and always challenge her.*

She gathered her courage and kissed Caden softly on the lips, and as they enjoyed the sweet kiss, Lena scratched her fingernails down her mate's neck. Not enough to break the skin, but enough to get her attention.

She heard Caden give the smallest of growls and knew she had achieved her first goal. "I think we should go back to your den and have an early night. What do you think, my Big Bad Wolf?"

Caden grabbed Lena's bag and her hand and led her to the apartment stairs. "Let's go."

When they made it down to the sidewalk, Lena noticed an unfamiliar person striding toward them, a storm cloud in his face.

Caden stepped between this stranger and Lena. "Kurtis, out for an evening walk?"

"Yes, Caden. I thought I'd take the evening air, although the stench of human threatens to ruin it." Kurtis looked directly at Lena when he said that.

Caden grabbed him and slammed him up against the wall of the building. "Learn some manners, you mutt. That human is my mate, and you will respect her as the Second's mate or you will be sorry. Understand me?"

"You took a human for a mate? This pack really has lost its way. You will pollute our pack."

Caden's face had shifted. Her rage was frightening as she held her claws inches from his face, ready to strike.

"Caden, stop. Just ignore him. It doesn't matter." Lena rubbed Caden's back, trying to soothe her anger. "Just leave him, Cade, and take me home to your den. Please?"

Caden let herself shift back to skin. "You are lucky today, Kurtis. Learn some respect or the next time you'll be sorry."

Kurtis smiled as he watched them get into their car and called after them, "You are about to get your arrogant tail bitten right off, Caden."

❖

The journey to Caden's had been quiet, but Lena could feel the anger and aggression rolling off her mate. They walked into the den and Caden dropped Lena's bag with a bang. "Why are you so angry?"

"Because he disrespected my mate right in front of me. Why do you think?"

"What does it matter? Not every wolf in the pack is going to accept a human. I'm fine as long as the ones that count do."

"They will accept what I or Dante tell them to. I am pack Second, and the Second's mate will be treated accordingly. You wouldn't understand," Caden said and began to walk off.

Lena grabbed her hand to stop her leaving. "What? Because I'm a human I don't understand? You're dismissing my views because I'm a human?"

Caden turned around. Her eyes had started to turn the first shades of yellow. "I'm not discussing this any further." She ripped her shirt off and said, "I'm going for a run."

Lena jumped in front of her mate and put her hand on her bare torso. "You're not running out on me because of some person… wolf…*whatever*, who doesn't even matter."

Caden took a breath. She put her hands on Lena's shoulders and looked directly into her eyes. "No, I'm leaving because my wolf feels hot and aggressive and wants to fuck you. That's why. Now let me go."

Lena tried not to show her slight shock at those blunt words or any nervousness that she felt and reminded herself this was what she wanted. The real Caden, the Caden who was a werewolf. She took off her glasses and placed them on the end table before walking up close to Caden and stroking her fingers down her chest.

"Don't play with me, Lena. Let me go."

Caden sounded frustrated and near the edge, so Lena placed little kisses over her chest while her fingers slipped under her belt buckle. "I'm not playing, Cade. I want my Big Bad Wolf."

Caden's eyes were wild and yellow now with lust. This was what Lena wanted. She wanted Caden to take her so badly.

"Leave me now, Lena, I mean it." Caden was breathing hard.

Lena could see how hard her mate was fighting her. *Challenge her, always challenge her dominance.* Lena remembered Eden's advice and knew what she had to do.

She pulled Caden down to her, so she could whisper in her ear, "Trust me to be strong enough. I love you, all of you."

When she finished speaking, Lena dragged her nails across her mate's chest. Caden roared in disbelief at what her human mate had done.

Lena saw that she had drawn blood. "I'm sorry, I didn't mean—"

Caden ripped the dress from her body before she could finish speaking and carried her to the rug in front of the fire. "You wanted the Big Bad Wolf, my mate? You've got me," Caden said.

She bit off Selena's bra while her claws ripped off her panties. She sucked her way around her mate's breasts, allowing her fangs to graze the side.

"Oh God, Cade…"

"Is this what you wanted, mate?"

"Yes. I want everything." Lena tried to put her uninjured hand on her mate's back, but Caden held it above her head.

"You challenge me? I am your dominant wolf, and I will prove it." Caden moved between her mate's legs and opened herself up. Her engorged clitoris slipped easily into the mating position. She groaned as they started to move together, and Lena moaned along with her.

"Cade, I can feel you. I can feel you."

Caden's thrusts got faster as her ego was stroked, and Lena struggled in pleasure. "You're mine, Lena, I want to bite you." Caden knew she couldn't bite, but she drew her teeth along her claim mark, freshening the wound.

"Cade, harder," Lena demanded.

Caden was happy to oblige, and her thrusts got faster and harder. She could feel herself readying to shoot her essence into her mate and growled, "You're mine. Tell me you're mine."

Lena looked up at her with dazed and submissive eyes. "I'm yours, only yours. Fill up my belly."

Caden was caught off guard with that request, and within seconds she started to come. Her hips were powering and slapping into her mate, and with a final howl, she came.

Caden collapsed onto Lena, and Lena wrapped her arms around Caden's back. "Thank you, Cade, thank you for giving me everything. I love you."

"I love you. It's not enough—I have more to give you, mate." Caden grew hard again in seconds and flipped her mate over onto her front.

"What are you doing, Cade?" Caden sank her teeth into Lena's buttock and she squealed in pleasure. "Cade…"

Caden smiled when Lena raised her ass and presented herself for her pleasure. She growled and thrust her throbbing clitoris between Lena's butt cheeks. She held the back of her mate's neck down and began to pound her hips into Lena. "I'm going to fill you up, mate."

Lena gripped the rug in front of her and moaned in higher and higher pitched tones. Caden slipped two fingers inside Lena, and she heard her deep guttural scream as her orgasm threatened to spill over.

"I'm going to fill up your belly, mate, fill it up till it's full. I wish I could give you a cub."

Lena screamed out her orgasm, and the sound of her mate's pleasure made Caden roar and explode into Lena. "Mine."

## Chapter Twenty

Caden returned from her morning run and grinned from ear to ear at the scent that welcomed her home. In a short period of time, Lena's scent had mingled with Caden's, to create the comforting warmth of home and pack.

After last night, any lingering doubts that Caden had about taking a human for a mate dwindled away to nothing. Lena took all the passion she had to give her and gave just as much back in return, as the marks she had found this morning on her own neck and chest could testify to.

Her pleasant memories were disturbed when she heard her mate banging around upstairs and sensed her anxiety. Caden immediately bounded up the stairs, into the bedroom.

Lena, dressed only in a towel wrapped around her body, was frantically looking through her purse and overnight bag.

"Lena, what's wrong?"

Lena jumped back in fright. "Don't sneak up on me like that," Lena snapped.

Caden immediately covered the distance between them and took Lena into her arms. "What's wrong?"

"I can't find my pen case, I've looked everywhere. I need it."

Caden could not only feel and scent Lena's anxiety, it was written all over her face. She lifted her overnight bag and took the pen case from the side pocket. "You put them in your bag, remember?"

Lena took hold of the case and began to ritually count the pens out. After she was satisfied they were all present and correct, she let out huge sigh of relief.

There was something wrong, and Caden was determined to find out what it was. "Come and sit with me." She sat on the bed and pulled her mate onto her lap. "What's wrong?"

"Why do you think there's something wrong? I'm fine. I'm just going for a shower." Lena tried to stand, but Caden kept her in place.

"Oh no, there's something. Before I went out for my run, you were snug and content in bed, and now you're desperately looking for your pens. You do that when you're stressed."

Lena sighed in resignation. "How can you know me so well?"

"You are my mate. I know everything about you, so tell me." She rubbed noses with her in a tender and sweet way that seemed to put Lena at her ease.

"It's the picnic today. I'm nervous."

"Why would you be nervous?" Caden didn't see any problems that would concern her.

Lena laid her head on her mate's shoulder and said, "You said it was a pack picnic. Everyone there will be werewolves, and I will be the only human."

"But you've met a lot of those wolves and like them."

"Of course I like them. It's just, it'll be the first time everyone will know that we're together, and I know your secret, and you know I panic around a lot people, and what if some act the same as that Kurtis guy…"

Caden stopped her rambling with a kiss. "There are very few in our pack like Kurtis. He is a jealous, envious wolf. Anyone you meet will be delighted to meet you, and you need never worry about anyone doing anything inappropriate, even if I'm not near you. No wolf would dare to disrespect the Second's mate. My scent is now all over you."

Lena smiled. "I have my very own guard wolf now?"

"You have had me ever since I saw you on the forest floor, my mate."

Lena held on to Caden's neck and kissed her softly. "I'm so lucky to have you, my Big Bad Wolf."

"I'm sorry, but your Big Bad Wolf is all hot and sweaty from the chase, and I need to shower." Caden wrapped her arms around her mate, and nuzzled her neck.

"I don't care." Lena pulled her towel off and dropped it to the side of the bed.

Caden's hands started to wander her mate's body, squeezing her breasts, and teasing her hardening nipples.

Lena traced Caden's face with her finger, and Caden snarled, threatening to bite the appendage.

Lena laughed. "Those big wolf teeth do make a mess of my neck and chest, not to mention the yelp I gave when I sat down this morning."

Caden couldn't help but feel proud at having marked her mate, and she chuckled remembering the particularly strong bite she'd given her buttock. "You didn't seem to mind when I gave them to you, and in fact you gave me plenty in return. I wish they didn't heal when I shifted. I would wear them like a badge of honor at the picnic today."

Lena's smile and burgeoning arousal faltered a little, and her fingers tapped nervously as they always did when she was working up to ask something.

"Hey? What has you worried, Goddess?"

"My mind is trying to make me feel guilty about enjoying your bites. It tells me that it's bad, dirty somehow to enjoy it, but I do. I crave your nips and bites, and when you do, it feels like the bite is connected to my…you know, down there."

Caden smiled at the sweet, bashful comment. "Please don't feel bad. It's part of the way we make love. Your body, your nerves, and your sex organs react to my saliva and the bite because we are mates. It is quite natural, I assure you. That's why after the mating ceremony, the two wolves bite each other. It seals our bond, and we carry it till we die."

"I won't turn into a werewolf or anything, will I?"

Caden laughed out loud. "Oh, Goddess. You have been watching too many movies. No, the only way a human can turn is if they mix blood with a werewolf—a great deal of blood. You're quite safe."

"You wouldn't want me to?"

Caden's face and tone of voice became serious all of a sudden. "No, I wouldn't. Not ever. It's a difficult thing to go through."

Lena breathed a sigh of relief. "Oh, good, I was worried, and I didn't want to disappoint you."

"You never could." Caden flipped her mate onto her back and descended for a kiss.

"Cade? I know you can't yet, but show me where you would bite me, and maybe we could practice with a little nip?"

Caden's lip lifted to a sly smile. "You are a naughty girl, Miss Miller."

❖

The picnic was in full swing when Caden and Lena arrived. As they walked across the grass, wolves smiled and saluted as they passed. "What a beautiful place, Cade." Lena had never seen a happier group of people, than the wolves around her.

Little kids played games and chased around them, while the older ones played baseball in the center of the meadow. "I'm glad you think so. I want you to stay."

"I'm not going anywhere without you. I've found my hunter, and I want to build a den with her."

Caden put her arm around her mate's shoulder and gave her head a kiss. "I'm glad. You still want to ask Dante?"

"Yes, I want to have a mating ceremony with you as soon as we can. I want to belong to you forever."

"Well, she's busy playing baseball just now, but maybe we can ask later?"

Lena looked over to the baseball game and saw Dante hoist Megan in the air so she could catch the ball. "Look at all the adults playing with the kids. It's nice. My father never played with us."

Caden pulled her mate into her arms, "Family is everything to wolves. Nothing makes a wolf happier than playing with the cubs—it's how we teach them how to be wolves."

"You would be a wonderful pater, Caden. I wish I could have a cub with you."

"We will have a cub one day," Caden assured her. "There are plenty of cubs out there who need a good home, and even if it wasn't born to us, we wouldn't love it any less."

That earned Caden a kiss on her lips. "You are the perfect wolf, you know that?" Lena nuzzled in closer to her mate.

"I'm awfully glad you think so."

"Caden." Lena knew who that voice belonged to without turning: the Mater. "Bring Lena over to see us."

*Us* turned out to be a table full of smiling submissive wolves, and they were beckoning Lena over. Caden nodded at Lena's questioning glance, and as she hurried over to join them, she wondered why Caden looked so concerned. It must have been her imagination.

"Sit down, Lena, I thought we'd never get rid of Caden." After a brief greeting, Caden was packed off with Conan to play with the other cubs. "You already know Stella, and this is Ava, baby Hannah, her sister-in-law Kyra, and Dante's mother, Iris. Vance will be here soon—he and Flash are running late."

Lena fiddled with her glasses nervously. "Hi, it's nice to meet you all. Your baby is beautiful, Ava."

"Thank you. Would you like a hold?"

Before Lena could respond, she found her arms full. "I'm not very good with babies. Am I holding her all right?"

"You're doing fine. Just support her head," Ava told her.

They all smiled to each other as they watched Lena coo and talk to the baby. "Hi, Hannah. You're a pretty girl."

"She has a pretty good pair of lungs too," Ava joked.

"So?" Eden said. "How are things with Caden? Wolfie things, I mean."

Stella laughed and said, "Going by the love bites on her neck, I'd say things were going well."

Lena knew she was blushing brightly. "Yes, things are good. She trusts that I won't break just because I'm a human, and in fact… No, I shouldn't say anything."

They all huddled closer, and Eden said, "Oh no. First thing you have to learn about den talk is there are no secrets from each other. That's why it terrifies the dominants so much, keeps them on their toes. Right, girls?"

The women nodded and smiled, encouraging Selena to talk and feel comfortable. Having never mixed well with people or ever having had close girlfriends, it was a strange experience to now be sharing secrets with these women. But she felt they were on her side, and that was something very new for her.

"Caden and I are going to ask Dante, the Alpha, for permission to have a mating ceremony."

There were squeals from her new friends, and Eden jumped up to carefully hug her, as she was still holding the baby. "I'm so happy for you, Lena."

"Can you believe it?" Stella said. "Our committed bachelor of a Second, going to be mated."

"Do you think your pack will have any problems with me being human?" Lena asked.

Eden looked to Iris, the pack matriarch to explain. "Lena, my dear, the Great Mother decides before we are born who our mate will be. It doesn't matter who that person is, be they male, female, human, or wolf. We trust her judgment completely and only care that the couples are happy."

Lena looked down at the baby in her arms, and said, "Will I make her happy, though? I won't be able to give her a cub."

Iris smiled enigmatically. "Caden's grandmother was my friend, a close friend. She was a remarkable woman who saw things others did not. When I asked her why she had told Caden her wolf mate didn't exist, she simply answered that it was the truth, but despite that her granddaughter would have a very happy life. I can only conclude that you are the one to make her happy."

"You really think so?" Lena asked.

"I do. Don't spend your time worrying about what you can't do. Concentrate on what you can do."

Ava grinned as she added, "Besides, the Wolfgang pack is going to be overpopulated anyway, with our Mater likely to be pregnant straight through to menopause."

"Ava." Eden pretended to be shocked but couldn't help but laugh along with her friends.

Lena looked around the faces of the happy, smiling women, and thought, for the first time in her life, *This is where I belong. I've found my home.*

It was an idyllic day, and Caden couldn't remember being happier. She was playing baseball with the cubs, Dante was by her side with Conan in her arms, and Lena was sitting with the people she loved, watching her and looking happier and more relaxed than she'd ever seen her.

The pack was accepting her as one of their own, and it meant the world to her. She should have been concentrating on the game, but she couldn't help but gaze at her mate lovingly.

The wind blew the hem of Lena's dress up a few inches and Caden gave a low rumbling growl when she saw the bite mark she had made there only that morning. She had bitten down, just as Lena had begged her to, while she made her come with her fingers. Each time she made her mate come, Caden's hunger didn't seem to wane. She wanted Lena again and she wanted her now.

Caden felt fire spread all over her body, and her claws started to emerge. Just as she started to move toward Lena, Dante stood in front of her. Conan was in her arms, chewing on her T-shirt.

"Second? Are you with us?"

"What?" Caden looked around quickly. She had completely forgotten they were in the middle of a game. Cubs laughing and shouting, the sound of the ball hitting the bat, adults cheering, nothing had roused her from her distracted state. The players were all dispersing from the field in search of food. "Did I miss the whole game?"

Dante laughed and handed her a bottle of water. "Yes, you missed it. You spent the whole time staring at your mate. You, my friend, are totally drunk on love."

"I think I am. It's so confusing. I just want to be near her, touching her, all the time, but it's never enough. No matter how many times I touch her, I just want her more each time. It's like never being able to quench my thirst."

Dante put Conan on the grass and allowed him to toddle around. "You've got the hunger, my friend. You'll never lose that hunger, but once you bite and your wolf is secure that she's yours, you'll be able to control the hunger better."

Caden scrubbed her face with her hands, trying to rid herself of the clawing frustration her wolf felt. "I'm like a cub, unable to control myself."

"I'm your Alpha. I feel what you feel, and that's why I came over to calm your emotions. This is Lena's first pack event. She's finding her place among us and among the submissives. Calm your wolf and let her be. Your time alone with her will come soon enough."

Dante was right. Lena was relaxed and happy for the first time in her life, and from the smile on her face and her laughter, it appeared as if she was making true friendships for the first time in her life.

"You're right, thank you. Will you give us permission to be mated as soon as possible?"

Dante pulled her into an embrace. "Nothing would give me greater pleasure. You and I are strong leaders, but we are given strength by our mates. The heart of our pack will now be complete, and with a strong heart there's nothing our pack cannot face."

It was then that Dante's cell phone rang. It was Blaze.

## Chapter Twenty-one

"Here he comes, Alpha."

Leroux and Ovid watched a black van approach them on a desolate plot of wasteland, a few miles from their base. They were accompanied by two cars full of fully armed Lupa wolves, for protection.

Leroux looked in her side mirror and saw the van for herself. "Let's just hope, for Kurtis's sake, that he has delivered what we wanted."

The van stopped to the side of them and the wolves from the security team got out and surrounded the van.

"He looks terrified," Ovid said.

She watched Kurtis carefully. He was as white as a sheet and he held the steering wheel with a death grip. Beside him was his son, and next to him, his mate. She was thin and sharp featured, and looked less frightened and more determined than he did.

"What is it about Wolfgangs, Ovid? They cower and hide behind their mates like they have no teeth."

Ovid laughed and got out of the car to walk around and open Leroux's door. "And he thought he could be your Second."

Leroux smiled and slapped her on the back. "I'll have no other Second but you. We're just using his jealousy and hatred to get what we want. Now, let's inspect our package."

They walked to the back of the van where Kurtis and his family were standing. Leroux immediately stood in front of Kurtis's mate and said, "Are you going to introduce me to your mate?"

Kurtis gulped and said, "Of course, Alpha. This is my mate, Dorcus, and my son, Jasper."

She didn't even give the boy a second glance but took Dorcus's hand and kissed it chivalrously. "What a beautiful wolf. Have you been hiding this treasure in Wolfgang land, Kurtis?"

Dorcus giggled and blushed. She was clearly excited by very dominant wolves, and Leroux could scent interest.

"Thank you, Alpha," she gushed. "Thank you for allowing us to join the Lupas. Kurtis has been consistently overlooked by Dante each time a place among her elite wolves has become available."

"That's enough, Dorcus," Kurtis snapped. "Leroux doesn't want to hear all our troubles."

"Now, now, Kurtis. There's no need for that, but Dorcus, your mate and I do have some business, so why don't you take your cub and sit in my car, hmm?"

Once they were escorted away, Leroux indicated for Ovid to open the van. Ovid threw open the doors, and there in the back were two terrified-looking cubs, a boy and a girl, bound and gagged, tears rolling down their cheeks.

In an instant, Leroux grabbed Kurtis and smashed him so hard into the van it made a dent, and held her claws at his throat. "Those are not the Alpha's cubs. You promised me her two oldest cubs, Kurtis," she spat.

Kurtis looked terrified. He averted his eyes submissively and said, "I couldn't get them, but I got the sheriff's daughter, Tia, and Flash's son, Marco. They are Dante's closest friends after the Second. She will go on the hunt for them, I promise."

Leroux knew that already, but her heart had been set on causing Dante as much pain as possible. In an instant, though, Leroux masked her fury with a smile. "You are quite right, Kurtis. In fact, Dante is so disgustingly noble that she would probably go on the hunt for the weediest runt in her pack, but the sheriff and Flash are the next most dominant wolves, so I'll take that."

She let Kurtis go and he breathed a big sigh of relief. "Thank you, Alpha."

Leroux cupped his face in a deceptively gentle gesture and

said, "But if you ever fail me again, Kurtis...Well, I don't really have to say, do I?"

"Never again, Alpha."

Marco and Tia chose that moment to squeal as best they could through their gags, and Kurtis glanced back at them.

"It's too late for second thoughts now, Kurtis. You've betrayed your pack, your kin, and there's no going back, because Dante will tear your throat out. You have new loyalties now."

Leroux turned to Ovid and pointed to the other car. "Second, take Kurtis to ride with my wolves."

Kurtis looked panicked. "But my family is—"

What a weak runt he was. "They are riding with me. Off you go, then."

When Ovid escorted him away, Leroux looked at the two terrified cubs in the back of the van again and roared, enjoying the fear she induced. She slammed the door shut and laughed. "Come and get them, Dante."

The elite wolves and their mates started to gather around the Alpha, who'd put the call on speaker. "Blaze, calm down. Tell me what we know."

"They've taken our cubs. Flash called as soon as he realized they were gone. They have my baby cub."

Dante saw Flash and Vance speeding across the grass. "Blaze, stay calm. We'll get our cubs back. Go to the war room, and we'll meet you there."

Flash and Vance were beside them in an instant. "Alpha, Marco and Tia are gone. She took them," Flash said.

Vance had tears falling down his cheeks. "They were just hanging out at the park while we got the picnic ready, and we were going to pick up Blaze on our way, but they were gone. They were just gone, Alpha. This note was left taped to the slide."

He handed Dante a note which read: *Missing something, Dante? We have your cubs. Come and get them, if you dare.*

She crumpled up the paper in her hand and said to Caden, "Second, have my wolves go home to their dens, and order the elite wolves to the war room. Leroux is back and has taken first bite."

❖

Dante stood at the head of the conference table, with Caden at her right hand. The elite wolves all sat before them, except Flash and Blaze, who stood, unable to calm themselves.

"Flash says the scent is strong from where they were taken. I will lead a hunting party with Flash, Blaze, and Caden. Xander, I want you to stay and take command. Organize twenty-four-hour patrols around the border of the county. No one stands down until we have the cubs back."

"Yes, Alpha," Xander said.

Flash banged his fist on the table. "Can we go now? Our cubs are out there in the hands of a wolf who kills without mercy. We're wasting time."

Caden growled and was in Flash's face instantly. "Mind your place, Flash. We will get your cub back, but we must make sure our pack land and families are secure while we are gone. Do you understand me, Wolf?"

Flash lowered his eyes in submission. "I'm sorry, Second. I just want my cub back." Then he turned to Blaze, who was barely keeping his rage under control. "I was supposed to keep them safe, Blaze. I failed."

Blaze pulled Flash to him. "You have not failed, we are going to get them back, and when we do, you and I will tear her apart."

It was good to see the dominant wolves settle this tension themselves, because Caden knew they would need unity and obedience out on the hunt.

Dante addressed her wolves one final time. "Our pack has been attacked, and we will bring those responsible to justice. Xander, I leave the remaining wolves under your command."

"Very good, Alpha," Xander said.

"Good hunting, Wolves."

❖

Dante and her wolves had been following the cubs' scent in a truck for around two hours. Before they left Wolfgang County, they'd discovered Kurtis, a low-ranking wolf, and his family had packed up and left. She was sure they had something to do with this attack. Kurtis's grandfather had been Second and had betrayed Dante's own grandmother. The betrayal had nearly killed Dante's grandmother, and now it looked as if his kin had done the same.

Caden looked in the rearview mirror and saw the terrified looks of two frightened parents who had lost their cubs, and she couldn't imagine how she would feel in their place, fearing for the safe return of a cub or a mate.

It had been so hard to leave Lena. She had never gone on a hunt before, leaving her love behind. She was desperate to have Lena in her arms, protected and safe.

"How are you bearing up, Second?" Dante asked.

"Me? I'm okay. I just want to get the cubs back where they belong."

"It's the first mission you've been on with a mate waiting behind," Dante said.

Caden glanced at her quickly and returned her eyes to the road. "My wolf is clawing my insides to shreds. I want to be with her, around and over her, keeping her from harm. I don't know how you've done it all these years, Dante, especially when Eden's been pregnant. I simply don't know how I could do it."

"It drives me crazy, but that's part of being Alpha. I have to make decisions and take actions for the good of the pack, and I pray to the Great Mother she will be kept safe."

Caden's burden had been made easier by Eden insisting on Lena staying with her while their mates were gone. She hated to think of her mate alone in their den.

"I'm so happy the Mater and Lena get on so well. She doesn't make friends easily and has been lonely for most of her life. Eden has been so welcoming to her."

"That is why Eden was born to be Mater. She mothers the pack and makes any newcomers feel part of us. But she genuinely likes Lena, and we're both so happy for you, Second."

"Thank you for allowing our mating ceremony to be held as soon as possible."

Dante smiled and smacked her best friend on the shoulder. "Nothing would give me greater pleasure. As soon as we get the cubs back and dispose of this Leroux problem, the pack will rejoice in Lena becoming a Wolfgang."

"Thank you, my friend. Then let's get the cubs and get back to our mates. My hunger is growing." Caden smiled.

The strong scent Dante, Caden, and their wolves had been following brought them to the perimeter of a large run-down ranch and house. They left the truck and shifted to pelt. They stalked the perimeter of the land until they were close enough to get a look at the front of the property.

Dante signaled for the others to stop and observe the guards covering the front door of the house. Caden held her snout high in the air and inhaled all the scents, painting a picture of the surrounding area.

*Status report, Second?*

*The front is well guarded, Alpha. We should make our way round to the back and find a way in there.*

*That's my thinking. Blaze—take Flash and loop round to the left and meet us at the back of the property. The Second and I will take the right.*

*Yes, Alpha.*

Once they had moved off, Caden asked, *What's wrong, Alpha? I can feel your concern.*

*You know me too well, Second. There's something not right. I can feel it.*

*How so?*

*Do you not think it's all been too easy? Why pick a spot only a few hours from Wolfgang pack land, if Leroux didn't want us to track them? The scent was so strong, she made no effort to cover her tracks.*

*You think this is a trap?*

*It may be, but we have no other choice than to walk into it, Second. The cubs are depending on us.*

The two wolves padded quietly toward the back of the old farm building. There was no sign of any of Leroux's wolves, and that made Caden uneasy. She spotted Blaze and Flash up ahead and signaled them to stay down while she checked the back door.

She crept up to the back door and listened carefully to what was happening inside. There was no movement, which was worrying in itself. She pushed her snout through the door, which was ajar. Immediately she could scent both cubs and Leroux strongly.

*Alpha, Leroux wants us in there. Whatever the trap, it's set in that structure.*

*Caden,* the Alpha replied, *signal Blaze and Flash. We're going to give Leroux what she wants.*

❖

Lena watched Vance look up at the clock, his eyes red with tears. "Flash and I normally go up to bed at this time, and we look in Marco's bedroom and watch him sleeping soundly, not a care in the world. It's my favorite time of day, because I know he's safe."

He broke down in tears again, and Stella joined him. She put her arm round his shoulders, while Lena and Eden looked on.

"Why didn't I just insist Tia come with me? I had to leave early to set up the food, and I just left her to play with Marco," Stella said.

"The Alpha's hunting party will bring them back. You can be sure of that," Eden reassured them.

Conan was fussing, picking up on everyone's stress. "Bear, Mama."

Eden sighed. "I forgot his cuddle bear. He's not going to settle without it. Stella, could you take him until I run back to the den to pick it up?"

"You can't go outside, Eden," Stella said. "Who knows who's out there?"

"Stella, Xander hasn't come across anyone on her patrols as yet, and we have the best security in the world. Our perimeter is secure. Anyway, I'll only be five minutes. If I don't get the bear, Conan won't sleep."

"Why not send one of the guards?" Vance suggested.

"They wouldn't know where to look. I need to go."

Lena, who had kept very quiet, said, "I'll come with you. Keep you company. I could do with some air."

"Okay, sure. Stella, if we're not back in an hour, send out the search parties," Eden joked.

Outside Stella's there were two guards at the door, and others patrolling the grounds. One of the young wolves on the door stopped them before they went any farther. "Mater, the Alpha's orders were that you weren't to leave Stella's den."

Eden sighed. "But, Jinx, my cub needs his cuddle bear. Lena and I will only be five minutes. You can tell the Alpha it was my fault."

Jinx looked extremely distressed at the thought of disobeying the Alpha's orders. "I can't let you go, Mater. Please tell us where it is, and we'll get it for you."

"Jinx, I am your Mater, and I will go back to my den, but you may accompany us if you like."

Jinx considered this for a minute and agreed. "Of course, Mater." Then she called over two more wolves and told him they wouldn't be long. "Stay at your post, no matter what."

"Yes, Jinx," they replied.

Eden said to Lena, "So much trouble, just to find a cuddle bear. I hope Conan appreciates this."

Dante and Caden crept softly into the house and followed the cubs' scents. They came to a door and took position on either side.

*On three, Second. One, two, three.*

The two wolves burst through the door and found themselves in darkness. After a few seconds, the light was switched on to reveal the cubs tied to chairs and gagged, in the middle of the room. Standing beside them was Leroux in her human form, looking completely relaxed.

"Dante. You join us at last, and, Caden, wonderful to see you."

Dante growled and bared her teeth, looking as intimidating as possible. *We've come for the cubs.*

Marco and Tia strained at their bonds, looking as if they were trying to tell them something. Marco finally reached Caden telepathically. *Tell the Alpha. It's a trap.*

*Calm yourself, cub. We will handle this,* Caden assured him.

"What a pathetic pair of cubs these two are. They've been crying for their mommies the whole time. Pathetic whelps." Leroux casually stroked Tia's head.

Dante and Caden both growled a fierce warning, and Dante warned Leroux, *Don't touch them. Caden, untie them and take them outside.*

Caden shifted to skin and approached the chair.

"Oh, allow me." Leroux began to untie them, and as soon as they were free, Tia leaped into Caden's arms, and Marco held on to her sleeve. She handed the cubs over to Blaze and Flash outside and came back into the room.

Leroux sat in one of the now-vacated seats and crossed her legs. "So, Dante?"

*You think I don't know this is a trap? I don't walk into traps without a plan.*

Leroux started to laugh. "Oh, I assure you, I have no other Lupa wolves than the ones you've already seen at the front door, and I'm sure your arrogant wolves would be quite efficient in defending you against them. No, I have different purposes."

Caden growled and said, "Let me tear her apart."

*Hold your wolf, Second. Have patience.*

Dante shifted to skin and stood tall and intimidating.

Leroux taunted Dante. "My, what a physical specimen you are. All the bitches you encounter seem to think so. Eden, Suzy."

"Suzy Mitchell?"

Leroux stood and casually walked over to her opponent. "Yes, you were all she could talk about—she was like a bitch in heat for you. What happened? Did you fuck her and never call back?"

Caden watched their back and forth silently, ready to protect the Alpha should she need her help. But this was Dante's battle to fight.

Dante growled and pulled back her lips into a sneer. "Never. I am loyal to my mate, as I should be. I may not have liked Suzy, but you tore her apart, like all the other humans you've encountered recently."

"You've been keeping track of me? How flattering. What can I say? Her constant whining about you became annoying."

"You're very confident for a wolf I left for dead and who has scars all over her body. You really think you're going to survive another fight with me?"

"You did leave me for dead, with injuries my wolf couldn't heal overnight. But you are not going to fight me today. Our battle lies in the future, when I have my strength back, and my pack mates have all rejoined me."

Dante grabbed Leroux's throat and began to squeeze. "Do you think I'm going to let you walk away today, just because we retrieved the cubs?" She slammed Leroux up against the wall, causing the plaster to crack and fall. Dante's teeth and eyes shifted, making her look terrifying. "You took two of my wolves, and you touched my mate. I'm going to rip your limbs off, one by one, then let Blaze and Flash rip you to pieces."

Leroux grasped at Dante's hand, struggling for air. "Yes…I clawed open Eden's mate mark and tasted her blood. She…tastes so sweet."

Dante lifted Leroux off the floor and flung her through the air. She smashed into the wall and crashed to the ground. In an instant Dante was over her, teeth bared and ready to strike. "Any last words, Mutt?"

Leroux coughed and spat blood. "After our last fight, I was broken. I was so badly injured, but recovery gives you a lot of time to think. And I thought, I don't want to simply kill Dante and take her riches, that's not enough anymore." She smiled as the blood ran down her chin. "I want to break you, Dante. I want you to hurt and live a long life, feeling that hurt every single second, minute, and hour you spend on this earth." Leroux raised her hand and glanced at her watch. "And the method of your torment should be happening any minute now."

Caden had a sinking feeling in the pit of her stomach, and she could sense her Alpha felt the same.

"What do you mean?" Dante roared.

"Didn't you wonder why I made this so easy for you? I needed to get you out of Wolfgang County."

A look of horror passed over Dante's face. "What have you done?"

"Tell me, Dante? What do you prize above everything?"

The answer hit Caden like a lead weight. *Eden.*

Dante didn't say a word, but shifted and burst out the door. Caden shifted as well and was fast on her heels.

## Chapter Twenty-two

*Alpha. Stop.* Caden chased Dante down and leaped in front of her. *Out of my way, Second. They have my mate. This was all a ruse to get me out of the county.*

*I know, but we can get there faster in the truck. Try and keep the fury from clouding your judgment, Alpha.*

Dante growled but turned and ran back to the others. She and Caden shifted and quickly pulled their clothes back on.

"Get in, wolves. Our land and our mates are under attack," Caden said as she jumped behind the wheel, Dante beside her in the passenger seat.

Blaze, Flash, and the two crying and shocked cubs got in the back, and the truck zoomed off into the night.

"We must get Xander and my elite wolves to the Mater," Dante ordered.

Caden called Xander's number and it rang out. "She must be out on patrol."

"Try the sheriff's office, Second," Blaze said. "My deputy should be there."

"Anything?" Dante asked.

"The line's busy, I can't get through."

"Fuck." Dante smashed her fist off the dashboard. "Keep trying. We need to get our message to them."

"Alpha, this is our fault," Tia's small voice said. "We shouldn't have walked up to Kurtis's van. Jasper said he wanted to show us something."

"Kurtis." Dante roared. "His family betrays us again. He and Leroux will pay for whatever harm she has caused."

❖

Eden and Lena were in the nursery when they heard some commotion from downstairs. They crept along the landing and saw their two guards and one intruder lying on the floor.

They both gasped.

"Oh my God," Lena said.

"Leroux. It must be."

"Is this an attack from the Lupa pack? Caden was telling me about them."

"Yes. We have to get back to the cubs. Stay behind me, Lena," Eden ordered.

"But you're pregnant, Eden."

"I'm also a wolf, Lena. I have a better chance than you, especially with that broken arm."

Lena nodded, and they crept down the wide staircase. Seeing no one around, Eden crouched to check the intruder and, satisfied he was dead, turned her attention to the first wolf guard. "He's dead." She placed a hand on his chest and whispered, "May the Great Mother bless you on your journey. Run free in the Great Forest, Wolf." Eden shut her eyes for a few seconds to honor him.

Lena saw the other guard move and pull herself up against the wall. "Eden, Jinx is alive."

They rushed to her side. "Jinx, are you all right? You need to shift," Eden told the young wolf.

"I can't, Mater. They have crossbows with silver bolts. I'm poisoned."

"Cowards," Eden said angrily.

Lena was confused. From what Caden had told her, wolves could heal from most injuries by shifting to pelt. "What does that mean, Eden?"

"The traditional way to kill a werewolf is to shoot a silver bolt to the heart. The silver then enters the bloodstream in seconds, and death follows immediately. These weapons have been left in the past by all the civilized wolf packs, but the Lupas are not civilized. Jinx put up a great fight and was shot in the side, and we wolves can't shift while there is silver in our bodies. It means the silver and any tissue around it must be removed if the wolf is to heal."

Jinx groaned in pain. "I'm sorry I failed you, Mater."

Eden stroked the young wolf's head. "You did not fail me, Wolf. You nearly died trying to protect me. They're coming."

"Who's coming?" Lena said in panic.

"Leroux's wolves. I can hear them. Jinx, if we're to have any chance, we need the element of surprise. This is what we'll do."

Eden's white wolf stood defiantly in front of the bodies and Lena, who was right behind her. A dark dominant female wolf walked in, holding a crossbow pointed right at her. She smirked when she saw Eden ready to defend herself.

"The Wolfgang Mater, I presume? Allow me to introduce myself. I am Ovid, Leroux's Second, and who is the mousy-looking human behind you, Mater?"

Lena figured if she was going to die, she might as well die being true to herself. "I am Selena, the Wolfgang Second's mate."

Ovid began to laugh loudly. "My, my. Leroux was right. The Wolfgangs have sunk to low depths. The Second has a human for a mate? Well, it's just all too perfect, then. I can destroy the entire heart of the pack in one go. Dante and Caden will be crushed."

Eden growled. *You are a coward, wolf. Are you going to shoot two submissives with a silver bolt? What kind of weak dominants do the Lupas breed?*

Ovid growled low in her throat. "I am not going to shoot you, but someone else is. Get in here, Kurtis."

*You traitor, Kurtis. How could you betray your pack?*

"Because Dante and those before her have made us weak. It's time to change."

Ovid pointed to his crossbow and said, "It's time to prove your loyalty to the Lupas. Shoot the Mater."

Lena jumped in front of Eden and shouted, "No. You can't do this."

"What bravery! Who knew humans had any?" Ovid pushed Lena clear across the room. "Do it, Kurtis. Now," Ovid ordered.

Kurtis walked up to Eden's wolf and directed the crossbow to her heart. His hand shook with the recognition of what he was about to do.

*Look me in the eye when you shoot me, Kurtis, because I don't think you have the courage to shoot that bolt.*

Kurtis turned his head away from her and prepared to squeeze. Just then, Jinx rose up and barreled toward him.

Kurtis dropped his arm and ran out the door. The confusion gave Eden the distraction she needed to pounce on Ovid.

Ovid shifted to pelt in a second and swiped Eden across her shoulder, leaving a deep, bloody gash.

Lena ran forward to get between the dark wolf and her friend. "Eden, no!"

Dante, Caden, Blaze, and Flash jumped from the truck and ran into the Alpha's den to find a terrifying scene.

Eden lay on the floor in skin form, blood flowing from deep scratches and bite wounds. Next to her, Lena lay with gashes down her right side. Dante fell to her knees and howled her rage to all who would hear her.

Caden followed suit and howled along with her.

"Cade," Lena murmured.

"You're alive," Caden said.

Dante checked Eden's neck for a pulse. "Flash. Get the EMTs here now."

"Yes, Alpha."

Tears rolled down Dante's face. "There's still a chance. Please, Great Mother, keep her alive. We need her."

"Cade? It hurts," Lena said.

Caden stroked her mate's brow. "Just lie still, Goddess, I'm here now."

"Jinx saved us."

Dante looked up as one of her wolves checked Jinx's pulse and shook her head. "We will mourn her as a hero when we have gotten our mates to safety."

Caden looked between Lena's and the Mater's bodies. Both lay in a pool of blood still flowing from the deep gashes they both had on their shoulders and arms. There was so much blood.

She held her face in her hands and cursed the Lupas who had done this. *Oh, Great Mother, no.*

❖

The Mater and Lena were brought straight to the hospital. The Mater was rushed into surgery to treat flesh that was grazed by a silver bolt.

Lena was in a hospital room after having her wounds stitched and drugs administered. Caden sat at her bedside, waiting to get Lena's blood test results and for her mate to wake up.

Lena's blood had mixed with the Mater's. If there was sufficient transfer, if she was turned, there was a chance she wouldn't survive the change.

Caden brought Lena's hand up to her lips and placed a soft kiss there. When she looked at her mate now, hooked up to a drip with machines beeping in the background, she looked so fragile. *How could you ever go through the change, my Goddess?*

There was a knock on the door and Dr. Riley, who had been doing Lena's test, came in.

Caden jumped up immediately. "Any news, Doctor?"

"Yes, we have the test results, Second."

"Well?"

Doctor Riley looked down at Lena's notes before saying, "Ms. Miller was infected by the Mater's blood, but we managed to irrigate the wound sufficiently so only a small level of infection occurred."

Caden ran her hand through her hair. "What does that mean? Is she going to change?"

"We don't believe so, no. The level of pathogen wasn't high enough to alter her genetic material entirely, Second."

Caden breathed a huge sigh of relief. "So she'll be okay?"

Dr. Riley smiled. "I believe so. She may experience some minor changes in temperament, but we expect that's all."

Caden slumped into her chair and scrubbed her face with her hands. "Thank you, Great Mother, and thank you, Doctor. How is the Mater?"

The doctor looked altogether more nervous at that question. "Dr. Jaycen is with the Alpha now."

"Please, tell me."

"The Mater will recover but she lost the cub. It wasn't strong enough to fight the silver coursing through the Mater's blood. I'm sorry, Second." As the doctor told her this news, a loud painful roar erupted in another part of the hospital, and then the sound of furniture and glass being smashed.

"The Alpha." Caden rushed from the room.

❖

Caden shifted and followed the trail of destruction and the Alpha's scent down to the edge of the forest. She saw the Alpha up ahead, roaring, slashing, and smashing her claws repeatedly on a huge tree trunk.

It was potentially suicide to approach a dominant wolf in such a state of grief, but she had to help her friend.

Dante scented her and turned around to face her. She looked terrifying, snarling and growling. If Leroux had been here, she would have torn her apart.

Caden approached slowly and submissively. Her eyes lowered,

tail between her legs, ears back, everything to show she was not a threat.

*Alpha? Let me help you, please. I know you want Leroux's blood. We will get it.*

At the mention of Leroux's name, Dante launched through the air and knocked her Second to the ground. She snarled and snapped at Caden's face, blinded by her rage.

Caden did the only thing she could do, and that was to offer her throat. *Alpha, I give you my throat, but please let me help you.*

The Alpha's stormy eyes started to clear, and she saw her friend beneath her. Dante walked back and shifted to skin.

Caden followed suit and kneeled down beside her Alpha, who had her head bowed and was breathing heavily.

"Alpha, I'm so sorry."

Dante's dark hair was slick with sweat, and her muscles taut with fury. She lifted her head and Caden saw tears of grief rolling down her Alpha's face. "How do I tell her, Cade? How do I tell her when she wakes up that our cub is dead?"

Caden had no clue what to say. She couldn't imagine having to break that sort of news. "I don't know, Alpha, but I do know when you do, you will be the Mater's strength, and she will need you more than ever."

Dante wiped her face, trying to pull herself together. "I know. I have to be strong for her and the cubs."

They both stood, and Caden saw a look of cold, hard determination come over her Alpha.

"I might not have been able to protect Eden today, but I swear to the Great Mother, I will find Leroux and tear her apart, piece by piece."

❖

Blaze and Flash found Dante and Caden in the forest clearing by the river. When Dante saw who they had captured, she charged toward him.

"No, no! Please, Dante," Kurtis screamed.

She stopped inches from him and snarled, "Let him go, Wolves."

Kurtis fell to his knees and started to sob. "Thank you, oh God. I thought you were going to kill me. This was all a misunderstanding."

"Stand," Dante said.

Kurtis stood on wobbly knees and looked down submissively. Blaze and Flash stood behind them, barely restraining their rage. Caden stood at her Alpha's right hand.

"No, I'm not going to kill you."

Blaze and Flash started to protest, but Dante silenced them with a growl. "I'm not going to kill you. I just wanted to look into your eyes first, then make sure you die a fair and honorable death. Blaze? As you are higher ranked than Flash, you have the honor of killing this traitor. Flash, you must hold your wolf."

"Yes, Alpha," they replied.

"No, Dante, please," Kurtis begged.

Dante signaled to Caden to follow her and they turned and padded away. "Have at it, Blaze."

Kurtis starting screaming. "I hate you, Dante. I hope your bitch and that bastard cub inside her die."

Dante stopped, and Caden said, "Leave him, Alpha. Let us go back to our mates."

As they walked off, all they could hear were the sounds of snapping jaws and squeals of pain.

Caden didn't know how Dante would cope with the pain of losing a cub, and nearly her mate, but one thing she knew for certain was that she and the Mater would survive, with the love and support of the pack.

## Chapter Twenty-three

Smoke rose to the clear dark sky from two funeral pyres, set in a large forest clearing. As many of the Wolfgang pack as could crowd the space were there to witness and mourn the passing of two young wolves.

At the front the first family of the pack stood together. Dante held tightly to her mate, who was still healing after her horrific injuries. Eden kept baby Conan close in her arms, and Megan held on to her pater for reassurance. Dion kept one hand on her mom, while holding Tia's hand with the other. The sounds of grief and the crackle of the fire echoed across the clearing.

Beside them, Caden and the elite wolves and their mates stood in order of precedence. Caden held Lena in her arms, breathing in the scent that brought calm to her wolf.

Dante walked forward and approached the fallen wolves' families. She embraced each wolf in turn and said, "Thank you for your sacrifice."

"Caden?" Lena whispered.

"Yes, Goddess?"

"I've never experienced anything like this. The atmosphere, the sense of loss, every wolf is sharing in it equally. It's closer than family."

Caden gave her a soft smile. "That's what pack is all about. We are a collective force. We live and die together. Every cog and every wheel is needed to make us work. We are nothing without every wolf around us, and you are part of that now, Lena. You are pack, and you will never be found wanting again. I will love you and protect you until I stop breathing."

Lena looked up and placed a kiss on Caden's cheek. She knew she had found her place of safety, her place of acceptance, but she would never have believed she would find her liberation in the strict regime of a werewolf pack.

Dante addressed her pack. "My wolves, we come together to honor Jinx and Kai, two wolves who laid down their lives for their pack mates, and pack land. We will never forget their bravery or sacrifice. As they make their way to the everlasting hunt in the Great Mother's forest, it falls to us to make their sacrifice worthwhile. An act of war was committed against the Wolfgang pack, and I know you will all stand with me as we take our vengeance on those who have sought to harm our peaceful way of life."

Dante turned and faced the glowing pyres and thumped her chest in salute. "Good hunting, Wolves."

The rest of the pack followed suit and joined in as Dante led them in a long haunting howl.

❖

Lena was getting dressed for her special day in one of the Alpha's guest bedrooms with the help of her new close friends, Eden and Stella. She was looking at her dress in the mirror, and all she could hear was her mother's laughter. *You can't wear something like this, my baby elephant. You'll look ridiculous.*

Her dress was a long forest-green elven-style dress with a long train of chiffon. Eden and Stella had helped her choose it and assured her it was the traditional dress for a wolf wedding. When she chose it she was high on excitement and loved the dress, but now on her mating day her anxiety was taking control and destroying her confidence.

She broke down in tears. "I can't do this. I look horrible and I'm just going to embarrass Cade."

Eden was beside her in a second and held her in her arms. "Stop that now. It's just nerves. Stella, would you excuse us a moment?"

"Of course, Mater."

When she left, Eden got her a tissue and said, "Here, dry those tears. You have got nothing to worry about, Lena. You look beautiful. I wish you could see what Caden and all of us see in you."

Lena wanted to believe her, but after a lifetime of beating her down, her fears were hard to let go of. "I try, but it's hard. Caden should have a wolf, a wolf like you or Stella."

Eden caressed Lena's cheek tenderly. "As Dante's mother told you, the Great Mother picks out a mate before we are born. So if you didn't accept your love for her, and hers for you, she would be alone for the rest of her life. Is that what you would want?"

She hadn't thought of it that way, and Lena did trust that Caden loved her. She always showered her in affection and utter adoration. But leaving her own gray, bleak world and entering this bright, lush forest wonderland sometimes left her wondering if it was all just a dream, that she might wake up in her apartment in Salt Lake City alone.

"No, I'd never want that. I love her. I just need to be enough for her, and to be part of your world, Mater."

Eden put her hand on Lena's chest. "Lena, you saved my life and risked your own in the process. You are brave, honorable, and good. The Alpha and I will always be in your debt. Without you, we might have lost each other as well as our cub."

The emotion in Eden's voice brought fresh tears to Lena's eyes. "I wish I could have done more."

"No, you risked everything for me. We shared my blood, and it now runs in your veins. We are bound forever in friendship. No one deserves to be one of us more than you. You are pack. Understand?"

Lena wiped away her tears and found a surge of strength from inside her. "Yes, I understand. I'm ready, Mater."

❖

Caden strode purposefully into the sacred forest where the bones of their ancestors were buried. A platform was set up among a clearing in the trees, and the sunlight streamed down through the leaves above.

The pack stood around the platform and parted to allow Caden through. Behind her, the elite wolves followed in procession. They were all dressed the same, in white open-necked shirts, black trousers cut off at the shin, green velvet capes with silver clasps, their feet bare. Caden's cloak had gold braiding and a gold clasp to signify her rank.

She reached the bottom of the platform and saw Dante sitting on a wooden throne. Dante's cape was trimmed in thick fur.

Dante looked down at her and winked. "Who are you and why do you come here today, Wolf?"

Caden replied in a loud booming voice, "Alpha, I am Caden, Second of the Wolfgang pack, and I come here today to be joined with my mate, Selena Miller."

Even as the words came out of Caden's mouth, she still couldn't believe it was happening. She never in her wildest dreams imagined that she would be doing this or saying these words, but she wasn't in the slightest bit scared. This moment was what she was born for, and she couldn't wait for the next phase of her life to start.

Dante waved her up onto the platform. "Approach, Caden, Second of the Wolfgang Pack."

Caden walked up to the top of the platform and bowed her head. Dante rose from her ceremonial throne and opened her arms out wide to speak to the assembled pack.

"My wolves, Caden has come before us today to join with Selena Miller. Selena, if you wish to join with Caden, Second of the Wolfgang pack, come forward now."

The pack around the platform split into two and a line of submissive women and men, all mates of the elite wolves, walked forward and branched off to the side of the platform, leading the Mater and Lena into the clearing.

Caden gulped hard when she saw Lena. She was the most beautiful she had ever seen her. Her hair hung loosely in ringlets, and a crown of small white flowers lay atop her head. The forest-green dress trailed off in a train at the back, but in front it was shorter, to show her bare feet.

"I can't believe she's mine," Caden said softly to Dante.

"She is, my friend. She is yours forever," Dante replied.

Eden led her up onto the platform and gave Lena's hand to Caden to hold, then took her place at Dante's side.

"You look stunning, Goddess," Caden whispered to her, and Lena blushed.

Dante held up her hand. "Are you Selena Miller?"

"I am."

"And do you wish to be joined to Caden, the Wolfgang pack Second?"

Lena looked at her mate nervously, and Caden gave her hand a squeeze of support. "I am Selena and I wish to be joined to Caden."

Dante smiled happily. "Then let us begin."

Eden handed Dante the oathing stone that Caden and Lena had picked out. On top were two mating rings, each set with a beautifully cut version of the rainbow moonstone Caden had given her. Dante took the stone and held it up in the air. "May the Great Mother bless this stone and these moonstone rings, and may she bring happiness to Caden and Lena, and many happy years together."

She then offered the smaller of the rings to Caden. Caden lifted it and had to take a few deep breaths to calm the emotions inside her. She and Lena hadn't slept under the same roof for a week as per tradition, and it had been torture for her not to be near Lena. Now they were going to be joined and Lena would never be separated from her. The wave of happiness was overpowering. She lifted the ring and asked for Lena's hand.

"Selena Miller, I pledge to be a true and faithful mate, to protect you from all harm with my life, to love you, and I promise that you will never go without food or shelter. Will you be my mate?"

Lena gave her that smile that turned her heart to mush. "I will be your mate, Caden. By taking your ring, I promise to be a faithful mate, to care for you, to love you, and to give you everything you need."

Caden slipped on the ring and kissed her cheek. She smiled with pride as she watched Lena look down at her ring with wonder.

Lena then placed the larger ring on Caden's finger, making their pledge final.

*This is it. You've done it, Wolf.*

Dante asked them both to take the oathing stone in their hands. "The oath you take today is indivisible. Do you both swear in front of your pack to never break the vows you make today, and to keep them till death and beyond, when you enter the Great Forest?"

"We do swear, Alpha."

"You are now mated and can enjoy all the privileges and responsibilities that brings."

Dante reached out and took Eden's hand and pulled her close. "Today, my wolves, the heart of our pack is complete. While Caden and Lena kiss to seal their bond, let us come together and proclaim our joy to the Great Mother for bringing Lena to us."

The Alpha threw her head back and howled, and all the other wolves followed suit.

Caden pulled Lena to her and said, "I have you at last, my Goddess."

"And I have my hunter." Their lips came together and they both moaned. Lena pulled back and breathed heavily, "Take me back to our den."

## Chapter Twenty-four

While the rest of the pack feasted and celebrated, as tradition dictated, Caden and Lena set their oathing stone by a tree selected by Caden's ancestors. Their stone sat atop a mound of others, and it struck Lena that she was part of something now, part of a long line of family, of pack, and as much as it hurt that her own birth family rejected her, she now had new family, a pack who would always support her.

Caden pointed to some of the older stones. "This was my mother and pater's stone, and this Grandpa and Grandma's. I never thought in a million years I'd be doing the same thing."

Lena slipped her arms around her mate's neck. "And are you happy you are?"

"Can you not tell by the stupid grin on my face?"

She rested her head on Caden's chest. "I know you are. I feel it every time you look at me."

"Now for the last part of the mating ritual." Caden stood back and started unclasping her cloak.

"What is it?" Lena wondered why she was stripping down to her skin, out here in the forest. She wasn't going to…or was she?

"I am going to take you back to our den. The den is now yours to do with as you please. I'm going to make improvements and make it bigger, but—"

Lena silenced her with a kiss. "Take me back to my den, Wolf."

Caden growled and started to undress quickly. She piled her clothes up and shifted. No matter how many times Lena saw it, the process still gave her the same sense of awe and just a little bit of fear, but as soon as Caden was in her wolf form fully, she felt safe. The wolf would never hurt her.

She held on to her wolf's ruff, and they walked in quiet companionship, until they arrived at the den.

Caden shifted back to skin in an instant and stood up slowly. Lena gasped as she did. The sight of her mate, muscles taut and eyes wild, made her hot.

Lena's breathing began to shorten as Caden approached her. Caden nuzzled her neck and growled. "I want you, Goddess. I want to make you scream."

She grasped Caden's shoulders and dug her nails in. "And I want to make you howl, Wolf."

Caden picked her up and carried her upstairs to the bedroom.

Lena was ravenous for Caden. She felt hot and in desperate need of an orgasm. One thing she had noticed since she'd mixed blood with the Mater was that her sex drive had risen exponentially. Maybe it was a combination of that and meeting Caden, but every time she was in her presence, all she could think about was Caden, raw and needy. Thrusting into her and making her come.

"Take it off," Caden said looking at her dress.

Lena carefully took off her glasses and flower crown and laid them to the side. Caden was looking at her with hot, predator eyes and was barely in control. As she took off her dress, she heard Caden's low growl, and she was instantly wet and throbbing inside.

She quickly disposed of her underwear and paused before she unclasped her bra. There was still some small part of her mind that was anxious about the way she looked. Caden stepped closer, placed one hand on the back of her neck, and caressed her cheek gently with the other. "Don't you know by now how beautiful you are? I worship you, Goddess."

"Thank you for seeing me, when no one else did." She took off her bra and dropped it at her feet.

Caden's wolf teeth erupted and she ran her tongue over her elongated canines. "I want you, mate."

Feeling confident, Lena took her nails and scratched Caden's torso, and that broke her mate's restraint. Caden lifted her and threw her on the bed, before crawling up her body and claiming her lips aggressively. Lena's legs parted and Caden's sex slid into place quite naturally.

Caden dragged her teeth down Lena's neck, causing her to grasp at Caden's shoulders and wrap her legs around her hard, muscled ass.

"Oh God, Caden, bite me."

Caden could feel Lena's wetness on her hard erect clit and couldn't help but start to thrust. "I've missed my mate this week. I have so much to give you," Caden said.

She kissed and sucked at Lena's breasts, Caden's favorite places to touch and bite, kiss and lavish with attention. They were so full, so female and fertile. Lena writhed under her.

"Caden, please?"

Her hips started to thrust in response to the need in Lena's voice. "I'll give you what you need, always. I can scent how ready you are, mate."

Caden latched onto the mating spot on her neck and kissed and licked, preparing the area. She slowed her thrusts, and Lena groaned.

"Don't stop, Cade. I love you."

"I love you, Goddess, and I'm going to make you mine." She grasped Lena's chin and rumbled a growl, commanding her mate to submit.

Lena looked away and bared her neck. "I'm yours."

Caden ran her tongue the length of her neck and said, "I have pledged to protect and provide for you before our pack, and now I claim your body and your soul as mine evermore." Caden bit down hard, and Lena gave a high-pitched groan, while her slick, hot sex undulated, begging Caden to thrust.

The pain and pleasure sensation was so overwhelming that Lena felt light-headed and almost passed out. As Caden's saliva dripped from her canines into the fresh wound she had made, Lena felt a powerful heat race from the wound and travel to every cell in her body.

Warmth and pleasure crashed through her cells, and slowly she began to become aware of Caden's thoughts.

*I love you, Goddess.*

Caden pulled her teeth from Lena's flesh and lifted her head to howl to all who heard that Lena was now hers, and off-limits to everyone but her.

Lena should have been scared, watching her own blood drip off Caden's fangs as she howled, but she wasn't. She felt complete for the first time in her life. She was Caden's mate and that was her rightful place.

She reached up and tenderly trailed her fingers down Caden's chest. She used her mind to communicate with Caden. *I love you so much, Caden.*

Caden looked down at her quizzically. *You can hear me?*

No one quite knew the effect the mating bite would have on her. The Alpha hadn't known humans to feel the full effect of a mate before, but the Mater's blood now flowed in Lena.

*I can feel everything, Caden. Your love, your heat, your want. Take what you need, Wolf. Fill up my belly.*

Caden howled and began thrusting hard and fast. "I'm going to fill you, mate. Take it for me?"

*Always*, Lena vowed.

Caden placed Lena's legs over her own shoulders to get as close as possible. The sound of slapping flesh and Caden's moans brought Lena to the edge of her orgasm.

"Fill me now," Lena shouted as her orgasm tumbled over and heat and pleasure rushed throughout her body.

Caden gave a howling cry as she came hard, and Lena felt the warmth of her essence enter her body.

Her mate collapsed onto her and shook. "I've never felt anything like that before in my life. I love you, Goddess, and I can't survive without you."

Lena took Caden's hand and placed it on her heart. "Your strength gave me the courage to come out from the shadows and become the person I was always meant to be. I could never have done it without you. And I will never leave your side. You have given me a family and your heart. I love you."

Caden kissed the moonstone ring on her finger. "You've given me a reason for being, Selena Miller, and I'm going to treasure you forever. You have completed me."

They lay quietly, enjoying the sounds of the forest outside the window, as Caden's bite weaved their hearts and their souls into one.

## About the Author

Jenny Frame is from the small town of Motherwell in Scotland, where she lives with her partner, Lou, and their well-loved and very spoiled dog.

She has a diverse range of qualifications, including a BA in public management and a diploma in acting and performance. Nowadays, she likes to put her creative energies into writing rather than treading the boards.

When not writing or reading, Jenny loves cheering on her local football team, which is not always an easy task!

Jenny can be contacted at jennyframe91@yahoo.com, or visit her website: http://www.jennyframe.com.

# Books Available From Bold Strokes Books

**A Touch of Temptation** by Julie Blair. Recent law school graduate Kate Dawson's ordained path to the perfect life gets thrown off course when handsome butch top Chris Brent initiates her to sexual pleasure. (978-1-62639-488-9)

**Beneath the Waves** by Ali Vali. Kai Merlin and Vivien Palmer love the water and the secrets trapped in the depths, but if Kai gives in to her feelings, it might come at a cost to her entire realm. (978-1-62639-609-8)

**Girls on Campus**, edited by Sandy Lowe and Stacia Seaman. College: four years when rules are made to be broken. This collection is required reading for anyone looking to earn an A in sex ed. (978-1-62639-733-0)

**Heart of the Pack** by Jenny Frame. Human Selena Miller falls for the domineering Caden Wolfgang, but will their love survive Selena learning the Wolfgangs are werewolves? (978-1-62639-566-4)

**Miss Match** by Fiona Riley. Matchmaker Samantha Monteiro makes the impossible possible for everyone but herself. Is mysterious dancer Lucinda Moss her perfect match? (978-1-62639-574-9)

**Paladins of the Storm Lord** by Barbara Ann Wright. Lieutenant Cordelia Ross must choose between duty and honor when a man with godlike powers forces her soldiers to provoke an alien threat. (978-1-62639-604-3)

**Taking a Gamble** by P.J. Trebelhorn. Storage auction buyer Cassidy Holmes and postal worker Erica Jacobs want different things out of life, but taking a gamble on love might prove lucky for them both. (978-1-62639-542-8)

**The Copper Egg** by Catherine Friend. Archeologist Claire Adams wants to find the buried treasure in Peru. Her ex, Sochi Castillo, wants to steal it. The last thing either of them wants is to still be in love. (978-1-62639-613-5)

**Capsized** by Julie Cannon. What happens when a woman turns your life completely upside down? (978-1-62639-479-7)

**A Reunion to Remember** by TJ Thomas. Reunited after a decade, Jo Adams and Rhonda Black must navigate a significant age difference, family dynamics, and their own desires and fears to explore an opportunity for love. (978-1-62639-534-3)

**Built to Last** by Aurora Rey. When Professor Olivia Bennett hires contractor Joss Bauer to restore her dilapidated farmhouse, she learns her heart, as much as her house, is in need of a renovation. (978-1-62639-552-7)

**Girls With Guns** by Ali Vali, Carsen Taite, and Michelle Grubb. Three stories by three talented crime writers—Carsen Taite, Ali Vali, and Michelle Grubb—each packing her own special brand of heat. (978-1-62639-585-5)

**Heartscapes** by MJ Williamz. Will Odette ever recover her memory, or is Jesse condemned to remember their love alone? (978-1-62639-532-9)

**Murder on the Rocks** by Clara Nipper. Detective Jill Rogers lives with two things on her mind: sex and murder. While an ice storm cripples Tulsa, two things stand in Jill's way: her lover and the DA. (978-1-62639-600-5)

**Necromantia** by Sheri Lewis Wohl. When seeing dead people is more than a movie tagline. (978-1-62639-611-1)

**Salvation** by I. Beacham. Claire's long-term partner now hates her, for all the wrong reasons, and she sees no future until she meets Regan, who challenges her to face the truth and find love. (978-1-62639-548-0)

**Trigger** by Jessica Webb. Dr. Kate Morrison races to discover how to defuse human bombs while learning to trust her increasingly strong feelings for the lead investigator, Sergeant Andy Wyles. (978-1-62639-669-2)

**Wild Shores** by Radclyffe. Can two women on opposite sides of an oil spill find a way to save both a wildlife sanctuary and their hearts? (978-1-62639-645-6)

**Soul to Keep** by Rebekah Weatherspoon. What won't a vampire do for love… (978-1-62639-616-6)